Into the Mist

Elizabeth Sinclair

Medallion Press, Inc.

Printed in the USA

DEDICATION:

To my dearest friend, my adopted sister and my mentor, Vicki Hinze. Your friendship, love and guidance are my miracle. Thank you.

Published 2008 by Medallion Press, Inc.

The MEDALLION PRESS LOGO
is a registered tradmark of Medallion Press, Inc.

Names, characters, places, and incidents are the products of the author's imagination or are used fictionally. Any resemblance to actual events, locales, or persons, living or dead, is entirely coincidental.

Printed in the United States of America
Typeset in Adobe Garamond Pro

ISBN# 1933836423
ISBN# 9781933836423

ACKNOWLEDGEMENTS:

My continued thanks to my friends and invaluable critique partners: Dolores J. Wilson and Vickie King. I'd be lost without you.

To my husband, Bob, for his continued faith, love and support. I love you.

PROLOGUE

Assistant Librarian Irma Peese looked around the dimly lit Tarrytown Library. Outside, the blowing snow had piled up in deep drifts against the buildings and across the streets. Disappointment dogged Irma's steps. She always looked forward to the annual Christmas story hour the library sponsored. This year she'd been especially excited to take the place of the resident storyteller, Anna Hobbs. Anna couldn't navigate the deep snow with her walker and had to reluctantly bow out.

The evening had started off well, but the laughter of the children had ended abruptly when a parent had arrived and warned Irma that the blizzard howling outside the building was getting worse and the children should be getting home while the parents could still travel on the treacherous roads.

After they'd all left, only Irma and her small family, her daughter, Meghan; son-in-law, Steve Cameron; and granddaughter, Faith, had remained behind. They would have left, as well, but there was an important task to be taken care of first.

Irma stacked the rest of the books she'd picked out but never gotten to read to the children that night and moved them to the library book cart. Monday would be soon enough to put them back on the shelves.

She glanced lovingly at her family. It wasn't all that long ago that Irma had had no family; she had wandered aimlessly through Central Park as a bag lady searching for wounded souls. That one of those souls would be the man who would love her daughter for all time had never crossed her mind. But then she'd found Steve, a pediatric oncologist, sitting on a park bench, wondering why the children who came into his care died and he was helpless to stop it. Irma had believed him to be just another lost human being questioning the strength of true love and the existence of miracles.

Now. . .

Meghan and Steve were deep in conversation over an architectural magazine. They'd been planning an addition to their family and were thinking about putting another room on the Gateway Cabin. From their hand movements, there seemed to be some point of contention in making that decision.

Irma smiled. She had no doubt that in the end it

would be a mutual decision, as everything in their lives was, and born of the deep love they bore for each other.

Leaving them to their quandary, Irma wandered to the table where Faith had just finished her latest rendition of Santa Claus and his sleigh and had started another picture. She'd already completed several drawings of the jolly old man and his reindeer, which now hung in a place of honor on the family refrigerator.

"Very nice," Irma told Faith as she leaned over her shoulder to inspect the latest Christmas masterpiece.

"Thank you, Ahmee," Faith said politely.

Irma shifted her attention to the piece of paper on which Faith had already drawn what looked like a river and mountains. "What have we here?" she asked, leaning over the girl's shoulder and studying the drawing. "If I'm not mistaken, that's a picture of the Hudson Highlands."

"Yup," the child said, smiling up at her grandmother. "It's where Rip Man Winkler went to sleep for days and days." With the tip of her black crayon, she pointed at the tiny stick figure she'd just completed, reclining on the side of the mountain. "See? There he is, just sleeping away."

"I see him." Irma chuckled and slid into the chair beside Faith, slipping her arm around the child's slim shoulders. "Actually, sweetheart, Rip Van Winkle slept on the mountain for twenty years."

Faith turned her mother's big blue eyes on her

grandmother. "Really?"

Irma kissed her rosy cheek. "Really."

"How come?"

"Well, no one really knows. Strange things happen in the Highlands. It's a very special, magical mountain, where wonderful things happen that no one can explain."

For a moment Faith was quiet. Then she turned to Irma again. "Like in Resnance?"

A gentle smile crept across Irma's face. "Yes, darling, like in Renaissance."

She wasn't surprised that Faith knew about the misty village hidden in the glen just beyond the Gateway Cabin. After all, her mother and father were the Gate Keepers, and she knew that Irma was one of the Guides who took the needy souls to the cabin. Many times, Meghan had told the child the story of the village and how it came to be. Over the years, it had become Faith's favorite bedtime story.

Faith yawned. Irma glanced at the big clock above the librarian's desk. Almost ten thirty. Late for the child to be up. But since her father and mother needed to be here when *she* arrived, they'd had little choice but to bring Faith with them.

Pushing her drawing aside, Faith climbed into her grandmother's lap and snuggled against her ample bosom. "Tell me the story of Emanuel, Ahmee."

Irma wrapped her granddaughter in her arms and

cradled her close to her heart. "Well, a long time ago, when the Indians still lived here in the Highlands, people came from across the ocean to find a new place to live where they could worship as they wanted to. Two of those people were—"

"Michiah and Rachel Biddle," Faith finished for her.

"Yes," she said and squeezed Faith lovingly. "Michiah and Rachel Biddle built a cabin." Irma tickled Faith's side. "The very cabin where you live now."

Faith giggled and squirmed impatiently. "Hurry up and get to the Emanuel part, Ahmee."

Irma laughed. "Ah, but you can't get to that part without knowing how Emanuel came to be."

A noise at her side made her look up. Steve and Meghan had come to join them. They each took a seat on the other side of the library table and leaned toward Irma, as eager as the child to hear the story.

"Not long after the Biddles had finished their cabin, Rachel gave birth to a baby boy."

"Emanuel," Faith declared, and everyone laughed.

Irma looked down at her granddaughter's sweet face. "You know this story as well as I do. I'd better warn Anna Hobbs that she might lose her job as storyteller one of these days."

"Aw, Ahmee." Faith leaned away from Irma and cast a look of incredulity at her. "I'm not old enough to have a job."

Irma laughed and hugged Faith. "I guess you're right." She sighed in total contentment and continued. "Emanuel was named after Michiah's great-grandfather. They were a very happy little family. They farmed the land, and when Emanuel was old enough, he and Michiah hunted for food in the woods. One day, when Emanuel was twelve, his mother became very ill. Michiah was very sad. He was afraid Rachel would die, and since he loved her so very much, he didn't know how he could go on living without her.

"Michiah was so sad that he couldn't even work the farm anymore. He spent every day wandering in the woods alone. One day he found a hill and climbed it and got to his knees and prayed for Rachel to get well. He did that every day for a long time. But each day, when he returned to the cabin, Rachel was still very sick. The next day, he'd go back to the hill and pray again, hoping that one day, when he went home, his prayer would have been answered, but it never was.

"Michiah had almost given up when he went to the hill one last time. This time, he noticed a mist in the glen below the hill. It was not like any fog he'd ever seen in the glen before. This mist was thick and white and had a strange light glowing inside it. As Michiah watched, the glow seemed to get brighter and brighter. Curious as to what the strange thing that glowed so brightly was, Michiah went down the hill and walked into the mist."

Realizing Faith hadn't moved or spoken in the past few minutes, Irma glanced down at her granddaughter. Faith was asleep. "Hmm, seems I've lost my audience."

Meghan cleared her throat, drawing Irma's attention. "Not entirely," she said, smiling. "Please go on. I never get tired of hearing this story."

"Where was I?"

"Michiah had just gone into the mist," Steve prompted, the expression on his face as eager as Faith's had been.

"Michiah was sure when he emerged from the mist that he'd been gone so long his family would be worried about him. He was even afraid that Rachel had died while he was gone and that Emanuel had been left to fend for himself. But as soon as he stepped outside the fog, his heart swelled with happiness, and he knew Rachel was well again. He hurried home to find his wife cooking supper for the first time in days. When she scolded him for leaving that morning and not returning for lunch, he was confused, but too elated to find her well to question her."

Irma shifted Faith to a more comfortable position. The child never stirred.

"The years passed, and the family continued to live happily in their cabin. Recalling the absolute love he'd found inside the mist, Michiah returned to the hill often, hoping to find it again. When Emanuel began asking questions about where his father went so often, Michiah told

7

his young son what had happened to him. Entranced by his father's tale of this place where such love and peace could be found, Emanuel began accompanying his father to the hill to wait for the mist to reappear. But it never did.

"Then, two days before his fourteenth birthday, Emanuel's parents both died from a fever that had stricken many people in the valley. Inconsolable, Emanuel wandered into the woods to the hill where his father had told him he'd seen the strange mist. There, at the very top of the hill, he buried his parents side by side. Soon after that, Emanuel vanished from the settlement."

Irma glanced down at her sleeping granddaughter, then to Steve and Meghan. "Many said the Indians killed him and threw him into the Hudson River. Others say the wild animals got him and devoured his body." She winked at Meghan. "But *we* know what really happened to him."

Meghan grinned, then sat up straight, looked at the clock, and stretched her cramped muscles. She yawned, making her look much like Faith. "It's nearly midnight. Are you sure tonight was the night?"

Irma looked at her daughter and raised an eyebrow. "Is he ever wrong?"

Meghan shook her head. "Not to my knowledge."

The words had just passed Meghan's lips when the sound of the latch falling into place on the front door to the library echoed through the silent room.

CHAPTER 1

We are each of us angels with one wing.
And we can only fly by embracing each other.
—Luciano de Crescenzo

December 23, Tarrytown, New York

*B*lood! All over her blouse, coat, and skirt. Where had it come from? What had happened? Terror, colder and icier than the biting winds whipping around her legs, clawed at her insides. Was the blood hers? Or was it someone else's, someone she'd hurt, someone. . .

Horrible scenarios of the possible source of the blood skittered through her mind. The terror grew until she felt as if she'd choke on it. Shivers that had no connection to the numbing wind chilling her face made her shiver and draw her coat closer to her body.

Frantically she looked around her. For what? Anything that would give her answers. She saw nothing through the wind-driven snow but dark buildings lining a quaint little street, Christmas lights twinkling gaily on long strings draped across the deserted road—and her. Not even a car passed that she could flag down.

With a desperation born of the unbridled panic of not knowing, she began walking aimlessly, oblivious to the snow blowing down the neck of her coat and the unrelenting cold permeating every inch of her body. She scoured her mind for details that seemed to hover just beyond her grasp. Though she strained to retrieve them, the closer she got to the answers, the more they scattered like frightened, elusive butterflies and left her with. . .*nothing*. No idea who she was, where she was, how she'd gotten there, or how she'd come to be splattered in blood.

Reminded of the stains covering her clothing, her mind reverted back into paralyzing panic.

Blood! My God, all this blood. Where had it come from? What have I done?

Terror rose up in her throat and nearly choked her. Tears blurred her vision. She felt as though she'd gone to sleep and awakened to find her nightmare was real. She began to shake uncontrollably, and not as a result of the numbness that had taken over her feet or the icy frostiness that had claimed her body.

Wait, she admonished herself, in a desperate attempt to get a grip on her fear and confusion. *Calm down. Think.* But her mind remained as blank as an unused sheet of paper.

Help. I need help. Surely, when she found someone, they'd be able to help her understand what was happening to her. In this weather, she couldn't have just wandered into town. She must live here. If that were true, then it logically followed that the people who also lived here would know her.

But she didn't know where to go to find any of those people. How could she, on these deserted streets? She didn't even know where she was or where she lived. How could anyone help her?

Hollow desperation flooded her. Hopelessness overcame her, and a new spate of tears blurred her vision. Still, as if driven by some unseen force, she plowed on through the drifting blizzard toward. . .what? Once more she stopped and looked around her, frantically searching for something, anything that looked familiar. Again. . .nothing. It was as though she'd been picked up and set down in a strange town, with her memory wiped clean of anything beyond this moment in time.

Forcing herself to concentrate, she prodded her mind

for answers until her head throbbed so painfully that she felt as though it would burst open like a ripe peach. Gritting her teeth, she bore the pain. It was worth it if she could just find one thread of memory, one tiny little thing that she could cling to. But she found nothing. Her mind was like a blackboard that had been erased.

Her stomach heaved in response to her throbbing in her skull. She rubbed her aching temple and felt a slick stickiness on her skin. Drawing her hand slowly away, she stared down at her fingertips. More blood. Could all this blood be hers?

Head wounds bleed profusely.

She squinted against the pain in her head and tried to focus.

How had she known that? She searched the blankness inside her mind for an answer, but none came. *Why can I recall that and not my name or my address or. . .*

She pressed the heels of her hands against her pulsating temples.

"Someone, please help me," she pleaded to the frozen landscape.

Frustration blossomed inside her and grew until she wanted to run screaming into the night to find someone who could tell her what was happening, who she was. Was the blood all hers, or had she done something unthinkable? If she'd hurt someone else, she had to find them, get them help, make it right.

Then, just ahead of her, through the wall of swirling snowflakes, she saw subdued light coming from a window of a large, brick building. The light splayed over the snow like a bright pathway, as though showing her the way. Through the window, she could see a couple of people inside. She hurried toward the beacon, stumbled, slipped on the snow-covered walkway, and fell into a drift. Clawing her way to her feet, she righted herself, ignored the icy snow that had gotten inside her coat collar, chilling her to the bone and making her wet blouse cling to her skin, and trudged on purposefully in the direction of the light.

At the end of the walk leading up to the front door, a large, white sign with bold, black lettering protruded from the snow. *Tarrytown Public Library.* As if an invisible thread were connected to her, she felt herself being drawn toward the building. With hope singing in her heart that surely someone in there would be able to tell her who she was, she hurried to the door, opened it, and stood poised on the doorstep.

Blessed warmth rushed out at her and almost stole her breath. Snow swirled in ahead of her and melted instantly on the polished hardwood floor, leaving small, shimmering puddles that reflected the dim lighting. The aromatic fragrance of cinnamon mixed with fresh-cut pine accosted her. In one corner stood a large Christmas tree decked out in paper chains and candy canes. On the wall behind the tree, red construction-paper stockings hung, each bearing the name of its owner in gold glitter. Pots of poinsettias sat on each of the highly-polished tables scattered about the room.

Gathered around one of the tables on the far side of the room were two women, a man, and a little girl. The child was sleeping peacefully in the older woman's arms.

She stepped gingerly inside and closed the door. The sound of the heavy, wrought-iron latch falling into place made all three people turn to her.

"I—" she began. "Can you help me?"

"Oh my word!" For a moment, Assistant Librarian Irma Peese studied the terrified girl shivering uncontrollably in the middle of the library floor. Her face was as pale as the snow coating her entire body. The girl was covered with spatters of blood, and a large cut, probably the source of the blood, marred her temple. The look of stark fear on her face brought Irma to her feet.

Irma glanced at Steve. "Get me some wet paper towels." Then she turned to Meghan. "Take Faith." Gently, she transferred her sleeping granddaughter to her daughter's arms, then rushed to the girl's side, took her arm, and led her to a chair.

Moments later, her son-in-law rushed back to her

side with a wet paper towel and handed it to her. "Here, Irma," he said. "Wipe away the blood so we can see how bad it is."

Irma took the paper towel and began carefully wiping away the blood on the woman's forehead. "My, but you've got a nasty cut here, dear." She glanced at Steve. "Stitches?"

He studied the cut, gently probed the edges, and then shook his head. "It looks worse than it is. It's really shallow. Just a good-sized bandage should do."

Irma turned to her daughter. Faith was now awake and standing beside her mother, staring at the young woman with large, inquisitive eyes. "Meghan, go into the librarian's office and bring me the first-aid kit." When Meghan rushed off to do her bidding, Irma looked down at the young woman's pale face. "What on earth happened to you?"

"I. . .I don't know," the girl said, her voice low and almost apologetic.

"Well, no need to worry about that right now. Let's see to that cut and get you cleaned up first." Irma proceeded to gently wipe the blood from the girl's cheeks and chin with a clean paper towel. She looked at Steve and then nodded toward her granddaughter, who was still staring wide-eyed at the injured woman. Faith didn't need to see this. "Steve, why don't you take Faith home, and we'll meet you there in a bit."

"Are you sure you won't need me?"

Irma shook her head. "As long as she doesn't need any stitches, I'm sure Meghan and I can handle it, dear."

"Irma," Steve said, lowering his voice. "Is she the one?"

Irma nodded almost imperceptibly. "I think so. Now, you get Faith home. It's past her bedtime." She leaned down and placed a warm kiss on the child's rosy cheek and then brushed the tangle of ash-blond curls from her face. "See you in the morning, love."

"Nite, Ahmee."

"Tell Meghan I'll see her at home." He took Faith's hand and led her toward the door. "Come on, sweetie. We'll go to the cabin and make hot chocolate for when Mommy and Grandma come home."

"Can the lady have some, too?"

Irma looked at Steve. They exchanged silent glances. Irma nodded. Her heart had told Irma almost the instant she'd looked up and seen the woman standing there that this was the girl Emanuel had sent word about, and she'd be getting more than a cup of hot chocolate at the cabin. She'd find a beginning to a new life.

"Of course, she can, sweetie, if she wants to," Steve said. He winked at Irma and then ushered his daughter out the door and into the snowy night.

"Drive carefully," Irma called after them, and then

went back to her chore. When she was satisfied that she'd gotten most of the blood off the young woman's forehead, Irma stood back and looked down at her. "We'll put a bandage on that cut just as soon as Meghan comes back with the first-aid kit."

"Thank you," the young woman murmured, her eyes downcast, "but I can't take up any more of your time. You should be going home with your family. I'm so sorry to have bothered you." She started to stand, but wobbled like a child's top just before it fell over sideways to the floor.

Irma grabbed her arm and eased her back into the chair. "It appears as if you're not going anywhere just yet. Now, you sit down and let me see to that cut. This storm is no place for anyone to be wandering around, injured or not. I have all the time in the world. I was just closing the library. Tonight was the annual Christmas Eve story hour."

Irma glanced out the window at the blizzard, hoping that her young audience members had made it home safely. This night in particular was very special because it was the night Irma told the story of Rachel and Michiah and the miracle of the mist, just as Anna Hobbs had done at Christmastime for the last twenty-five years. But since the children had to leave early, she'd had only her small family as an audience.

"The children got here before the storm started but had to leave early." She made a *tsk-tsk* sound, shook her head, and then centered her attention back on the stranger. "What's your name, dear?"

The woman looked at her with a blank expression and then promptly burst into tears.

Irma smiled warmly, wrapped the young woman in her arms, and murmured assurances to her. She hadn't felt quite this helpless since the night she told Meghan she had witnessed her own mother's rape and then left Meghan in the safety of Emanuel's care to protect her from the evil of the world.

"Now, now. No need for tears. If you don't want to tell me your name, you don't have to."

Slowly, the girl raised her head and sniffed loudly. She peered up at Irma from a pallid face, her large, green eyes wide with fear and confusion. "It's not that I don't want to. I just can't remember what my name is," she said around a heartbreaking sob.

Irma smiled to herself. *Amnesia.* Emanuel certainly found unique ways to administer to the spiritually needy.

Just then, Meghan appeared with a white box bearing a large red cross and handed it to Irma. "Here's the first-aid kit you wanted, Mom."

Irma took the box, set it on a table, and opened it. "This young lady tells me she doesn't know who she is,

Meghan." After sending her daughter a speaking glance, she removed a square of white gauze from its paper wrapper and applied a dot of antibiotic salve to it.

Meghan smiled knowingly. "Then perhaps we can help her."

Irma smiled. "I wouldn't be at all surprised."

Hope brought a sparkle to the woman's lackluster eyes. "You can help me? Really?"

"Everything in good time, my child," Irma said as she laid the gauze on the woman's forehead, then secured it with two strips of adhesive tape. "First of all, we need to find out your name."

She looked from one to the other, her lovely eyes large, frightened, and puzzled. "But I—"

"Look in your pocket," Meghan urged.

When the young woman looked to Irma for confirmation, Irma nodded. This reminded her of the day she'd first told Steve about the Gateway Cabin. He'd been hesitant, too. . .until he'd discovered the envelope where Irma had written the directions to the Gateway Cabin, the envelope he'd thrown in the trash and that had magically reappeared in his pocket.

"Do as Meghan asks, dear. Look in your pocket."

Irma and Meghan waited silently while the woman dug into her coat pocket and pulled out a small, rumpled, white piece of paper. She handed the paper to Irma.

Irma scanned the sheet. It was a receipt for several tubes of oil paint from a store called The Artist's Palette. The upper corner had been torn off, but today's date was still visible and just the first name—*Carrie*.

* * *

The interior of the Camerons' cabin closed around Carrie like a mother's womb, enfolding her in its warmth and love. Though her memory was still tantalizingly beyond her reach, she had no trouble recognizing a house decked out in all its splendor to celebrate Christmas.

A huge blue spruce spread its abundant branches and took up the entire bay window. Glittering strings of tinsel; rainbow-colored lights; garlands of fluffy, white popcorn; and an abundance of all sizes and shapes of shiny ornaments graced every limb. Beneath the tree lay colorfully wrapped packages tied up with bows and just waiting for the recipients to discover what was concealed inside. Over the blazing fireplace, a swag of fragrant pine adorned the mantel, permeating the house with its rich aroma. The coffee table held a cut-glass bowl overflowing with pinecones interspersed with gold and silver balls. The blazing fireplace's reflection danced brightly in the bowl's prisms. Candles burned on every surface, spreading a homey warmth throughout the room that no electric lamp could attain.

Carrie could feel in her bones that love, laughter, and happiness resided within these walls and that the people who lived here were special. Yet all the wonderfully calming emotions she sensed here felt so very foreign to her. Why?

Meghan deposited a tray laden with four mugs topped with snowy whipped cream on the coffee table. She handed Carrie one of the steaming mugs. The aroma of rich chocolate drifted up with the steam and made Carrie's taste buds water. She had no idea when she'd last eaten, but from the hollowness inside her, she had to assume it had been some time ago.

"Faith insisted I give you hot chocolate because she just knew you were very cold and would catch your death if I didn't." Meghan laughed. "I think she may follow in her father's footsteps and be a doctor someday."

Carrie looked around to thank the child.

"She's gone to bed," Meghan explained. "She has a big day ahead of her tomorrow. We're going to the city to help feed the homeless, and then she'll be staying with her grandmother for Christmas Eve."

When Carrie frowned at the idea of the child being anywhere but at home with her parents on Christmas Eve, Meghan smiled. "It's a tradition. She and her grandmother make popcorn balls and decorate Irma's tree, then bright and early on Christmas Day, they show up here to open presents and have a big family breakfast. My mother only lives a mile or so down the road from here."

Irma and Steve came in from the kitchen, and each picked up a cup of hot chocolate from the tray. The peaks of whipped cream that had poked up above the rim of each mug had begun to melt. Irma seated herself beside Carrie, and Steve flopped into the big recliner, pushed on the arms until the footrest popped up, and then crossed his ankles and rested the cup of hot chocolate on his flat stomach.

Carrie sipped at her cup, licked the sweet whipped cream from her upper lip, and waited for their inevitable questions, the questions she wouldn't be able to answer.

Steve dropped the footrest and leaned forward, his elbows resting on his thighs, the mug cradled in his hands. "So, tell me, Carrie, what exactly do you remember?"

She set her mug aside and folded her hands in her lap. The warm, cozy feeling the house had produced in her dissipated and was replaced by the cold, empty hopelessness she'd experienced before.

"Nothing before I found myself standing on the street, I'm afraid." She looked from one to the other, and the desolation lying in the pit of her stomach grew. "You said you could help me remember," she reminded them.

"No, we said we could help *you*," Meghan said softly.

"But doesn't that mean. . ."

Irma laid a hand on her arm. "It means we'll help you find yourself. Your *true* self."

Carrie shook her head. The throbbing in her temples had begun again. "I don't understand."

Meghan smiled. "What if we told you that there was a place where you could go and not only learn who you are, but what you are? A place where miracles happen and dreams come true?"

Unreasonable fear gathered instantly in a tight ball in the pit of Carrie's stomach. Her throat closed off, preventing her from saying anything in response. She gripped her hands together in her lap until her fingers hurt. Whatever had possessed her to come here with these people, with all their crazy talk about miracles and dreams coming true? For all she knew, they'd murder her and throw her body into the woods for the animals to feed on.

The fear that had grown in her stomach spread to enfold her entire body in its icy embrace. Never taking her gaze from them, she stood very slowly and edged around the couch. She forced a weak smile to her lips. "Thank you for everything, but I think I'd better go," she said, easing toward the door.

Irma quickly intercepted her and put an arm around

her shoulders. "Where will you go, child?"

Carrie stiffened. "I. . ." Her voice quavered, making it hard for her to form words.

"Don't be frightened. We're not going to harm you," Irma crooned softly as if to a baby.

Almost instantly, Irma's words seemed to reach down inside Carrie and replace the fear and panic with calm and. . .trust? What was there about this woman that made Carrie feel as though she were a child being reassured by a loving parent?

"No one will force you to do anything you don't want to do," Steve added, going to stand beside his wife and pulling her to his side. "It has to be your choice, Carrie."

Hesitantly, Carrie weighed their words. Looking from one to the other, she could see without exception the honesty and gentle love shining from their eyes. Oddly, she felt as though that emotion was something she hadn't seen in anyone's eyes for a long time.

The hopelessness came back. If her life had been that bleak and loveless, that empty, did she really want to remember any of it? Maybe she should forget trying to remember and just go forth from this moment and build new memories, happy memories.

"There is no future without a past," Irma said.

Irma's words unnerved her. It was as though she'd been reading Carrie's thoughts. But that was impossible.

Wasn't it? Whether or not she'd read her mind, Irma was right. No matter what her past held, how could she go forward without knowing where she'd already been?

And really, how much worse could it be than this limbo she'd found herself in? Knowing the worst had to be better than knowing nothing at all.

"This place. . .the one you spoke of, where is it?" Carrie could hear the tremble in her voice.

A radiant smile spread over Irma's face, making her look like an angel. "Nearby. We'll take you there if you'd like."

Carrie hesitated for a moment, and then, knowing instinctively that Irma wanted only what was best for her and that she'd trust this woman with her life, she nodded. "Okay."

On the mantel, the interior of the small, green lantern began to fill with a fine white mist, evidence that an Assignment was due to arrive within the mystical village of Renaissance.

* * *

Earlier the same evening, somewhere in the mist of time. . .

Clara Webb stood to the side while Emanuel drew up a chair to the kitchen table. When he was comfortably seated, she placed a steaming mug of strong coffee in front of the village Elder.

He smiled up at her. Her heart twisted. Sadness lurked in his usually bright, gray eyes tonight. Due to her long-standing love for this man, Clara felt his sadness more acutely than anyone else in the small village. But she'd never voiced that love. He was already charged with such a heavy burden to bear. All these needy souls, all looking to him for help. She wished she knew how to lighten his load. But then, he probably wouldn't let her. If she even offered, he would simply tell her that he had chosen to walk this road long ago, and that the burden was his alone to bear.

"Ah, Clara," he proclaimed, pulling her out of her reverie, "you always know what I need to warm my soul. I'll have plenty of time to enjoy this before the village goes into the first Transition stage." Then he sighed. "But I must admit that at this time of year, I do so miss Meghan's sugar cookies."

Clara chuckled and placed a plate of golden-brown sugar cookies in front of him. "I expect she knew you'd be missing her cookies, so when Alvin went to the cabin yesterday to tell Irma about the arrival of another Assignment, Meghan sent these back with him."

Assignments, the troubled souls from the world outside the enchanted village of Renaissance, came and went periodically, each with their own special emotional burden, each seeking peace. Most times, the Guides who lived in that outside world sent the Assignments to the village, but this time, Emanuel knew of this particular arrival before anyone else did. To ask him how he knew would be fruitless. Emanuel always knew things to which the rest of the residents of the village weren't privy, and no one ever asked the why or how of it. His uncommon sight was simply accepted for what it was: a blessing.

Emanuel smiled over the cup's rim at the woman who wove the cloth for the village of Renaissance. He moved aside an angel cookie and chose one of the frosted bells.

"The first Transition stage? Will there be more than one Assignment this time?" Clara knew it was rare that more than one troubled soul came to the village at a time. When Emanuel nodded, she asked, "Will they arrive together?" She refreshed his coffee.

He took a bite of the golden-brown cookie, then set both the cup and the unfinished cookie on the table and leaned back in his chair. "Ah, yes, the Assignments. No, they won't be arriving during the same Transition. One is being prepared as we speak and will arrive soon. The other will not come until Christmas Eve. I've decided that the first one will be yours. Only you can give her the special care she'll need, Clara." He frowned.

The snowy-haired woman slipped into the seat across from him. Outside her window, she could see that a fine mist had begun to gather. It would take a while for the mist to thicken and herald the Transition of the village from mystical to material. Shortly after that, the mist would part, and they would welcome another soul in turmoil, an Assignment, into their midst.

Emanuel's obvious despondency tore at her heart. She didn't know for certain why she felt his emotions more acutely than the others in the village did, but she had come to believe it was because her love for Emanuel was different from their emotional bond to him.

"This troubles you. Why?" she asked, her full attention concentrated on the man sitting across from her.

His bushy eyebrows drew together in concern. "I have to wonder why people mistreat each other so badly and then label it as love. Such a peculiar contradiction of the word." He shrugged and rubbed his large hands together. "But that's a worry for another day. We've more urgent concerns to occupy our minds at present. Your Assignment's life has been especially hard, very hard. She's lost her direction as a result. She needs to rediscover herself, to renew her faith in the person she has always been, a strong, goodhearted woman. And she needs to find the strength to face and relinquish all that has turned her life into a hell on earth. In short, she needs to rediscover love, Clara."

This Assignment indeed sounded special, and in dire need of the peace she'd find here in the village.

Clara nodded toward the gathering mist outside the window. "And the other Assignment? Who will get that one? Surely you won't be giving both of them to me." Dividing her attention between two Assignments would severely disadvantage one or the other.

He shook his head and patted her hand. His long beard swayed gracefully back and forth across his chest. "No, no. I want all your efforts aimed at healing this one's needy soul. The other one will be Alvin Tripp's."

That announcement surprised Clara. "Alvin's? But why?"

Alvin, the Traveler, was Renaissance's connection to the world beyond the perimeter of the village, the messenger between Emanuel and the Guides who found the wounded souls and sent them to Renaissance to heal. Ever since Alvin had come to them after the tragic loss of his wife, Clara had never known Emanuel to charge Alvin with the care of an Assignment.

"Alvin and our new Assignment have much in common. I believe in this instance that the Healer, as well as the Assignment, is in need of being ministered to." He patted Clara's hand. "I have put this off long enough, my dear. Alvin cannot go on forever shouldering this heavy burden, a burden that is not his to bear." He smiled wistfully. "Perhaps there will be three souls who find peace very soon."

29

Clara should have known that it hadn't escaped Emanuel's notice that Alvin kept to himself. That he only accepted responsibility if it didn't directly entail another human being's welfare. Sometimes Alvin's self-imposed isolation just tore at her heart. He had so much to give, if he could only find peace within himself. She could easily see the wisdom of Emanuel's choice, but would Alvin? However, she had learned long ago that Emanuel's wisdom often found its roots in things of which she had no knowledge.

A loud knock sounded on the door. Clara hurried to answer it. A very tall, very husky, middle-aged man, dressed in buckskin and smelling like crisp, fresh air, took up a good deal of the opening. His face, weathered by the elements through which he loved traipsing, was nearly hidden behind his unruly, dark brown hair and a beard that sprouted from his cheeks and jaw like an overgrown huckleberry bush.

"Evenin', Clara."

"Hello, Alvin."

He nodded in the direction of the table. "Emanuel."

"Good evening, Alvin." Emanuel motioned to the chair at his side. "Please, join me for a cup of Clara's outstanding coffee."

Clara smiled to herself. If Emanuel had a weakness, it was his love of coffee, and true to his diplomatic nature, he often made the proclamation that the coffee in which he was indulging at the moment was the best he'd ever had. She'd once asked him about it, and he'd smiled and explained that whatever cup of coffee he was drinking at the time was, indeed, the best he'd had, since it was also, at that moment, the only one. She knew it was just one small facet of the abundance of love he showered equally on those around him.

As Alvin started to take a step forward, Clara, though more than a foot shorter than him, stopped him with a firm hand to his broad, muscular chest. "Mind you wipe your feet," she admonished and kept a discerning eye trained on him until he did.

Satisfied that her gleaming floor would not be tracked up with the mud from the woods where Alvin had undoubtedly spent his day, she stepped back and made way for him to move past her into the room.

Between her weaving loom nestled in the corner near the blazing hearth and the imposing figures of both Alvin and Emanuel in her small kitchen, the keeping room seemed to shrink considerably. Clara hustled about, getting Alvin coffee. When she had it poured and placed in front of him, she joined the men at the table, eager to see Alvin's reaction to having his first Assignment.

"I have a job for you," Emanuel said, favoring his friend with a smile.

Clara saw no reaction from Alvin, but that didn't surprise her. Little that was said to him or happened around him stirred much of a response in Alvin, besides this was a request he'd often heard from the Elder in the past.

"Where will you be sending me this time?" Alvin asked without preamble or a change of expression.

"You won't be leaving the village this time, my boy." Emanuel pointed out the window at the gathering mist. "A new Assignment will soon enter the village, but there is also one due tomorrow evening. I'll be going to meet him in the woods above the Glen. Steve and Meghan will be bringing him to me."

A warm glow surrounded Clara's heart at the mention of the two people who had found love inside the village despite almost insurmountable odds. Both of them had learned the meaning of faith and trust and that the one true miracle was love.

Alvin had just taken a drink of coffee and swallowed hurriedly. "Figured it was the Assignment when I saw the mist as I came across the square." He glanced at Clara. "Yours?"

"Yes, Alvin," Emanuel broke in, sending Clara a silencing glance. "This one is Clara's, but the Assignment coming tomorrow night is yours."

Clara turned her attention from Emanuel to the burly woodsman. The large hand gripping Alvin's coffee cup had stopped halfway to his mouth and every ounce of color had drained from his normally ruddy face.

CHAPTER 2

The next morning in Clara Webb's cottage...

For a moment Carrie panicked. Disoriented and half-asleep, she had no idea where she was. An unfamiliar room surrounded her. The old chest of drawers in the corner; starched, white curtains blowing in the balmy breeze from the open window; and the hand-worked, multi-colored quilt folded neatly over the foot rail of the bed had never been part of her bedroom.

Then recollections of the night before flashed through her mind. She remembered Irma guiding her through the snowy night and into a glen shrouded in a strange, brightly glowing, white mist. Though Carrie had initially held back, Irma had reassured her with a calm voice that banished all fear and replaced it with the kind of security only a true friend can command. Carrie had allowed herself to be ushered into the mist. Though

33

the mist had glowed like a thousand candles, she had felt only comforting warmth. Instantly any residual fear or hesitation had been completely removed. It had felt like coming home after a long, exhausting journey. In her heart, she had known it had been the right thing to do.

Then she and Irma had stepped out of the mist and onto a small, rustic footbridge. On the other side of the bridge lay a village that seemed to have dropped from a fairy tale, illuminated by a sliver of pale yellow moon. Despite that lack of light, she had been able to make out the flowers abounding everywhere, even though, where she had just come from, it was the dead of winter. A mixture of their heady fragrances had filled the air. Quaint gaslights had illuminated the single, narrow dirt street curling through the scattering of thatch-roofed cottages.

Standing alone on the footpath on the opposite side of the bridge, apparently waiting for her with an outstretched hand, had been a woman who looked like everyone's image of their grandmother—except she seemed to have passed through a time warp.

Her white hair, which was almost concealed beneath a mobcap straight out of Colonial times, framed her smiling face. She wore a white muslin blouse and a long, dark skirt covered by a full-length, white apron. Her feet were encased in black shoes with large silver buckles that reflected the moonlight.

"This is Clara Webb, the village Weaver," Irma had told her. "You'll be staying with her during your time in the village."

"Welcome, my dear," Clara had said in a voice that oozed over Carrie like maple syrup on a hot summer day and left behind it a residue that reminded Carrie of her grandmother's love.

Carrie had barely had enough time to register that she'd recalled a small tidbit of her past before Clara had taken her hand, and Irma had vanished back into the mist. Left with little choice, Carrie had followed Clara to one of the cottages where the kindly woman had urged her to eat something and then took her to the loft and put her to bed, as though she were tending to a beloved child.

The bed had felt wonderful last night, warm and cozy, but this morning, it felt even better, and Carrie found herself very reluctant to leave her haven against the cold. She snuggled deeper into the heavenly, warm folds of the down comforter. From somewhere outside her cocoon the rich aroma of coffee brewing and bacon sizzling in a frying pan wafted temptingly to her.

Her tummy growled with hunger. She could almost taste the bacon and feel the warm coffee slipping down her dry throat.

How frustrating that she automatically remembered inconsequential things like the smell of bacon and the taste of coffee, while important details of her life remained tantalizingly just beyond the edges of her memory.

She sighed, rolled onto her back, and stared unseeingly at the peaked, open-beamed ceiling. She had no idea what would happen to her here, but if it helped her to finally grasp more than just the fringes of her memory, as Irma, Steve, and Meghan had promised, then she would be patient.

Throwing back the heavy comforter, she slid from the abnormally high bed and dropped to the floor, surprised that the room was comfortably warm. Her bare feet hit the pine boards before she saw a small set of steps that had been provided to get down from the bed. On a chair near the door lay her clothes—freshly laundered, meticulously ironed, and neatly folded. The bright red splotches of blood were gone from her white blouse, as well as all traces of the dirty smudges that had covered her brown skirt last night.

Dressed and barefooted, Carrie made her way noiselessly down the ladder from the loft.

"Good morning, my dear."

Carrie swung around and found Clara with her back to her. True to her designation within the village, Clara was deeply engrossed in working her loom and producing a long swath of dark green cloth.

"Morning," she said shyly, remaining at the foot of

the ladder, unsure of what she should do next.

Clara continued to guide the shuttle to and fro on the loom. The *clickity clack* of the loom working its magic as it produced yard after yard of material broke the heavy silence in the room. Totally in awe of her surroundings, Carrie took the opportunity to look around her.

From the hand-hewn ceiling beams to the wide pine flooring, this entire place could have fallen out of a travel brochure for Williamsburg, Virginia. The keeping room, as she had known instantly it was referred to, like the loft and the woman who lived here, smacked strongly of a bygone era.

An unfinished, wrought-iron crane held a large, blackened teakettle over the blazing fire. Steam spewed from its spout. Next to the fieldstone hearth, a pile of logs half-hid a crudely made straw broom leaning against the stone fireplace. On the other side of the hearth, a black iron frying pan sat waiting to be used on the only close-to-modern thing in the room—a woodstove. A polished, well-used trestle-style table took up much of one end of the room and the loom filled the other. The highly polished pine floor was partially hidden beneath a rainbow-colored, handmade braided rug. Candles were placed strategically to spread a warm glow around the room, which was void of any sign of electricity. Like her bedroom, large hand-hewn beams crisscrossed the ceiling and held up the floor above. Muslin curtains framed the open, mullioned windows and fluttered in the soft, warm breeze. Outside the windows, flower boxes dripped with a blanket of pink petunias.

The smell of pine tickled Carrie's nose. She suddenly remembered that it was Christmas Eve, and like the Gateway Cabin, the cottage abounded with holiday decorations. Garlands stretched their greenery across the doorway and hearth and filled the air with their intoxicating scent. Candles nestled in beds of fresh pine dotted with pinecones. A much smaller tree than Steve and Meghan had in the cabin stood beside the window. Instead of the bright lights and shiny ornaments, Clara's tree held small, white candles at the tip of each branch, popcorn and cranberry strings, and sugar cookies. On top was a wooden star.

"Best eat before it gets cold," Clara said without turning around.

Carrie started and turned her gaze back to the trestle table. On it a plate of crisp, brown bacon; perfectly fried eggs; and golden, buttery toast awaited her. Beside it sat a mug of steaming coffee.

For a moment, Carrie could only stare in awe at the food. She could have sworn the table had been empty when she'd come down the ladder, and yet Clara hadn't moved from the loom in that time. So where had the food come from? She glanced at Clara, who continued weaving the seemingly never-ending swath of dark green cloth. Carrie's stomach growled, and instead of continuing to wonder where the food had come from, she sat down and dug in.

* * *

Clara peeked over her shoulder, smiled to herself, and turned back in time to catch the shuttle and slide it easily between the threads stretched over the frame of the loom. When things started happening that the Assignments couldn't logically explain, they looked so puzzled and surprised. Clara loved that. Just as she loved watching that puzzlement and surprise turn to wonder and then, eventually, to calm acceptance. Her breakfast was only the first of many things in Renaissance that Carrie would question, but have to come to accept.

Such a sweet thing this Carrie was, Clara thought. But, unfortunately, Emanuel was right. Carrie had no idea who she was or what she was, and it had nothing to do with her amnesia. It had to do with losing her soul, her courage, and her inner strength. Little did she know, her soul wasn't entirely lost. Just misplaced. And God willing, Clara would help her put herself together again into the wonderful woman she was before—well, before her life went sour.

Clara caught the shuttle and laid it aside. Glancing out the window toward the babbling stream that ran alongside the pathway and then made a sharp right turn to pass behind her cottage, she smiled and gave a faint nod. It was time for Carrie's first memory to return. She turned to Carrie, who had just finished the last bite of her breakfast and was gathering her dishes to take them to the washbasin on the table beside the sink.

"Leave them, dear. I'll see to them shortly. You've more important things that need your attention." She rose and went to Carrie. Laying a hand on her shoulder, she motioned with the other at the window overlooking the backyard. "I think you might want to take a walk outside. Perhaps to that large rock beside the water. I like to go out there sometimes when things become too heavy for my mind to bear. It helps me to put order to my thoughts."

Carrie paused in the midst of stacking the mug on the plate and starred at Clara with confused eyes. "But—"

"Shush. I'll not have an argument. Now, off with you," Clara said softly, and after urging the young woman to her feet, she guided her out the back door.

* * *

Carrie stepped off the stone steps onto the cushiony grass. A few feet away, the clearest water she'd ever seen gurgled and babbled its way zealously over various size rocks as it cut a zigzag path through the green lawn. Beneath the surface Carrie could see silvery fish swimming about. Occasionally, one would leap from the water and snare an unsuspecting insect, then drop back with a splash.

Along the path that ran adjacent to the stream, a well-tended flower bed teeming with a rainbow of blossoms spilled a myriad of sweet scents into the breeze and enticed dozens of bees and butterflies to savor the treats hidden within their colorful petals. Leaving the insects to their busy work, she strolled along the water's edge until she came to the large rock Clara had mentioned. With a sigh, she lowered herself to it and dug her bare toes into the sun-warmed, damp grass.

As she stared into the moving water, Carrie shook her head. How could she remember the insects' names—bumblebee, monarch butterfly, dragonfly—but she only knew her own name because of a slip of paper she'd found in her pocket? She didn't even know for sure that it *was* her name. But for the time being and until she found out differently, she was willing to be Carrie.

Unconsciously shoving her hands deep into the pockets of her skirt, she felt something small and smooth. Hesitantly, she drew it out and stared down at it. Crudely carved from a black stone, it resembled a tiny bear about an inch long and an inch high. It bore an inlay of another reddish stone that ran in a line from its mouth and terminated in an arrow shape about mid-chest near its heart. Its eyes were inlaid turquoise.

For a long time, Carrie studied it, turning it over and over in her fingers, feeling the slick surface of the warm, polished stone. Slowly the memory emerged. *Shashtsoh,* the grizzly bear. The line of red was a heart line and indicated a brave heart. Nana George, her part-Navajo maternal grandmother, had given it to her after she'd come back from a vacation in Arizona. Carrie had thought she'd lost it years ago. To find it in her pocket now was very strange, but very comforting.

"The Native Americans believe that the bear is the bravest of their forest brothers," Nana had said as she lay dying. "Keep him close. When I am gone, his courage and strength will help guide you down the true path of your life."

Why had her grandmother felt that way? Carrie racked her brain for an answer, but none came. All she saw were the blank pages of memory. Carrie bowed her head, closed her eyes tightly, gripped the small bear in her fingers, and concentrated with as much energy as she could. But nothing came to her except the dull throbbing behind her eyes.

Be patient, my sweet girl.

Carrie started. Her eyes popped open, and she looked around for the person who had spoken. But she soon found she was alone with only a robin for company. The robin looked at her. Blinked and flew into a nearby maple tree.

It will all come back to you soon. For now, you must concentrate on you, what you need, who you are, not as a name, but as a woman.

That voice again. Was it inside her head or coming from a real person? Again Carrie scanned the area around her. Still no one. Then who—

Suddenly she recognized the voice. "Nana George? Is that you?"

But the only sounds she heard were the buzzing of the insects and the twittering of the robin high above her.

* * *

Later that evening, while helping Clara with supper and still contemplating what had happened by the stream, Carrie glanced out the window. "It's getting foggy out."

"No, dear. That's the Transition beginning."

"Transition? What's that?"

Clara took her hand and seated her at the table.

"When a troubled soul, such as yourself, comes to the village, the village must come into a material state to admit that person. That process is called a Transition."

Carrie frowned. "A material state? But isn't it material already?"

Clara laughed softly. "Renaissance exists in the mists of time. When it's needed, it then takes on its material state to welcome the troubled within its embrace."

"Then is this some kind of dream? Since I'm not really here, I can leave anytime simply by. . .waking up. Right?"

Shaking her head, Clara grasped Carrie's hand. She dropped her gaze to their hands, made a soft *tsking* sound with her tongue, and then spoke as if to herself. "This is always the most difficult part." Then she shook herself as if to clear her thoughts. "Get to the point, Clara." She raised her gaze and fixed it on Carrie. "I can assure you, this is not a dream from which you will awaken. You *are* really here, and I'm afraid you can't leave."

Oddly, that she couldn't leave didn't alarm her. Carrie wasn't at all sure she ever wanted to leave here. This place, Clara, the cottage, all felt so secure and safe, and she didn't know why, but that seemed to be very important to her.

Clara squeezed Carrie's fingers. "The village is a permanent home to just the few of us who live here. For others, such as you, this is but a stopover in time. Like a short nap in the middle of a long, tiring day."

Again, Carrie was taken aback that Clara seemed able to read her thoughts. But she had too many questions to ask to dwell on that one fact. "How did this place, this village," Carrie asked, waving her hand to encompass all beyond the window, "come to be?"

Clara smiled. "That's a question almost all the Assignments ask, but none quite as soon as this." She adjusted her seat and then appeared to settle in to relate the beginnings of Renaissance. "Way back, when this area was being settled by religiously persecuted immigrants from England, a newly married couple, Michiah and Rachel Biddle, made their home here. They built a cabin just beyond the glen. Shortly after that, Rachel gave birth to a son, Emanuel." A warm glow lit Clara's eyes when she spoke the name. "When Rachel became ill and almost died, a distraught Michiah came to the hilltop to pray for her life. While there, he noticed a glowing mist gathering in the glen and ventured into it. When he came out, his wife was well, and he related to his young son the peace and the love he'd found there. After both his parents passed away, the teenaged Emanuel, despondent and determined to find this place his father had told him of, sat on the hilltop for weeks, waiting for the mist to appear. When it did, he walked into it, and no one from the outside ever saw him again. Since that time, Emanuel has lived within the mist and helped heal tortured souls."

Carrie had seen the village Elder, a man named Emanuel, pass by the house earlier and Clara had told her who he was. "Then the man I saw today is his ancestor."

Clara shook her head and smiled. "No, my dear. That *is* Emanuel."

"But that can't be," Carrie protested, her eyes wide. "That would make him—"

"As old as time," Clara said. Her blue eyes twinkled. "But then, time is relative, isn't it, my dear?"

"And the Camerons' cabin?" she asked. Even as she asked, she was certain that the very idea that this might be the same cabin that the Biddles had built was too far-fetched.

"Michiah's and Rachel's cabin," Clara said softly. "The Gateway to the village. Steve and Meghan are the Gate Keepers, and Irma is a Guide. They help the needy find their way here."

Carrie was stunned. But even before she could ask more about the cabin, another question tumbled into her mind. "What if I hadn't found the library when I did?"

Clara smiled, but said nothing.

Then Carrie recalled the glowing path of light that seemed to guide her to the front door of the library and the inexplicable pull she'd felt urging her along the path.

"I was guided there, wasn't I?"

Clara nodded. "By Emanuel."

"But why? And what if I'd refused to come?"

Clara smiled knowingly. "Over the years, I have learned not to question Emanuel's wisdom. You'll find he doesn't take no for an answer often, and this was one time he would have firmly stood his ground. The need he felt in you was much too urgent."

CHAPTER 3

Christmas Eve, the Gateway Cabin. . .

D r. Frank Donovan pulled his snow-covered car in beside the cabin that was the home of his two best friends, Dr. Steve Cameron and his wife, Meghan. For a long time, Frank sat in the car staring at the cabin that Steve had renovated to meet the needs of his family. A new bedroom had been added for their daughter, Faith; another small room would soon be added for future Camerons; and the living room had been enlarged to include an expansive bay window. Normally, the window abounded in green plants that Meghan nurtured like a second child, but today a massive, twinkling Christmas tree engulfed the entire space and spilled a rainbow of colored lights over the snow outside.

How he envied the Camerons. They had everything

he'd ever wanted and almost had, until—

He forced the thought from his mind. Thinking about it only dredged up the guilt, and that depressed him. If he sank any deeper into that black abyss, he was afraid he'd never claw his way out. To rid him of the guilt was, after all, why Frank found himself sitting in his car outside the Camerons' cabin in a blizzard on Christmas Eve.

Steve had told him about the cabin and its special qualities, and a mysterious place that lay in the woods beyond the cabin; a place, Steve had said, that could heal Frank and help him to get on with his life.

He didn't believe a word of it, but what the hell? He'd tried everything else, and since he'd had to call for another surgeon to take over for him during two heart surgeries last week, he knew it was past time to kill the demons that haunted him. If it meant putting an end to the ever-present sound of the screeching of tires, the crunching of metal, and the echo of Sandy's screams, and the nights when he awoke bathed in a cold sweat to a room filled to overflowing with despair, loneliness, and self-loathing, then he'd be a fool not to try it. If gaining that end meant giving Steve the benefit of the doubt, then so be it.

Steve had told him of his trip to this special place and that it helped him understand his role as a pediatric oncologist and the loss of young lives with which he had to contend almost on a daily basis. If it could bring Steve the same kind of peace of mind, then maybe, just maybe, there was hope for him, as well.

He shivered and glanced at his watch and realized time had gotten away from him. He should have been here an hour ago. With the lousy road conditions from the blizzard that had covered the southern part of New York State the night before and all day today, and with the heavy holiday traffic, he should have left earlier. But he didn't, and he knew why. Afraid to acknowledge the false hope it might give him, he had put this off as long as he could.

Resignedly, Frank opened the car door and climbed out. He made his way toward the front porch. The freshly fallen snow crunched under his boots. As though his feet contained lead weights, he slowly climbed the steps until he reached the porch and stood outside the rough-hewn door. He stomped the snow off his feet, then raised his hand and knocked.

Moments later, Meghan and Steve stood in the open doorway, *welcome* written all over their faces. The enticing aromas of cinnamon, new pine, and freshly baked cookies wafted out to greet him. A crackling fire spread homey warmth through the room, warmth that reached out and beckoned to him to come inside.

Steve wrapped his arm around his wife and smiled. "We were beginning to think you wouldn't make it."

Frank leaned against the door frame and stared at his closest friend, uncertain whether or not he should go inside. "I almost didn't. I still don't see what all this is going to accomplish." He glanced around him at the very ordinary-looking cabin. "This cabin may have been the thing that brought you back to life, but I think I'm beyond resurrecting."

"It was not the cabin, but what is out there," Steve said, motioning with his free hand toward the thick wall of trees surrounding the cabin. "And no one is beyond resurrecting, my friend. This place will teach you that, if you let it." Steve snuggled Meghan closer to his side. "There's a miracle waiting for you there. All you have to do is open your heart to it."

Miracles. Hogwash.

Perhaps because his sentiments had been written plainly on his face for her to see, Meghan smiled at her husband, then at Frank. "Faith and trust, Frank, that's all you need."

As he looked at the two of them, a painful twinge squeezed Frank's heart. He remembered when Sandy had smiled up at him like that, her beautiful blue eyes full of adoration and trust. *Trust.* The word lay heavy on his conscience, and though he hadn't spoken it aloud, bitterness filled his mouth. His shoulders slumped. Sometimes he felt as though they bore the weight of a thousand tons of lead. How misplaced Sandy's trust had been, and he'd proven that to her in the worst way possible.

Resigned, Frank stepped into the light just beyond the threshold.

Steve's expression told him how terrible he looked. He wasn't stupid, and he'd seen his own reflection in the mirror that morning. He knew lines etched his face, he had dark circles rimming his eyes, his mouth had forgotten how to smile, and his mismatched clothes bespoke how little attention he'd paid to how he appeared to other people. In short, he looked like hell. He should just turn around and go home instead of inflicting his misery on these two wonderful people on a night when they should be surrounded with love, happiness, and peace on earth.

Steve must have read his mind. Without another word, he took Frank's arm and hauled him the rest of the way inside and then closed the door behind them. Resigned to being there, Frank began unbuttoning his coat.

Steve stopped him. "We're going out again in a minute, so you might as well leave it on."

"Out? Where? I thought I was supposed to spend Christmas Eve here with you." Then it occurred to him that they must be going tonight to that *place* that Steve had told him about.

Instead of answering, Steve and Meghan simply smiled conspiratorially at each other and pulled on their coats.

Moments later, during which time Frank had voiced several inquiries about their destination that went unanswered, they climbed toward the crest of a small hill. The newly fallen snow lay thick and white across the ground and muffled their footsteps, making it seem as though they weren't really there. Inexplicably, Frank glanced behind them at the indentations in the snow to confirm that they *were* actually there. He laughed at his own foolishness and turned back to the hill.

Then Frank saw him. A man stood atop the hill. Mist swirled at his feet, making him look as though he were standing on a cloud. A long, flowing, white robe, cinched at the waist with a ropelike belt, cloaked his large frame. The ends of the rope, tied in knots to prevent them from fraying, almost touched the ground. A snowy beard hung almost to his waist. Even from this distance, Frank could feel a strange kind of warmth emanating from the man's eyes. He smiled at Frank and held out his hand, but not to shake it. The hand lay palm up, much like a parent would offer his hand to a child to guide him through danger or over hazardous ground.

Unable to believe what he was seeing, Frank blinked several times, waiting for the image to vanish. But each time he opened his eyes, the man in the long robe was still there, smiling at him.

Despite the man's friendly demeanor, Frank drew back. "Who in hell is that?"

Steve laid a hand on Frank's shoulder. "That is Emanuel. He'll be taking you with him."

"Taking me where?" Frank tried to back away, but Steve blocked his way and held firm to his friend's shoulder.

"To a place the likes of which you have never seen before," Meghan said, her voice soft and dreamy.

Releasing Frank to pull his wife into his embrace, Steve grinned. "It's where I found Meghan, where my life turned around, and I became a whole man again." He kissed her cheek. "I promise if you go with Emanuel, when you return, your troubles will be gone. Isn't it worth trusting him for that?"

Frank hesitated. He wasn't at all sure about going anywhere with a dude who looked like he'd just stepped out of a biblical epic. Besides, where could they go? To his knowledge the only thing that lay beyond this hill was a small glen full of trees, and beyond that, the Hudson River. The man kept smiling at him, and it seemed to reach down inside Frank and tug at his resistance. Still, he fought the urge to take the extended hand.

He turned to Steve. "What about my patients, my job?"

"I've arranged everything. Dr. Carlson will take over

until you come back." Steve paused as though giving Frank time to think about it. "You have always trusted me as your friend before. Please take my word for it; you will not regret going with Emanuel."

Frank glanced at the robed man and then at Steve and Meghan.

"The choice has to be yours, my boy," Emanuel said softly, his voice sounding like the wind blowing through the pines.

Frank thought about it. What did he have to lose? If Steve was right and this guy could work miracles, then he had everything to gain. "What the hell? I can't feel any worse than I do now."

He covered the few feet separating them and took Emanuel's hand. Instantly, an overwhelming sense of peace washed over him. Emanuel smiled and ushered a dumbfounded, but docile Frank into the glen where an expanding, thick, glowing fog lay heavy over the snow-covered ground.

* * *

Inside the Gateway Cabin, the interior of Meghan's lantern glowed unusually bright. The increased brightness caught Steve's attention from where he sat on the sofa facing the blazing fire and cuddling his wife. "Look at that. What do you suppose is happening right now?"

Meghan snuggled down within his embrace and grinned. "Wonderful things," she said simply. "Two people are about to find themselves and each other, and if they allow themselves to heal enough to look, the one true miracle—love."

Chapter 4

With rising apprehension, as the man and Emanuel approached him, Alvin silently appraised his Assignment. He'd been told the man was a doctor, a pediatric cardiologist. At a distance he seemed youthful, too youthful, to be a surgeon who held tiny lives, literally, in the palm of his hand. But as the man drew closer, Alvin could see the lines that marked his handsome face, aging him prematurely, and the sadness that had taken up residence in his eyes. Alvin knew those telltale details all too well. On the few occasions when he'd allowed himself to look in a mirror, he'd seen them in his own face.

Clara had been right. Life had not been kind to this man, and his slumped, wide shoulders and shuffling step testified to the fact that the burden he carried was a heavy one that pressed unrelentingly on his soul. That realization, rather than easing Alvin's mind, caused him to straighten his spine and close down that portion of his memory that always brought a stinging pain to his heart. How could he help this poor soul find peace and self-forgiveness, when he could find none for himself?

He was afraid Emanuel had made a horrendous mistake in assigning Frank to him. When placing an Assignment before, Emanuel had never been wrong, but there was always a first time for everything, even for the village Elder. Alvin had nothing to offer Frank Donovan. Nothing except empathy and the hopelessness that reflected his own misery.

"Alvin," Emanuel said, coming to a halt before him, "this is Dr. Frank Donovan. You'll be his mentor for the duration of his stay with us." Emanuel's easy smile took away none of the tension in Alvin's body.

"Hi." Frank extended his hand.

Alvin nodded stiffly, but didn't offer to shake Frank's hand. Getting too familiar with this man spelled nothing but trouble for both of them.

Frank frowned and dropped his hand back to his side. He sent Emanuel a questioning glance, but the Elder was looking directly at Alvin.

"Are you sure about this?" Alvin asked.

Emanuel nodded almost imperceptibly. "Faith and trust, Alvin, faith and trust." He turned to Frank. "Alvin will show you where you'll be living while you're here."

For a long time, Alvin stared coldly at Frank and said nothing, then he merely inclined his head the slightest degree and turned to lead the way toward the most diminutive cottage set on the edge of the small, verdant town square. Without a word, Frank followed.

While they walked, Frank assessed the man who trudged on ahead of him. Upon his first glimpse of Alvin, Frank had thought about an old TV show he'd loved as a kid called *Grizzly Adams*. It had been about a mountain man who lived alone, dressed in buckskins, and sported a bush of facial hair. But that's where the similarities ended.

The TV actor had been private, but friendly, and had not used his facial hair as something to hide behind. Frank believed in his gut that this was not the case with this stoic man. Adams had interacted with people and the wild creatures of the mountains. Frank could see Alvin relating to the wild animals, but keeping any human at an emotional arm's length. Adams's eyes had sparkled with humor and life. Alvin's eyes were as dead as Frank's. This mentor of his was certainly an enigma.

Giving up on any attempt at understanding Alvin Tripp, Frank looked around him for the old man who had brought him here. Emanuel seemed to have totally dismissed them and was making his way to a little thatched cottage surrounded by a myriad of colorful flowers on the far side of the square. His long robe stirred up dust devils as he walked. Just as he stepped onto the threshold of the cottage, he turned toward them and caught Frank's gaze. The Elder studied them for a moment, and then he disappeared from sight inside the cottage.

Left to follow the retreating figure ahead of him, Frank hurried to catch up. He fell into step beside Alvin, and was struck immediately by how large the man was. Coming in at three inches over six feet, Frank was not a small man, but Alvin dwarfed him.

"So, how long have you been here?" Frank asked, trying to engage Tripp in conversation.

When Tripp continued to remain silent, Frank shrugged and took in the place that would be his home for an indeterminate length of time.

The mist that had surrounded the village on his arrival had dissipated. Streaks of sunlight lay like narrow golden paths across the row of thatched cottages. The dirt path that had brought him and Emanuel over the footbridge meandered between two rows of cottages that looked as though they had been snatched from a history book on Colonial America and plopped down here in the Hudson Highlands.

Vibrant blooms of a variety of flowers surrounded each cottage on all sides. The gardens reminded him of those that Sandy, his deceased wife, had labored over around their house. She'd taken such care with them, nursing seedlings into mature plants until they burst forth with color, seemingly at her command. Sandy hadn't had just a green thumb. She'd had a green hand. She could have stuck a dead twig into the ground, and the next day, it would have been a flourishing plant.

Pain sliced through his heart so strong his footsteps faltered. Angrily, he pushed the cloying memories away. Like persistent cobwebs, they clung, vying for his attention.

With renewed determination, he cleared his mind and concentrated on the village, which seemed to exist in a state of perpetual spring.

Spaced periodically between the cottages were light poles holding lanterns. Since he saw no sign of electricity, he assumed, when lit, they must be illuminated by candles. Aside from him and Alvin, not another human being was in evidence. Other than the cottages, there was no sign that anyone lived there.

A chill shivered over him. What a strange little place this was. What had Steve and Meghan gotten him into? As quickly as the doubt arose, it disappeared. Steve was his friend. He had never steered him wrong on anything before. Why would he start now? Still. . .

* * *

Emanuel sipped at the steaming coffee and looked intently at the flickering white candle in front of him. Clara watched him from across the trestle table, impatiently waiting for him to speak. She glanced out the window to where Carrie sat beside the stream in the waning sunlight.

Her impatience won out. "Are you going to tell me what happened, or are you going to study that candle for the rest of the day?"

As if rousing from a deep sleep, Emanuel blinked, and then raised his gaze to Clara and stared at her as if he'd just noticed her.

"I'm sorry, my dear. I was thinking about Alvin and wondering if I've made a mistake in assigning Frank to him." He sighed and set the cup down. "Perhaps I should have listened to you when you cautioned me against it."

Clara chuckled softly. "You forget that I deferred to your wisdom."

He glanced at her. "I know. But perhaps you should have stated your case more strongly and made me see the error of my judgment."

Clara touched his weathered hand. "Although I often foolishly question you, in all the years I've known you, you have never been wrong in your judgment."

Emanuel chuckled. "But without your questions I would have no reason to delve deeper for my answers, to weigh my own wisdom. You, my dear, are one of my greatest assets."

Clara waved off his compliment with her hand. "You have always found the answers to any problem within your heart. What does it tell you this time?"

For a long moment, the only sound in the room was the crackle of the fire burning brightly in the hearth.

"It's telling me that. . ." He thought for a time, seeming to choose his words carefully. "It's telling me that sometimes it takes another with the same wound to heal an afflicted soul."

She patted his hand and rose to refresh his cup. "Then perhaps you should listen to it." She replaced the coffeepot and resumed her seat. "Alvin has lived with his pain for far too long. You said so yourself. It's time he found peace."

* * *

Frank stepped over the threshold of the tiny cottage. The odor of disuse assailed him. The plain wood floor held no rug. A crudely made table flanked by four nondescript chairs resided somewhat sadly in the center of the room. A simple, pine cupboard stood against one wall. The fireplace held no fire, but lay as cold and unwelcoming as the cottage itself. Other than the rifle leaning against the wall near the fireplace, there were no signs that anyone inhabited the cottage.

Oddly, it reminded Frank of the apartment he'd moved into after Sandy's death. He couldn't bear staying in the house they'd built and furnished together, the house with the nursery upstairs that would never hold their child. It had been a constant reminder of all he'd lost through his own foolish stupidity and carelessness. He'd sold it, complete with all its contents.

"Your room is over there," Alvin said, bringing Frank abruptly out of his memories. "We're about the same size, so the clothes in the dresser should fit you. The pants might be a bit long."

"Won't you need your clothes?"

Alvin shook his head. "I've got enough." His assessing gaze slid over Frank's rumpled sports jacket and slacks. "Looks as if you'll be needing a change."

"Thanks." Silence stretched out between them.

"So. . .you live here?"

"Most days, when I'm not traveling for Emanuel."

"Nice place," Frank lied.

"It's somewhere to eat and lay my head," Alvin replied, noncommittally.

Frank almost laughed out loud. How many times, when someone asked him about his apartment, had he spoken those exact words? A place to eat, sleep, and do battle with the nightmares that visited him nightly.

"It seems like we have a lot in common," Frank said in an effort to still the voices of his memory and make conversation with his. . .landlord?

Alvin's head snapped up. He glared at Frank and then walked to the door. "I have things to do," he finally said. "If you get hungry, there's some food in the cupboard. Help yourself." Turning on his heel, he left the cottage.

Frank stared at the closed door, trying to recall what he'd said that could have elicited Alvin's reaction. Nothing rang a bell. He shrugged and went to explore the room that had been delegated to him.

Like the outer room, this one was barren, except for a single bed with a plain, brown quilt covering it and a dresser positioned against the wall with the only window the room boasted. Deep down, the plainness pleased Frank. No frills, no reason to become attached to it. A place to lay his head at the end of a long day.

Satisfied with the simplicity, Frank left the room and the cottage to explore the village. As he stepped from the cottage, deep shadows fell over him, and he realized that the sun had set behind the distant mountains while he'd been inside.

With a leisurely pace, he strolled past Alvin's cottage to the end of the village he had not yet seen. As he walked, he became aware of the sound of running water. A stream? Perhaps the stream that flowed beneath the footbridge leading into Renaissance. Quickening his pace, he headed in the direction of the sound that he now believed to be water cascading over rocks.

He rounded a large blooming lilac bush to find himself in someone's garden. Beyond the rows and rows of blooms was another cottage. Bigger than Alvin's and quite unlike it, it gave him a feeling of warmth, of acceptance, of welcome.

Looking up toward the curling smoke rising from the chimney, his gaze fastened on an image in one of the upper windows. A woman. Lit from behind, her hair seemed to glow like an iridescent, fiery veil surrounding her head and slim shoulders. She remained at the window for a long time. Frank felt her gaze on him, but he was unable to either move or divert his eyes. Instead, he drank in the sight of her. What he could see of her stole his breath. She was beautiful.

Something stirred inside him. Something that he hadn't felt in a very long time. Something painful that left him reluctant to acknowledge it. Life.

But this foreign feeling knew a very short existence. How could he stand here looking at this woman? How could he betray Sandy's memory like that? Swamped by guilt, Frank tore his gaze away.

What had he been thinking? He was not here to get involved with any woman in any way, no matter how slight. He was here to come to terms with the monster eating away at his insides.

He started back to Alvin's and found he could not resist one more glance over his shoulder. But she was gone. Though her absence gave birth to intense relief, the feelings the sight of her had evoked remained, warming dark places inside him that had known nothing except cold regret, icy guilt, and dark loss for far too long. The stinging pain of their rebirth was almost more than Frank could stand.

CHAPTER 5

Frozen in place and shielded by the window frame, Carrie stared into the night, unable to look away from the retreating man who had lingered beneath her window. Without being able to see his features in the waning light, she had nevertheless felt a sadness emanating from him, a sadness that seemed to connect her to him in some obscure way. That anyone could feel such overwhelming sadness wrenched at her heart, and she had to physically control the urge to dash downstairs and go after him to help him, to offer some kind of comfort.

"That's just crazy," she told herself, when he'd finally disappeared from sight and she was able to leave the window. "You have no idea who he is, what his problem is, or what you could possibly do for him. Besides, you have your own problems to sort through."

But even her self-reprimand wasn't enough to move

her thoughts away from the man. She dropped onto the edge of the bed and cast another glance toward the window. Why did she feel as if an invisible thread had spun out across the distance separating them and bound them together?

"Go to bed, Carrie," she told herself. "This whole day has obviously been a mental strain, and it's thrown your imagination into high gear."

Carrie stood and began to remove her clothes. By the time she had put on the soft cotton nightgown that Clara had given her and was snuggled beneath the heavenly down comforter, she had convinced herself she'd just experienced a surge of overactive imagination. Nothing a good night's sleep couldn't bring a little logic and clarity to in the morning.

With that, she closed her eyes, and feeling the world around her blur and darken, she gave herself up to the oblivion of slumber.

* * *

The distinct feeling of being watched awoke Carrie. Fighting off the dregs of sleep, she slowly opened her eyes. Her breath caught in her throat. Instantly, she was fully awake.

The room was dark, lit only by the moonlight

spilling through the window, but standing beside her bed, hovering over her, was the distinct silhouette of a man. Though his face was a blur, like the kind of thing they do on TV when a person wishes to conceal their identity, she had no trouble making out the fists doubled up at his sides and his stiff stance. Anger emanated from him as thick as the fog she'd seen on the footbridge.

Who was he angry at? Her?

He took a step closer to the bed. She cringed and backed deeper into the flimsy protection of the pillows. A scream for help started building deep inside her, but her voice was choked off by the terror building in her throat. She swallowed the scream, knowing instinctively that, if she were to allow it to escape, she would be punished by the man. That those clenched fists would come down on her without regret for the pain they'd inflict.

Despite the cold fear that gripped her, she could feel her gown sticking to the sweat covering her quivering body. By now, she was shaking so hard that the bed vibrated beneath her.

"Please," she whispered. "Please don't hurt me."

When he took another step toward her, she allowed the suppressed scream to burst forth.

* * *

Carrie bolted upright in bed. A light sheen of sweat coated her shaking body. Her saturated gown stuck to her legs, hampering her frantic attempts to scramble from the bed. Finally free of the clinging fabric, she clambered to the floor and backed into a dark corner. Her breath tore from her lungs in short, desperate gasps.

Her gaze darted around the room, straining to find the intruder. She saw the bear talisman her grandmother had given her lying on the night table and snatched it up. Clutching it to her chest, she continued to search the room for the faceless dream man. But she found no one. She was completely alone. No would-be assailant hovered ready to attack. No one lurked in the shadows. No one was about to strike out at her. She was completely alone.

Heaving a sigh of relief, she collapsed onto the bed. She'd been dreaming. But who had that faceless man been? Was he someone from her past? Someone she couldn't remember? Or was he just a figment of her tortured imagination? Maybe the man beneath her window?

Quickly, she hurried to the open window and peered out to the gardens below. They were shadowed and quiet. The sweet fragrance of lilacs drifted up to her. She listened intently. The only sound that came to her was the gurgle of the stream, the chirp of the crickets, and the occasional hoot of an owl. Despite that, she remained at the window for a long time, watching and waiting, jumping at every rustling leaf, every flower nodding in the slight breeze. But no lone figure moved amid the snarl of flowers and bushes.

She returned to the bed and buried her face in her hands. It couldn't be the man from beneath the window. The man at her bedside had emanated pure evil, and she'd felt nothing but sadness from the man outside. If, indeed, there had been a man outside her window, and he had not been just another ghost from her tortured imagination.

Frustrated, she racked her brain to see if any of the things she recalled about the faceless man in her dream would clue her in to his identity. But nothing came. His nondescript brown hair and average build could belong to anyone. Without a face to identify him, she had no way to answer her own questions.

Even though she decided that the man was more than likely a result of something she'd eaten for supper, the terror remained. It wrapped her like a chilled blanket, the cold seeping into her very bones. Perhaps he was just a faceless dream figure. But perhaps he was a whole lot more.

* * *

"Good morning, my dear." Clara smiled cheerfully at her as

Carrie stepped off the bottom stair into the keeping room.

"Mornin'," Carrie mumbled in response. She tried her best to add a smile, but her head throbbed, and every muscle and bone in her body loudly protested the lack of sleep.

"Bad night?"

"Hmm," Carrie mumbled in reply. Every movement, every verbalization, felt as though a thousand hammers pounded unmercifully at her temples.

"Have some coffee, dear. You'll be surprised at how much better you'll feel." Clara poured a cup of the life-giving liquid and set it in front of Carrie.

Eager for anything that would relieve the unrelenting pain slicing through her head, she took a tentative sip, and miraculously, the fatigue began to ebb from her body. With each successive sip, more of the tiredness left Carrie, eventually taking with it all signs of the merciless headache. She had no idea what Clara had added to the coffee, but whatever it was, she should bottle it. The old woman could retire to a mansion on the Riviera on what she'd make. But when Carrie looked around her, she couldn't imagine Clara in any other setting but this one. The hominess of the cottage suited her perfectly.

"That did the trick," she said, finally able to return Clara's smile. "Thanks."

"Always does," Clara said matter-of-factly and then

headed for the cupboard near the fireplace. "I have some-thing for you."

"For me?"

"Yes, Sara Spencer, the village shopkeeper, sent it over." From the cupboard she extracted a large, rectangular package wrapped in brown paper and tied with a string, and then carried it to the table and deposited it in front of Carrie.

Carrie looked at the package, then to Clara. "Why would she give me anything? She doesn't even know me."

"We all know you, Carrie, even if you don't know yourself." Clara's blue eyes sparkled. "If she sent it, she knows you need it. Sarah's stores are not always meant to nourish your physical hunger. Ofttimes they're meant to feed the soul and nurture the mind."

Puzzled by Clara's statement, Carrie untied the string holding the package together. Before she tore the paper off, she turned to Clara. "If you all know me, why can't you tell me anything about myself?"

"Those are things you have to learn for yourself. That's why you're here."

Still puzzled, Carrie let it go. Obviously, Clara was not going to tell her anything she didn't want her to know. Turning her attention back to the package, she slowly removed the paper. Inside rested a scarred wooden box about the size of a man's briefcase, its surface mottled with splashes of various colors of paint.

Carrie didn't stop to wonder how she knew how big a briefcase was. She'd grown accustomed to small bits of generic information popping up in her memory. Unfortunately, none of it helped her to remember the important things: who she was, where she'd come from, and how she'd ended up on that snowy street covered in blood.

Instead of dwelling on the unattainable, she gingerly opened the tarnished gold latch at the front of the box and lifted the lid. Inside the box, scattered about and obviously having been used, were tubes of oil paint, twisted and rolled up at the end like used toothpaste tubes. Beside them were brushes of various sizes, their handles stained with paint, their blond bristles clean and encased in clear plastic sleeves. On the bottom, an artist's palette, splotched with colorful blemishes, attested to its use.

Confusion and puzzlement drew her brows together. "I don't understand."

"It's yours, Carrie."

She glanced up at Clara. "Do I paint?"

Clara nodded and her mobcap wriggled and danced above her gray curls. "You used to."

"I used to?" The frown on her face deepened. "I don't understand. You mean I don't do it anymore?"

Clara sat beside her and took her hand, warming her cold fingers. "You haven't totally given it up, but your recent efforts have lost something. Once, long ago, you painted glorious pictures, Carrie. The pictures came straight from your heart. No one could look at them without seeing you and feeling your love for your subject. Recently, your paintings have lost that feeling. They've become harsh and devoid of that special love."

Carrie tried to absorb the information and process it into some form that would give rise to a memory, any memory. The fire crackled behind them. Birds chirped outside the window. She could hear Clara's soft breathing beside her. But the memories remained beyond her reach.

"Why did my paintings change so radically? Why did I stop?" she finally asked, looking imploringly at Clara for an answer.

But even as she asked, she could see Clara close down and knew no answer would be forthcoming.

"I'm afraid you'll have to discover that on your own, my dear."

Of course. Wasn't that why Irma and Meghan had sent her here, to find herself? To learn who she was, who she'd been, and who she could become? Carrie understood all that, but a hint would have been helpful to get her started down that path.

As if reading her thoughts, Clara pointed to a small, engraved plaque inside the lid of the box. The plaque read: *To Carrie Henderson, in recognition of her outstanding artistic talent, from her Fifth-Grade Art Teacher, Mrs. Virginia Carol.*

Remembering that the slip of paper she'd found in her pocket with her first name on it was from an art store, she smiled. "Is this me? Am I really an artist?"

Clara nodded. "It was presented to you as first prize in an art contest when you were ten years old. As you grew older, your talent matured into something very special. . .for a time. . ."

"But how did you get this?"

Clara said simply, "We have our ways."

Unable to totally believe what all this meant, Carrie stared at the box. This was a piece of her missing past. A part of who she had been. She read the words over and over, cherishing every letter. She wanted to tear the plaque from the wood and cradle it close. *Carrie Henderson.* She had a last name. She was *Carrie Henderson.* And she could paint. She was an artist. The knowledge made her feel like she did when she opened a longed-for gift.

As quickly as the elation had come, it vanished. She had no recollection of squeezing those tubes of paint, wielding those brushes across a brilliant white canvas and creating the pictures Clara had said she'd painted, or of being presented with what obviously had been a milestone in her life.

Overwhelming, depressing blankness filled her

mind. Tears burned behind her eyes, but she blinked them away. Feeling sorry for herself wasn't going to do anything to bring back the memories. What, she wondered, would?

Clara stood, walked to the cupboard where she'd gotten the paint case, and then pulled two white canvases and a wooden easel from it and handed them to Carrie. "Go outside and see if you can remember how to create beauty on a blank canvas."

Obediently, Carrie picked up the canvases, the easel, and the paint set. "But I. . ."

Clara took her hand and squeezed it tight, then released it and eased Carrie toward the back door. "It'll come. Have faith and trust, and it will come."

Without further protest, Carrie quietly left the cottage and headed for the rock by the stream, where she hoped to rediscover this small piece of herself.

CHAPTER 6

Frank opened his eyes and blinked. Where in hell was he? He gazed around at the unfamiliar surroundings and waited for the gauzy veil of sleep to dissipate. As it did, the events of the previous day sifted into his mind. He was in a cottage in a strange little village that had materialized out of a mist. He'd been assigned a mentor of sorts, Alvin Tripp, a man who had closed himself off from everyone around him, including Frank.

Sitting up and swinging his feet to the floor, Frank cocked an ear, listening for any sign of movement in the outer room. Silence. Tripp was either still sleeping or he'd already left the cottage. Resigned to spending the day by himself, he poured water from the pitcher into the plain white porcelain bowl and washed the sleep from his face.

After he'd donned the clothes Tripp had indicated he'd find in the old dresser, Frank stood in front of the

79

mirror. He smiled and smoothed his hands over the laundry-softened flannel. The red-and-black plaid shirt was too big, and the worn jeans had to be folded up at the cuffs, but they felt good. Homey, comfortable. Wearing someone else's clothes and waking up in someone else's house brought rise to a certain serenity.

Maybe that was the ultimate plan for him. Tripp would brainwash him into believing he was someone else, someone without a tortured past, someone who hadn't killed his wife and unborn child. Maybe the man would remove all memory of Sandy and the baby from his mind. Maybe that was the way he'd finally break free of his memories. But was that what he really wanted?

The smile melted from his face. He didn't want to forget Sandy or their baby. All he craved was to be free of the gnawing guilt that dogged him like a persistent specter. Taking on a new identity would not accomplish that. Besides, he didn't want a new identity. He liked who he was, and he loved being a pediatric cardiologist. All he really wanted was peace of mind, hope for a future with a little happiness, and maybe even a woman to love. Although right now the idea of loving anyone after Sandy seemed as remote as the African desert.

Unexpectedly, the woman he'd seen in the window the night before popped into his mind. Pushing her image away from him, Frank went into the outer room and found the meager breakfast Tripp had left him—a large slice of fresh-baked bread and a rosy, red apple. Frank got the unmistakable feeling that his so-called mentor was avoiding him. For a moment, he considered looking for Tripp, but then he tossed that idea. If Tripp didn't want to talk to him, who was Frank to hunt him down and insist? Certainly, if he did want to talk to Frank, he knew where to find him. This place wasn't all that expansive.

Grabbing the chunk of bread and apple from the table, he left the cottage.

Outside, the sun shown with a brilliance Frank had never seen before and comfortably warmed him through the flannel shirt. White, fluffy clouds dotted a sky so blue it almost blinded him to look at it. The heady fragrance of lilacs and roses drifted to him on the slight breeze stirring the trees, reminding him of his grandmother's garden where he'd played with all the innocence of a child who had no idea what demons crouched ready to invade his future.

Taking alternate bites of the apple's sweet, juicy flesh and the delicious bread, he chewed and strolled aimlessly along the path that gently meandered back and forth between the cottages, his spirit lighter than it had been in a very long time.

* * *

At the edge of the thick forest, Alvin kept an eye on Frank as he walked in the general direction of Clara Webb's cottage. Why had Emanuel given him this impossible task? How was he going to help this man?

The weight of his burden almost drove Alvin double. He needed answers, and there was one place he knew he had a chance of finding some. Determinedly, he aimed his footsteps toward the cottage just this side of the footbridge, the cottage that Meghan had once occupied until Steve had come to the village and their love had moved them outside Renaissance.

The cottage was now occupied by the new village Healer, Ellie Stanton. For reasons either unknown to him or ones that he didn't want to admit to, Alvin always found solace and comfort in Ellie's presence. But lately, he'd come to the realization that more often than not he gravitated to her for more than just spiritual guidance and the wisdom of her words.

* * *

Carrie made herself comfortable on the grass beside the stream. She propped the canvases against the rock, then opened the paint case and set it next to her. Automatically, she opened tubes, fanned out her brushes, and then deposited small globs of paint on the palette. She was ready to paint. But how? She had no recollection of even holding a paintbrush, much less creating anything recognizable with it.

For a moment, she gazed out over the stream and the surrounding forest in search of a subject to paint, and then at the blank canvas, not really sure what she'd do even if she did settle on a subject.

Then, when she'd just about given up, without consciously making a decision, she picked up a brush, dipped it into the black paint, and began to work. Seeming to have a mind of its own, the brush swirled across the canvas, bringing to life a figure of a man in an almost abstract setting. Around him she placed garish smears of red, yellow, orange, purple, and black.

Carrie's fingers gripped the brush handle as though it were a lifeline. Her clenched jaw set her teeth firmly against each other. Again and again she replenished the paint on her brush and continued to angrily apply more and more color to the canvas. With each brushstroke, she could feel the contact to her own skin, just as though each movement of the brush was a tiny razor blade scratching across her flesh.

At last, she applied the final slash of paint. Her breath came fast. Her heart beat heavy in her ears. She stared at what she'd done.

"Oh my God."

The brush dropped from her numb fingers. Her hands flew to cover her mouth in astonishment. She couldn't believe she'd actually created the grotesque picture before her.

Distorted, lightning-bolt-shaped splashes of bright red, orange, black, purple, and yellow cut brutally across the canvas. Black layered the top where a bright blue sky should have been.

The geometric angles were sharp and pointed, the colors dark and foreboding. This painting was violent, angry, and cruel, and at the same time filled with stark fear, agonizing pain, and a deep, dark sense of hopelessness. She saw many things in this painting, but what Carrie didn't see was any of the love and softness Clara said Carrie had always put in her paintings.

What was most disturbing could be found n the center of the painting—a man without a face. At his feet was a large, black hole, and just over his shoulder was a black-and-blue hand adorned with a wedding band and poised to push him in.

* * *

Frank's steps came to a halt. Without realizing where

his wanderings were taking him, he'd come back to the very spot in the garden below the window where he'd seen the woman the evening before. To his surprise and delight, a few feet from him sat that very woman, staring at a rather ugly painting propped against a rock at the stream's edge. From the paint tubes, brushes, and other paraphernalia scattered around her, he assumed she had been the artist.

"Interesting painting," he said, slipping through the bushes and walking to her side to get a closer look at both the picture and the woman.

"Oh!" She jumped backward, hand over her heart, and almost toppled over into the grass at his feet. He grabbed her forearm just in time to prevent her fall.

She looked up at him. Breathless, he could do no more than stare. Though the picture appeared even uglier up close, the woman was one of the most beautiful creatures he'd ever seen. With eyes as green as emeralds and hair that reminded him of sleek, reddish-brown silk, he had a hard time dragging his gaze away, but he forced himself to and concentrated instead on the painting.

"I'm sorry. I didn't mean to startle you." When she was steady again, he drew his hand away. "I was just admiring your painting."

"*Admiring* is hardly the word I would have used. It should be burned." Her voice slid over him, warming him and taking away all his trepidations about being there.

Frank laughed. "Okay, so I was being polite." He studied the painting, tilting his head this way and that. "It's really quite. . .weird." Immediately, he regretted his words. He glanced at the woman to see if he'd offended her. "I'm sorry. That was rude."

"Yes, it is weird." She pushed herself to her feet, picked up the painting, and held it at arm's length, then laughed. "And please don't apologize. That's probably the kindest thing anyone could say about it."

He turned to look at her. Her green eyes came alive with suppressed laughter. Her creamy complexion had taken on a hint of a pink flush of embarrassment. A breeze picked up a few strands of her hair from behind her ear and whipped them across her cheek. His fingers itched to push the hairs back, and then trail his fingertips down her smooth cheek. Before he could act on the urge, she captured the loose hairs and tucked them back in place behind her ear.

He gestured toward the canvas, groping for anything that would take his mind off his totally unexpected thoughts. "Why is he faceless?"

Her features seemed to melt into a troubled frown. When the laughter vanished from her eyes, he was instantly sorry he'd asked the question.

"I don't know," she said, just above a whisper. "I

guess he's faceless because. . .I dreamed him that way."

"I kind of feel sorry for him."

She turned to Frank. "Why?"

"Because he's obviously someone you are not very fond of, and from that hand ready to push him into the hole, someone for whom you wish bad things."

She turned back to the painting and studied it for a long time. "I certainly hope not, but you may be right."

"I'm Frank," he said, realizing he hadn't introduced himself. "Frank Donovan."

She smiled, and the light returned to her eyes. For Frank, the whole day got immeasurably brighter.

"I'm Carrie, Carrie Henderson. . .I think."

Frank frowned this time. "You think? Don't you know?"

The sparkle of those green eyes turned to the color of a misty drizzle on a depressingly cloudy day. "No, I don't. Or at least I'm not sure. People here have told me that's my name." She shrugged, and though he was sure the gesture was meant to be dismissive, something told him that she did not consider it as inconsequential as she'd like him to believe. She emitted a mirthless laugh. "Since I can't remember anything about myself, I have to take their word for it."

Amnesia? "Well, I like that name, Carrie Henderson. It fits you, so I hope they're right."

"Thanks." She smiled again, and Frank's heart sped up.

He took a deep steadying breath and dropped to the rock. The last time he'd been hit in the gut with this giddy, euphoric feeling, he'd been picking up Sandy for their first date. To cover the sudden surge of guilt that invariably came with the thought of his wife, he picked up a handful of pebbles and tossed them into the stream. They landed with a series of soft *plunks*. Concentric ripples fanned out from it like a series of chains on a silver necklace. Eventually, the movement of the ripples played out, and the surface of the water became smooth once more, allowing him to see his troubled expression in the water. Next to his reflection the woman's face shown back at him.

Carrie studied him while his back was turned. The way his hair lay in dark, loose curls all over his head gave him a boyish appearance. His gray eyes had appraised her in a way that told her he saw more than the surface of his fellow man. However, beyond his handsome face and muscular build, Carrie felt a definite calmness in his presence, and at the same time a sadness that lay heavy on his soul.

"So, Frank Donovan, who are you? Do you live here?"

Frank laughed. The sound made her smile.

"No, I don't live here. Like you, I'm an Assignment,

or so they tell me." He brushed the pebbles' soil from his hands, hands that looked gentle and caring, and then swung around on the rock to face her. "I'm a pediatric cardiologist at a hospital in the city." She frowned. "A children's heart doctor," Frank explained and then studied her for a moment. "You said you couldn't remember your name. Is it only your name you can't recall?"

She shook her head. "Oh, how I wish that were true."

"Do you know that when you shake your head like that, your hair catches the sunlight and it's almost as though a fire is buried within it?"

A deep heat permeated her cheeks, and she lowered her gaze. She ignored his outrageous observation. "Unfortunately, I can't remember anything at all of my past."

Even as she ignored his intimate remark, Carrie wondered what had prompted him to say such a thing to a woman he'd known for a grand total of several minutes.

Evidently following her lead to overlook his remark, he pointed at the strange painting. "And this, I take it, is an attempt at finding out something about your identity."

The thought that this painting could have anything to do with who she was sent shivers over her. "Yes, but I'm afraid it's just muddied the waters even more. Now I'm wondering if I *want* to find a past that belongs to someone who could create that."

He stood and stared at the canvas for a time.

"Psychology was never one of my strong points, but I'd say that is not the real you."

She laughed. "Please don't tell me that you think it's born of something buried deep in my psyche."

"We all have a dark side, I'm told. Maybe this is yours. You said you dreamed him without a face." She nodded. "There must be a reason you couldn't or wouldn't put a face on him. What else did you dream about? Maybe there's a clue hidden there."

She sighed. "If there was, then I don't remember it. All I recall is the faceless man standing over me. I know he frightened me." She opened her mouth to say more, but stopped.

A large orange and black butterfly had landed on her shoulder. Carrie stood stone still. It sat there for a few seconds, exercising its wings, and then it flew off into the flowering shrubs behind them. Carrie laughed like a delighted child.

As if punched in the gut, Frank sucked in his breath. A surge of the same feeling he had experienced the night before beneath her window coursed through him. Last night, he'd only guessed it was the return of life. Now, he was certain. This woman had him doing something he hadn't done in a very long time—looking forward to tomorrow.

Almost magically, Frank became acutely aware of his surroundings. The color of the flowers had become more brilliant, their fragrances headier; the gurgle of the stream reminded him of the laughter of children; the wisps of clouds dotting the sky were more vividly white, the sky itself a more dazzling blue. In short, like it or not, Frank Donovan was returning to the land of the living.

"Why don't you try painting something else? Maybe now that you've gotten that out of your system," he pointed at the garish painting, "you can paint something appealing to the eye."

Carrie glanced at the paint box, then at the second blank canvas. She picked up a brush.

CHAPTER 7

Alvin knocked on Ellie's cottage door. Moments later it swung open to reveal a lovely young woman dressed in an ankle-length, navy blue skirt and a white peasant blouse. Her long, blond hair hung in loose waves over her shoulders, framing her peaches-and-cream face, and her bright blue eyes danced with pleasure at seeing him. She seemed to have an inner merriment, which was an intricate part of why Alvin liked her so much.

"Alvin, how nice to see you." She moved to the side. "Come in, please."

Alvin stepped over the threshold and then went directly into the cottage's quaint living room. Many of the things that Meghan, the previous village Healer and this cottage's prior occupant, had kept there still remained: the clock with no hands that ticked away the time in the corner, the curio cabinet that held some of the mementos of Assignments who had passed through the former Healer's care, and the two well-worn armchairs that flanked the large, fieldstone fireplace. Even the basket containing a colorful tangle of embroidery thread still sat beside one of the armchairs, as if Meghan had just left the room for a moment, but would return presently.

But along with the remnants of Meghan's occupation of the cottage, Ellie had added her own special signature, and in doing so, had made the dwelling hers. A bright-colored, braided rug covered the pine floor in front of the hearth. Curled up on it and basking in the glow of the fire burning cheerfully behind him was a white dog, a stray that had wandered into the village and adopted Ellie, and whom she had christened Ghost for his habit of disappearing for days at a time and then suddenly reappearing on her doorstep. Curled comfortably amid Ghost's legs was an orange cat named Ginger. Neither acknowledged Alvin's arrival with more than a raised eyelid.

He strode to his customary seat in one of the armchairs and sat.

"Can I get you anything?" Ellie asked, coming to stand beside him.

Alvin shook his head. The only thing he needed didn't come in a cup or a glass, nor could it be laid out on a pretty plate. "I'd like to talk, if you have some time."

Ellie smiled and sank into the other armchair. She

curled her legs beneath her and pulled her skirt down to cover her bent knees and bare feet. "I always have all the time in the world for you."

Alvin met her gaze. He wished that were true. He'd like nothing better than to spend every waking moment with Ellie. But that was something that couldn't or wouldn't ever happen, so he was better off not even dreaming about it. Sweeping his mind clean of such empty wishes, he concentrated on his present dilemma.

"It's about my Assignment."

Ellie didn't experience any surprise at Alvin's announcement that he had an Assignment.

"Emanuel told me about Dr. Donovan," she said in answer to his questioning expression. She didn't add that she was in total agreement with Emanuel's decision to try to help Alvin by placing him in a position in which he'd have to help someone else facing a like predicament. From their first meeting, she'd known Alvin had something gnawing away at him, something that had been troubling him for a long time. But as long as he chose not to face it or share it with anyone, she was helpless to show him the way through the mire of his problems. She also knew that as long as Alvin had this shadow hanging over him, he could not go on with his life, a life of which she wanted very much to be a part.

For a long time, she didn't say anything and instead gave

Alvin the opportunity to gather his thoughts. Obviously he was deeply distressed and rushing him wouldn't help.

Ghost rose from the hearth rug, arched his back while he stretched his legs out in front of him, and then ambled over to her. Ginger turned onto her back with her paws in the air and ignored the removal of her comfortable resting place. The dog laid his head in Ellie's lap and turned his soulful eyes up to her in a silent plea for attention. Returning her gaze to Alvin, Ellie automatically scratched absently behind the dog's floppy ears.

When the silence had stretched out as long as Ellie was willing to allow, she cleared her throat, drawing Alvin's attention away from his contemplation of the floor at his feet.

"What about your Assignment is troubling you?"

Alvin made a disdainful sound. "Everything."

"Such as?"

Sitting up, Alvin leaned forward and rested his forearms on his muscular thighs. "Such as, Emanuel thinks I can help Donovan."

"And can you?"

"No."

"Why not?"

Alvin stared at her, his irritation at her lack of help clear in his expression. He opened his mouth, but then snapped it closed and shook his head.

Ellie patted Ghost's shaggy head and, needing her entire concentration on Alvin, mumbled, "Enough," to the animal.

The dog meandered back to the hearth rug, walked in a circle a couple of times, then flopped down beside Ginger, sighed heavily, and closed his eyes. The cat immediately snuggled into the arch made by the dog's curled body. Even from this distance, the cat's contented, rhythmic purrs vibrated loud enough for Ellie to hear.

Ellie shifted her gaze back to Alvin. Her heart ached for him. How she wished she could instill such contentment in the troubled man seated across from her. She cared deeply for Alvin, but until he looked inside himself and exorcised his demons, she could do nothing to ease his mind or his conscience.

"Alvin, the best way to help Frank Donovan is to get him to talk about what's caused him to feel he has to carry a burden that's not his to bear. Perhaps when he pulls it out of the darkness to which he's consigned it and faces it head-on, he can look at it through clearer eyes. Hiding from our troubles only magnifies them in our minds until they become so overwhelming that it seems impossible to get past them."

Frustration bloomed on Alvin's face. "And exactly how do I get him to do that? Maybe he doesn't want to talk about it. Maybe he feels like if he does, he'll have to go back and relive it all over again. Maybe he can't stand that kind of pain anymore."

Ellie knew Alvin had ceased discussing Frank and was now talking about himself. "That's a decision he and he alone can make." She smiled and stood. "Perhaps you should find him and encourage him to talk about it." She placed a hand on Alvin's arm and squeezed. "You won't know if you don't try, Alvin."

Alvin stood, convinced that Ellie had known he was applying what she'd said to himself. But even if she had, it didn't help him with his problem with Frank. "I'll have to think on it," he mumbled and hurried to the door.

For the first time since Frank's arrival, Alvin turned toward the one refuge that offered him any measure of contentment, if indeed a guilty man could find such a commodity. It seemed the only way he would get this albatross from around his neck was to get Frank to talk. Unfortunately, he knew how reluctant Frank was to talk about his problems. Alvin would go to any lengths to avoid talking about his past, and he couldn't believe that Frank was any more eager to talk about his. But if Alvin wanted back his quiet life in the village, he'd have to find a way to get Frank to open up.

Alvin crossed the small footbridge. He took one step off it and felt as he'd been hit in the gut by a tree trunk. Everything went off tilt. His world spun in crazy, circles. The only thing to which he could compare it was when he was a kid and he'd spin in circles and then walked drunkenly around his house, waiting for his balance to return to normal.

As the spirals tightened, his stomach began to heave. Just as he was sure he could stand no more of the rotation, little by little the tornado-like feeling lessened. When everything finally settled down and stopped rotating, his vision slowly cleared. To his astonishment, he was sitting at the table in his cottage. For a moment, he was stunned, and then the explanation for what had just happened became painfully clear.

He couldn't leave the village. There was only one reason for that. Assignments, once they'd entered the village, could not leave until they came to terms with what had brought them there. Alvin was not only a mentor for an Assignment, he *was* an Assignment himself.

Swamped suddenly by unreasonable exhaustion, Alvin went to his bed and lay down. Moments later, his eyes drifted closed, and his breathing became regular and deep.

* * *

Alvin pressed the cordless phone more tightly to his ear and stared blindly out the twelfth-floor window of the

Marriott that looked down on the bustling Los Angeles street below. His reflection in the window clearly portrayed his irritation with the person on the other end of the telephone connection.

"You said you'd be back in three days, and you've already been gone for more than a week. You promised me you'd be home tomorrow, and now you're telling me you want to extend your trip another day? Where does this end, Alvin?" His wife's voice choked with emotion. "When are you going to put us before that damned business you love so much?"

He straightened. "That damned business just bought you a new car, Alice." He knew he was being pigheaded, but his anger drove him on.

A long sigh came through the receiver. "Do you think I wouldn't trade that car in a second for a few uninterrupted hours with my husband?"

Alvin gritted his teeth. Didn't she understand that this business was his future—their future? It was still in its infancy. He had to work hard at it now so it would be easier down the road. Once he had a well-established clientele, he would be able to spend all the time in the world with her.

Will you? a little voice in the back of his head prodded.

He pushed the voice aside. "For God's sake, Alice, it's one lousy day." He sighed, exhaustion driving him to end the conversation. "I'm very tired, and I have an early day tomorrow and a dinner meeting tomorrow night. I'm taking a red-eye out as soon as the meeting's over. I'll be home tomorrow morning. We can discuss this then." Silence met his promise, a promise he'd made too many times before, a promise he knew in his heart she no longer believed.

"Alice?"

Nothing.

"Alice, talk to me."

"Why, Alvin? You won't hear a thing I say anyway."

The phone went dead.

* * *

The next morning, his anger forgotten, Alvin hurried down the hallway to their Greenwich Village apartment with a distinctive bounce in his step. He couldn't wait to tell Alice how well everything had gone. Not only had he secured a large shipment of his computer chips to one of the biggest computer manufacturers in the world, but he'd also been told confidentially by the president of the company that, if this new chip worked, Alvin's company had a good chance of becoming their exclusive supplier. Alvin had no doubt it would work. He'd spent many long nights testing it with his engineers before approaching Grayson Tech.

This meant so much. He and Alice would be able to take their long-overdue honeymoon. She could buy that house in Westchester she'd had her heart set on for months, and furnish it any way she wanted. Life was going to be good from now on.

As he started to slip his key in the lock, he whistled a nondescript tune. When the door swung open at his touch, the tune died away. Giving the door a tentative shove, he stepped inside the apartment. He stopped dead in his tracks. His suitcase slipped unnoticed to the floor, along with his suit coat and briefcase. Silence. So much silence.

Then a high, piercing cry rent the air.

"Nooooo!"

* * *

Alvin sprang up in the bed. The dream still played vividly through his head, so vividly that he had to look around to make sure he was no longer in the Greenwich Village apartment he and his wife had shared. He flipped his long legs over the edge of the mattress and planted his feet on the solid wooden floor. With a deep sigh, he covered his face in his hands, his elbows propped on his thighs.

The dream was back. The same one each time. The

one that stopped just short of allowing him to see everything. But he had seen it, and the memory, even if his brain wouldn't allow him to see it again, would always be with him, because he didn't know how to erase it.

After that horrible morning, he'd walked away from it all. There was no longer any reason for him to pursue his dream. He'd had the one thing that really mattered stolen from him, the one thing he treasured above all else—his beloved Alice. Shortly after that, he'd met Irma in Central Park, and she'd sent him to Renaissance. He'd been there ever since.

He'd so hoped when he'd gone a few months without experiencing the dream that it meant he was past being tortured with memories on a nightly basis. Obviously, he'd counted his blessings too soon. Or had he?

He knew Emanuel had the power to do many things. Had he intentionally caused Alvin to recall the worst nightmare of his life? The more he thought about it, the more certain he became that the dream had been a product of Emanuel's well-meaning guidance.

He slammed his fist into the mattress, and then rose and strode angrily to the door.

CHAPTER 8

L ulled by the gurgle of the stream and the perfume of the abundance of flowers surrounding them, Frank leaned back on his elbows in the grass and shifted a bit to the side to afford him a better view of Carrie's canvas and the picture she was creating. Once he'd urged her to try it again, she'd started hesitantly, but now seemed totally engrossed in her subject. She guided the brush across the canvas with an ease that told Frank, despite his being a novice about art and its creation, this was not a new process for her, even if she had no memory of it.

Progress was slow, and it didn't take long before he lost interest in the snail's-pace development of the painting. His gaze veered from the canvas and settled instead on the artist.

Carrie was without a doubt one of the most beautiful women he'd ever seen. His wife, Sandy, had taken his breath away, but Carrie made him forget to breathe altogether. As lovely as she was on the outside, he could see so much more in her eyes. Reflected in their green depths dwelt a gentle, compassionate, and loving woman. At the same time, he saw the shadows of a frail creature haunted by a past she couldn't recall.

He had to fight down an overwhelming urge to gather her close and protect her from her unknown demons. But he knew that, like him, she would have to find them and face them to be whole again, and until she put a face on her dream man and figured out his connection to her life, Frank had a feeling that would not happen, that her memories would remain tantalizingly just beyond her reach.

Frank knew no more about this guy's identity than Carrie did, but something deep down told him that whatever his connection to Carrie was, it was not good. Otherwise why couldn't or wouldn't she put a face on him? As long as she didn't know him, she would not have to face the atrocities of which she felt him capable.

He wasn't all that well versed in generalized amnesia and its treatment, but he did know that it was the brain's way of protecting a person from something particularly traumatic. In Carrie's case, it had to be something excessively traumatizing for her to have blanked out her entire life. He also knew that the return of her memory, if it came back at all, couldn't be rushed, and when it did come back, it would not be pleasant.

"Oh my!"

Carrie's exclamation drew Frank out of his dark thoughts. "What?"

She held the canvas up. "Look. It's so. . ." Her eyes sparkled, and her animated face had broken into a wide grin.

"Beautiful," he finished for her, not really sure if it was the painting or the artist that he was talking about.

Dragging his gaze from Carrie, he studied the painting. She had chosen the stream and its surroundings as her subject. Although the painting was still wet and would probably never hang in the Metropolitan Museum of Art, it replicated perfectly the landscape before them.

The soft colors, the misty feel of the village, the flowers, the stream with its little footbridge spanning it. It was all there, right down to the monarch butterfly that had landed on her shoulder. All perfectly reproduced. But in every brushstroke was a love that reached out to the observer.

"It's truly lovely, Carrie."

She grinned again. "Yes, it is, isn't it?" A small giggle escaped her. "I guess I am an artist after all."

"I guess you are, and a damned good one, I'd say."

For a long time, Carrie studied her work, her wide, lively smile telling Frank how pleased she was with both it and herself. Then, without warning, she set the canvas aside, then leaned forward and kissed his cheek.

She drew back a little and said, "Thank you for your encouragement."

Frank was stunned and for a moment could only stare at her. Her sweet breath feathered his cheek, warm and inviting. Before he could stop himself, he cupped her cheeks in his palms and gently drew her to him. Their lips touched, tentatively at first. Despite the fact that the kiss was sending shards of heat racing through Frank's body, her lips were cool beneath his.

When Carrie didn't protest, he slowly gathered her into his arms and increased the pressure of the kiss, still keeping it gentle. It had been a long time since Frank had held a woman in his arms and kissed her. It felt good, too good. But it felt oddly right, too. As right as it had felt holding and kissing Sandy.

The thought of his dead wife sent a cold chill down him. He pulled back and set Carrie away from him. What had he been thinking? He'd only know this woman for a few hours. Frank stared hard at Carrie, wondering what there was about her that had made him forget who and what he was, what he'd done, but most of all, that he loved Sandy.

Carrie had a bit of a problem getting her bearings. She had no basis for comparison, seeing as how she had no idea if she'd ever been kissed or what it felt like if she had. However, she believed that nothing could have been better than Frank's kiss. He was so gentle and the kiss so tender that it had left her as limp as a newborn kitten.

Then a terrible thought struck her. Did she even have the right to kiss him? She might be married or engaged. She might have children.

"I'm sorry." Frank looked shell-shocked, as if he had been thrown as much off kilter as she had. "I don't know why I did that. I had no right."

Carrie didn't know what to say. Did she regret it? No. Would she have let it go on? Yes. Definitely. Did either of them have the right? To her regret, she couldn't answer that question.

She looked at her hands, then at him. "Please, don't apologize. That would ruin. . ." What was she saying? She couldn't admit to him how much that kiss had affected her. "I was as much a part of the. . ." As she sought for words that would help her avoid saying *kiss*, she felt her cheeks heat up. ". . .of *it* as you were. It happened. That we can't change. But we can see to it that it doesn't happen again." Knowing she was babbling, she looked anywhere but at Frank. "We don't even know if I've betrayed someone." Then she heard him heave a resigned sigh, and she turned to him.

Frank nodded, looked away, then back to her. "I'd

like us to be friends, if that's okay with you."

Relief rushed through her. "I'd like that very much." The kiss may not have been a good idea, but she was not willing to let this man walk out of her life because of it. "And to seal the bargain, I want you to have this." She extended the painting to him.

"Oh, I couldn't."

"But you must," she said, forcing it into his hands. "After all, if it hadn't been for you, I might not have tried to paint anything else and stopped with that horrible first attempt." She pointed at the painting of the face-less man.

He laughed, and the sound rippled over her like a morning breeze. "Okay. Thank you." He smiled. "Can we meet here again tomorrow?"

The warm rush of pleasure returned to her insides. This time, her blood sang through her veins. "I'd like that very much."

* * *

Frank lay back on his bed, his arms crossed behind his head, waiting for sleep to come, but it remained as elusive as it had for the last few hours. His gaze drifted to Carrie's painting on top of the dresser where he'd propped it against the wall. The mist. The village.

The flowers. The thick growth of trees. All of it was so serene, so calming, so beautiful, just like the artist. But it wasn't just the subject or the artist. Something about the artwork itself was so real, as if any moment he'd hear the babble of the stream and smell the scent of the flowers. It made him want to sigh in contentment, a sensation that had become foreign to him of late, and he knew deep down it was because Carrie's hand had not only created the painting, she'd also painted her love of her creative talents and her subject into her art.

Yet, she'd also created that grotesque rendering of the faceless man. What was that all about? Where had such a painting come from? Certainly nothing that evil resided inside this sweet, sensitive woman who had painted the picture on his dresser. But it *had* come from Carrie. Carrie, the woman with hair the color of flames, eyes that sparkled like emeralds, and a smile that lit up the cold places in his heart.

Without warning, the kiss they'd shared escaped his subconscious and sneaked into his mind. He vividly recalled the shape and texture of her lips and how they'd conformed to his as if they'd been made especially for that purpose. He remembered how they'd tasted. So warm, so sweet.

Frank smiled at his whimsical musing, and then shook his head to clear it of all the nonsense. What in hell was wrong with him? He hadn't thought this way about a girl since high school. He was well past that age of dreamily longing for some attention from the girl in the next seat in study hall. For God's sake, he was a mature adult with a medical degree and a flourishing practice.

Then something caught his eye. A movement? In the painting? He propped himself up on one elbow and stared at the painting. Deep in the trees, he thought he saw a flash of white. He sat up and slid to the foot of the bed to get a closer look.

The flash of white came again between two of the tree trunks in the foreground. He leaned closer, and then jumped back when a woman stepped into the clearing on the bank of the stream. Her white gossamer gown flowed and swirled around her as she walked, as though captured by a gentle spring breeze. Long black ringlets cascaded down her back. She paused. Turning, she looked straight at Frank and frowned.

My God! It couldn't be? Was it. . .Sandy?

Frank blinked to clear his vision, but when he looked back, the woman was still there. He grabbed the painting from its resting place and stared hard at it. Sandy smiled. Not trusting his own eyes, he blinked again. The stream bank remained just as Carrie had painted it, and the only thing on it was grass and a splash of flowers. Sandy was gone. If she'd ever been there.

Frank collapsed on the end of the bed, the painting still clutched in his shaking hands. Was he going crazy? Had he actually seen his dead wife in the painting? Or had it just been a trick of the moonlight shafting through the window?

* * *

The next morning, Carrie almost floated down the stairs to Clara's keeping room. She'd had a full night's sleep, untroubled by faces she couldn't identify. Instead, her mind had been filled with dreams of Frank and a reenactment of their kiss.

"You look pretty chipper this morning," Clara offered, smiling mysteriously.

Carrie twirled in a circle. "I feel wonderful. The sun is out. The birds are singing. There's not a cloud in the sky." *And I'm going to meet Frank*, she added to herself, still unwilling to share this tiny bit of happiness with anyone else. "What more could I ask for?"

A shadow passed over Clara's face. "What more, indeed?"

Carrie paused in her exuberance. "Clara?"

The older woman sighed. "Perhaps you need to be looking for an answer to those dreams that trouble you."

"How did you. . ."

The mysterious smile returned to Clara's face. "I have my ways, dear."

She moved across the room and took her customary place at the loom. Soon the *whoosh* of the shuttle passing through the threads and returning to be caught by Clara, then the *click* of the loom snugging the fibers into place, filled the silence.

Carrie knew Clara had *her ways*, as she put it. If Carrie hadn't learned anything else in the brief time she'd been in Renaissance, she'd learned that not everything that happened here had an explanation, at least not one she could understand, and everything that happened had a purpose. She just hadn't figured out the rationale behind her nightmarish dreams. And today, she was not going to even try. Today, no matter what Clara or anyone else said, she would meet Frank, and she refused to let anything steal her happiness from her time with him.

Without further conversation, Carrie wolfed down her breakfast. After gathering her paint case and another blank canvas from the stack Sara Spencer had sent over from her shop, Carrie hurried out to the rock by the stream where she would eagerly await Frank's arrival.

When he finally came tromping through the bushes, she noted the way his shoulders seemed to sag today as if a tremendous weight had settled on them during the night.

"Is everything all right?" she asked tentatively. If it was something he didn't want to discuss, she didn't want to appear to be prying.

He smiled, but it lacked the easy spontaneity he'd displayed yesterday. "Everything's fine. Just fine."

The slightly sharp reply told her he did not want to talk about it. "Okay. I wasn't trying to pry. It was just a friend asking a friend." Hoping that he would eventually trust her enough to confide, she returned his smile.

Frank stared into her sparkling eyes, and instantly his day seemed brighter, his emotional burden lighter. He couldn't bear the thought of destroying her good mood by relating what he'd imagined the night before— that her painting had been the cause or, at the very least, the vehicle that had been responsible for his night of disturbing dreams.

Forcing a smile, he sat beside her on the rock. "What would you like to do today? I don't know about you, but I'm finding it hard to cope with all this leisure time."

"I'm sure you are. Your days must be very hectic at the hospital."

He sighed, realizing for the first time how much he missed being in the operating room. "Hectic" is putting it mildly. They often start in the middle of one night and end in the middle of the next, but I really love it."

Carrie studied the flowers growing near the rock.

"It must be wonderful to know you hold a life in your hands and that you have the power to—"

He bolted to his feet and held out his hand to her. "Let's take a walk in the woods."

Frank didn't want to get into a discussion about his ability to save lives. After all, the lives that had mattered most to him had been anything but safe in his hands. The image of Sandy in the painting ran through his mind. What was she trying to tell him? Had she been there at all, or had she just been a figment of his imagination, a product of the supper of bread and cheese Alvin had left for him?

Carrie looked down at her paint case. "Let me take this inside."

Frank grinned. "Do you really think it won't be safe here?" He looked up at the clear blue sky. "It doesn't look like rain, and I doubt there's a thief within miles of this village."

She giggled. The sound skipped over his nerves like fingers strumming the strings of a harp. How did she have the ability to change his mood so drastically simply by laughing?

"You're right, of course." She bent over and stood the case against the rock, then leaned the blank canvas against it. "Let's go."

* * *

Several hours later, Carrie and Frank sat on a fallen tree, resting. From their vantage point, they could look down on the village nestled snugly in the glen. A soft breeze carried the heady aroma of cedar to them as it blew through the pines above their heads. The resulting sound was almost like a sigh. Nearby, a squirrel scampered up a tree, causing a cascade of loose bark to tumble to the ground. They hadn't ventured far enough from the village to leave the eternal spring that embraced it, making it hard to imagine that just a few hundred yards away winter still held everything in its icy grip.

Carrie had gone quiet, deeply immersed in thought.

"Penny for your thoughts," Frank said, digging in his pants pocket and then holding out his hand. A bright copper penny rested in his palm.

Carrie stared at the penny, and then snatched it up. "Sold," she said, but then immediately fell silent again.

"Oh, no. You can't take my money, then renege on the deal." Frank shifted his position to face her squarely. His features softened. "Friends talk to friends."

"If that's true, then why did you sidestep talking to me about what was bothering you this morning?" When he opened his mouth, she read in his eyes the excuse that hovered on his lips and added, "And don't tell me *nothing* because I won't believe you."

Frank sighed, and then told her about the painting and seeing Sandy in it. "I can't make up my mind if I really saw her or if I'm just going bonkers."

Carrie laughed. "I've only known you for a short time, but I doubt you're going bonkers."

He stared at her. "Then how do you explain the part about seeing Sandy?"

She stood and walked to a large pine tree a few feet away. Turning and leaning her back against its rough trunk, she studied him. "A lot of strange things have happened to me since I came here. Seeing a moving figure in the painting is just one more to add to the list of the inexplicable." She glanced at a squirrel that scurried away at the sound of her voice, then back to Frank. "I think we should just accept what happens to us. Accept it at face value. Don't question it. There is probably an underlying reason for it. Just as there was a reason Sara gave me those paints, there was a reason you saw Sandy in the painting." When he opened his mouth to voice what she knew would be a protest, she stopped him with a raised hand. "Or *thought* you saw Sandy. How Sara knew about the paint case when I didn't and how she got it and why you saw Sandy are not important. What is important is that I discovered my name and a part of Carrie Henderson through the paints. You will learn something, too. I'm sure of it."

Frank looked at her with one eyebrow arched skeptically so that it almost blended with his hairline. "Yeah. I may learn I'm really a certifiable candidate for the funny farm."

Carrie frowned at him, her irritation with his flippant remark written clearly across her face. "Make fun, but I truly believe you saw Sandy and that there was a reason for it. The reason may not be clear now, but it will be. You'll see."

"Enough of this serious stuff," Frank declared, jumping to his feet and holding out his hand to her. "Let's walk."

Even as Carrie took it and joined him on the path they'd chosen to explore, deep down he doubted Carrie was right, yet at the same time, he prayed she was. He desperately hoped that seeing his dead wife last night marked the beginning of the healing process Steve had promised would take place here.

They had only covered a few yards when Carrie stopped. "Look!" she cried, pointing to a branch above them.

On the branch was a bird's nest, and sitting in the nest was a drab, olive-green female cardinal. As they watched, a bright red male came to perch on the edge of the nest. The male cardinal dropped the worm he had held in his beak into the female's mouth. In turn, she transferred it to the chirping baby birds waiting with their mouths open.

Suddenly, and without warning, the male cardinal

attacked the female, nipping at her head and swiping at her with his claws. Her high-pitched chirps echoed through the trees.

"That's the oddest thing I've ever seen," Frank said. "I'm not really big on ornithology, but I've never heard of a male bird attacking a female before, and seemingly for no reason." He tuned to Carrie. "Have you?"

Carrie was frozen. Stark terror filled her eyes. She had her hand clamped tightly over her mouth, as though to stifle a scream, and was backing away from the scene, shaking her head.

"No. No." The whispered words were barely audible.

"Carrie? What is it?"

She continued to back away, all the time shaking her head, her lips forming the word *no*. Her eyes were wide with fright. Her hands trembled. Suddenly, she turned and ran back toward the village, leaving Frank standing there staring after her.

CHAPTER 9

Carrie lay in bed, her blank gaze centered on the ceiling. Late-afternoon sunlight spilled through the windows and across the pine floor, bringing out the rich colors in the wood like threads of gold. But Carrie only absently noted her surroundings.

She was deep in thought about the birds and why she'd reacted as she had. Why had she run away? Why had she felt the pain the female bird must have felt as the male pummeled her with his beak? No ready explanation came to mind.

This is silly. Good grief, they were only birds. Why should it rattle her so much?

Though she tried to push it from her mind, it still continued to torture her thoughts. Obviously, Frank thought the bird's behavior odd. But for her it had been more than odd. It had been terrifying. Why had it sent such fear coursing through her? Fear strong enough to send her running back to the safety of the village and her room in Clara's loft. And poor Frank. What must he have thought about her crazy, frantic departure?

Then she remembered what she'd told Frank about accepting things that happened to them within Renaissance. Was this just another one of those things she *needed* to see and that would eventually come clear to her? Did this have something to do with the past that remained tantalizingly beyond her reach? The very thought that it did made her go cold all over.

Not for the first time, she wondered if she really wanted to remember any of her past life. If all she'd been shown so far was to remind her of all she'd forgotten, she must have led a truly frightening life.

Deciding she was giving far too much credence to a fight between two birds, she got up and grabbed her paint case. After propping a blank canvas up against the side of the window seat, she sat and opened the case. Without any prior thought, she began smearing paint over the canvas.

* * *

By the time Carrie set the paints aside, the sun had gone down, and the darkness of deep night had descended on the village. Light from the lampposts flickered over the deserted path winding between the cottages. The windows of the other cottages were black. An owl hooted in the distance, but no other noise was audible.

That night had fallen while she worked had gone unnoticed by Carrie. She'd only stopped long enough to light the candlestick Clara had left beside the bed; its flickering flame now spread a golden light over the room.

She stared at what she'd painted and smiled. A perfect likeness of Frank looked back at her from the painting. His black curly hair framed his face. His square chin was set in a stubborn line. High cheek-bones that told of a smattering of Native American blood somewhere in his ancestral past added a hint of rugged mystery to his face.

Then she noted his expression. His normally lively gray eyes were clouded, troubled, sad. Her heart ached to remove that indefinable sadness from his face. Why hadn't she painted him with a smile? Then she knew. It was because Frank's soul didn't smile. Because he carried a burden so cumbersome and so debilitating that it couldn't smile. But what was it? Did it have something to do with his dead wife?

She sighed and rose, knowing that until Frank was ready to share what troubled him, she would have to be content with supporting him along his journey and being there for him when the time came for him to face his problems. It came as a bit of a surprise that she felt so protective of a man she had just met.

Silly girl, she told herself. *You'd do the same for anyone.*

But it didn't gel. Frank wasn't just *anyone*. During the short time she'd known him, Frank had become special to her, very special.

Suddenly aware of how exhausted she was, she undressed and donned her simple cotton gown, then climbed into bed.

* * *

Someone was pursuing her. Carefully, she skirted the well-worn path and stumbled through the thick bushes. Thorns clawed at her clothes, and the muffled sound of tearing cloth sounded like a fire siren to her ears. She had to be quiet. If she wanted to live, she had to evade him. Her breath was coming in sharp, painful gasps.

Stopping behind a tree, she listened. Faint footsteps could be heard along with the breaking of twigs under heavily-booted feet. Her icy blood pounded through her veins. Clutching her hands together to stop their shaking, she held her breath, fearing that her labored breathing would give away her position.

Careful not to make any noise, she slipped into a dense thicket and plastered herself against the cold, moist ground. From there, through the lower branches of the thick bushes, she could see if anyone approached, but she was sure she would not be seen in turn. Minutes crawled by.

When she didn't hear anything, her fear began to subside. Still she remained as silent as death, crouched inside the protective, tangled undergrowth of the thicket. Waiting. Afraid to leave the cover of the bushes too soon. Afraid he lay in wait, watching, ready to pounce when she emerged.

It seemed she'd been there for hours. Her legs began to cramp. The cool, damp night air seeped into her clothes and skin, chilling her to the bone. Still she waited.

Then it came. The sound of those booted feet. First the sound came from her left, then in front of her, then to her right, then from behind. He was circling her like the predatory beast that she instinctively knew he was. Circling, waiting for his chance to capture his prey.

She peeked through the lower branches. The heavy hunting boots were directly in line with her vision. Carefully, she tilted her head up. Pale gray beams of moonlight streaked his face. Or the place where his face should have been. What she could see was like a camera gone out of focus. She knew he should have features, but she couldn't see them through the blur of colors.

He drew himself up to his full imposing height,

and then cupped his hands around his mouth. "I know you're out there, and I'll find you, Carrie. When I do, I'll kill you. Have no doubt about that."

* * *

Eyes wide, Carrie bolted upright in the bed. She was bathed in perspiration from head to toe. Her fingers clutched the bedclothes. She was shaking so hard, the bed vibrated beneath her. *He knew her name.*

Fear unlike anything she could imagine gripped her mind and body. Without thinking, she jumped from the bed and flew down the ladder and out into the inky night.

From the deep shadows of the trees, Alvin watched Carrie run across the front of Clara's cottage and down the lamp-lit path. For a moment he considered going after her, but then, when he saw the direction of her flight, decided against it. He hated it that she also had demons haunting her sleep.

* * *

Frank had just started to drift off to sleep when his bedroom door burst open. At first he thought it might be Alvin. But the moonlight that backlit the silhouette filling the doorway revealed it was a woman in a flowing gown of some kind.

Sandy?

Then she moved closer, and the moonlight bounced off her fiery auburn hair. He pushed himself to a sitting position.

"Carrie?"

Her name had barely crossed his lips before she had dashed across the floor and launched herself into his arms. Her skin was moist and icy cold, and she was trembling uncontrollably. Not until he felt the moisture on his face did he realize she was crying.

"What is it?"

She hiccupped and burrowed deeper against his shoulder. "He came. . .back. . .in my dreams. The man. . .with no. . .face. He came. . .back." She took a deep breath. "He said. . .he'd find me. . .and. . .kill me." She leaned back and looked at Frank. "He knew. . .my name."

Frank had never seen such terror in another human being's eyes. He enveloped her in his arms and held her as tightly as he could. "No one is going to hurt you as long as I'm around. No one."

"But—"

"No one," he repeated more firmly. He moved her away so he could look into her tear-stained, ghost-white face. "Listen to me. It was a dream, Carrie, just a dream. He can't hurt you."

Tears rolled down her cheeks, and the terror in her eyes made him want to fight this damned dream man who was doing this to Carrie, whoever the hell he was. But he couldn't fight dreams. He could only hold the dreamer and help her understand there was nothing to fear—and pray that he was right. After all, strange things did happen here.

"But he said he'd—"

"I know. I know what he said, but it was a dream, Carrie. Dreams can't hurt you."

He'd had to interrupt her. He couldn't bear the thought of hearing those words again. Carrie dead? My God, the thought tore through him like a freight train hurtling off its tracks. Desperately, he pushed the idea from his mind.

Gently, he kissed her forehead. "Trust me to take care of you, Carrie," he whispered into her hair. "I will not let anything hurt you." When her body relaxed, he knew before she spoke that he'd finally managed to ease her mind.

"All right." She snuggled closer. "I'll trust you, Frank."

Though her body had relaxed and her tears had slowed, her fingers still curled into his shoulders. Gently, he stroked her back until her sobs subsided and only a faint occasional hiccup emerged. Her body stopped shaking, and her grip on him eased, but she remained plastered tightly against him.

"Please let me stay with you."

Her plea reminded him of a child begging for protection from a nightmare. Not having the heart to send her back to Clara's, he slipped lower in the bed and drew her down with him, then pulled the blankets over both of them. Moments later, her even breathing told him she was asleep.

As he lay there trying to make sense of the dream man who kept haunting Carrie, his anger at this faceless entity escalated. When he was almost unable to control it, he tamped it down and centered his thoughts on finding sleep.

But sleep remained elusive, and it grew more and more so as he became increasingly aware of the slight curves pressed against him with only a thin, cotton nightgown preventing them from lying skin to skin.

His body stirred to life. With superhuman effort, he denied it what it craved. She had just experienced a trauma the likes of which he'd never before seen. This was no time to be thinking from his waist down.

But what he knew to be gentlemanly consideration for Carrie's plight and what his body wanted were two totally different things. By exercising more self-control than he dreamed himself capable of, consideration won out. He sighed and decided this night had suddenly acquired all the earmarks of being one of the most endless he'd ever endured.

* * *

The sun had not yet come up when Carrie awoke to find herself snuggled tightly against Frank's warm body. Shocked to find herself in Frank's bed, she extracted herself from the circle of his arms, and then slipped quietly from beneath the covers. As she stood there, the cool floor chilling her bare feet, she stared down at him and the imprint left by her head on the pillow beside him.

She'd spent the night in this man's bed, in this man's arms. Had anything happened? Color heated her cheeks. She didn't think anything had. Surely she would have remembered.

Carrie expected shame to overcome her, and was surprised when it didn't. Instead she experienced a rush of sensation completely foreign to her, that warmed her straight through and made her heart flutter. She recalled vividly his strong arms holding her and her face pressed against his broad, bare chest, his strong heartbeat echoing in her ear.

Frank remained deep asleep and oblivious to her having left his side. Contrarily, she wished he were awake so she could see how the past night had affected him. Was he angry that she'd thrown herself at him? Disgusted that she'd fallen into his bed?

Then she remembered how understanding and protective Frank had been when she'd come to him with her foolish fears of a nightmare that couldn't harm her. He would not judge her on this. This man was a good person who deserved to have his sadness lifted from his soul, and she swore, as she stood there, that just as he'd been there for her when she needed him, she would do whatever it took to free him.

Smiling, she leaned down, lightly kissed his lips and then slipped from the room.

* * *

Through slitted eyelids, Frank watched Carrie leave. Memories of her body pressed against him made him hard and left him aching with a need he hadn't experienced in a long time, a need that went bone- and soul-deep. Then his gaze drifted to the painting on the dresser, and he thought of Sandy, and the wanting vanished on a wave of shame. How could he desire another woman? How could he betray Sandy's memory like that?

Drawing the blankets over his head, he rolled over and closed his eyes. But behind his eyelids hovered an image of a lovely young woman in a thin, cotton night-dress with auburn hair and soft lips and a smile that could light up the heavens, but more importantly, his life.

* * *

From the edge of the forest, Alvin watched Carrie slip from his cottage and hurry down the lane to Clara's. He had no idea what had taken place that night between Frank and Carrie, nor did he want to know. That was their business, not his. What was his business was getting Frank to talk about his problems so he could get him out of Renaissance before Alvin was forced to live through his own hellish memories.

Hours later, when Alvin entered the cottage, Frank was just sitting down to the breakfast Alvin had left for him: coffee, bread, cheese, and an apple.

"Don't you people believe in eggs and bacon?" Frank asked, slicing off a generous hunk from the wedge of yellow cheese. He stared down at it, and then curled his nose. Shrugging, he popped it into his mouth.

Alvin took a seat across from him and poured himself a cup of the thick, dark coffee. "We don't keep any livestock in the village so we ran out of eggs." He took a sip from the cup. The blast of caffeine brought his body to life instantly.

"Isn't there a shop here?"

"Yes, but I have to bring most of the supplies from the outside."

Frank looked at him expectantly, and Alvin knew he was awaiting further explanation. He sighed and set the heavy mug back on the table with a loud *clunk*. "I've been a bit busy with *other things* and haven't left the village for a few days." He was not about to tell him that he couldn't leave the village, thanks to Emanuel. . .and Frank.

"If by *other things* you mean me, I didn't ask Emanuel to burden you with me. Feel free to turn me over to someone else to worry about anytime you want." Frank's voice held a resentful, clipped edge.

Instantly, Alvin was sorry for his statement. Frank was right. It wasn't his fault that by helping Frank to face his problems, Alvin was being forced to face his own demons. Emanuel had to take the full blame for that on his own shoulders. Alvin shook his head. "That wasn't right. I shouldn't blame you for my worries."

Frank's expression softened. "Would it help to talk about it?"

Alvin studied his hands for a moment, and then raised his gaze to meet Frank's. "Has it occurred to you that you're willing to take on that girl's problems and to talk about mine, but as yet you haven't addressed your own?"

Frank's face shut down. He picked up a paring

knife and began devoting undue, intense concentration to peeling the apple. "Nice apples," he said. "Do you get these outside the village, too?"

Having used it many times himself, Alvin knew evasion when he heard it. Shut down. Shut them out. Refuse to discuss it. Draw their attention away from you. Alvin picked up the second apple and turned it in his rough fingers.

"You know, Frank, apples are a lot like people. You don't really know what you've got until you get beneath their skin." He raised his gaze to Frank.

He stopped peeling and glanced at Alvin, then resumed removing the skin from the apple. "Spare me the philosophical garbage."

Alvin set the apple down. "Then talk to me."

"About what?" Frank asked, his dumb act not fooling Alvin for a second.

"About you. About why you're here. About what's eating a hole into your insides big enough for a truck to drive through."

Frank tossed the apple and the knife aside. "I killed my wife and unborn child. Is that what you want to hear?" His voice rose loud enough to be heard outside.

Alvin leaned back in his chair, tipping it up on two legs, and then crossed his arms over his stomach. "It's a start." He waited, but when Frank didn't offer more, he nudged him on. "How?"

Throwing him a scathing look, Frank stood and strode to the window. "How what?"

"How did you kill them, Frank?"

The question cut into Frank like a saber plunged into his heart. "It was snowing. I hit a tree," he finally mumbled. "My wife died instantly." Tears burned the back of his eyes.

He stared blankly out the window, but he didn't see the quaint little village. All he saw was snow falling in blinding sheets, a tree hurtling toward them, and all he heard were Sandy's terrified screams and then the high-pitched sound of crunching metal. Then silence.

"At least she died instantly," Alvin said, his voice weary and horribly sad.

Snatched from his memories, Frank turned back to the man hunched over at the table. "What?"

"I said at least she died instantly. My wife took hours to die in a hospital room." Alvin rose and abruptly left the cottage.

CHAPTER 10

After leaving Alvin's cottage, Frank wandered around the village for a while. He wasn't sure he wanted to see Carrie. It had nothing to do with what had happened the night before in his bed. He'd held Carrie, comforted her, and then let her go. Nothing more than one friend would do for another.

But it had everything to do with the fact that comfort had turned to desire. He had betrayed Sandy's memory. He had wanted another woman. Not just wanted, but longed for with an unbelievable intensity. How did he reconcile that with having loved Sandy more than any other human alive? Alvin's prying into the accident only served to underline that betrayal.

Then it came to him. Wanting didn't equal love. It had been a long time since he'd had a woman, and it was nothing more than his body reacting the way any full-blooded, healthy man's body would react if he had a half-naked woman lying in his arms. Still, he felt the tug of betrayal.

Suddenly, Carrie's words penetrated his brain. He'd been so wrapped up in her problems and his growing sexual attraction that they'd slipped past him until now.

I trust you, Frank.

The words bit deep into him. He picked up a dead twig and twisted it until it snapped. He didn't want her trust. He didn't want anyone's trust. Yet he'd asked Carrie to trust him. Why? Sandy had trusted him to take care of her and their unborn child, and look how that had ended. No. Carrie would have to see herself through this. He didn't want to be responsible for anyone else anymore.

But he cared about Carrie. How could he not be there for her? She had no one else. As he walked blindly through the village, a tug of war went on in his brain that soon had a dull pain jack-hammering in his skull.

Moments later, despite his vow to stay away, and as if his feet had a mind of their own, Frank found himself stepping into Clara's garden. Carrie sat in her usual spot beside the stream. He knew she was waiting for him. And he knew what he had to do.

"Morning," she said shyly.

"Morning."

"About last night," she blurted, giving him no chance

to speak. "I—"

He held up his hand. "No need."

Frank wasn't sure if she was about to apologize or not, but whatever she'd been about to say, he didn't want to hear it. He didn't want to see the sun shining down on her head like a halo or the way it picked up the red highlights in her hair and made them dance like flames. He didn't want to see the welcome in her eyes or the lift of her full lips in a smile that entwined him with a reminder of how sweet and soft they had felt beneath his.

What he wanted was to speak his piece, cut his ties, and run before he got sucked into another intimate situation, but his feet seemed glued to the ground. As he stood there gazing into her lovely face, he could feel his resolve to distance himself from her slowly crumbling. Before he lost his nerve or let her beauty override his intentions, he had to do what he'd come here to do.

"Carrie, I don't want to mislead you. I'm the worst person in the world to help you through this thing with your faceless man."

Mouth agape, she stared at him, obviously stunned by his change of attitude from last night.

"I have my own demons to extricate. Until I do, I can't. . .get close to anyone."

She dipped her head and clutched her hands together in her lap. "I understand."

But he knew she didn't. The light had gone out in her eyes. She felt abandoned, and he hated himself for being the cause.

"That doesn't mean we can't talk," he qualified, trying to take the edge off his abrupt declaration. "It just can't go beyond that." He almost added *for now*, but stopped himself before the words passed his lips. There was no *for now* about it. Was there?

He looked up at the clear blue sky. What the hell was wrong with him? His emotions were fluctuating like a flag in a shifting wind. One minute he wanted Carrie as far away from him as he could get her, and the next he couldn't bear the thought of being separated from her.

"Look." He squatted beside her and took one of her cold hands. "I'll be here for you whenever you need me, but don't trust me, Carrie."

She turned her face up to him. "Why?" Her moist eyes tugged painfully at his heart.

What could he say in answer to that? *Don't trust me because I kill the people closest to me?* "I can't seem to help myself, and if I can't do that, how can I help you?"

She smiled and covered his hand with her free one. The sun got brighter. "We can help each other."

Frank's insides churned. Was she right? Could this fragile, troubled woman help him find his way through the web of guilt the accident had spun around him? Was there, indeed, a light at the end of this cold, dark tunnel he'd been in for so long?

Carrie squeezed his hand. "Clara told me that the Assignments come to the village with a load of emotional baggage. Maybe sometimes, we have to help each other carry the load. Maybe we're supposed to help each other."

Was she right? Was that what this was all about? Was he reading far too much into his relationship with Carrie? Were they just meant to help each other find the answers they both so desperately sought?

"Let me help you with whatever's troubling you," she said softly. "And you can help me. It doesn't have to be any more than that, if that's what you want. A friend helping a friend over some rough spots in the road."

Although he wouldn't characterize what either of them were going through as anything as trivial as *rough spots*, Frank had known for a long time that his burden was becoming heavier than he could bear alone. After all, wasn't that why he'd come here, to lighten the load? What harm could it do to let her help him find the way to peace of mind and he, in turn, could do what he could to help her? It didn't have to be more than that. It wouldn't be more than that. He'd make sure of it.

Still, he hesitated. He glanced past Carrie to the opposite riverbank and started. On the other side, Sandy stood near the water's edge, smiling and nodding her head, as if telling him to go ahead. He blinked, and as before, she had already disappeared.

Contentment washed over him. He smiled and nodded. "Okay, we'll help each other."

Carrie waited, but although he had agreed to their mutual assistance, he did not offer to tell her about his troubles, and she didn't push. When he wanted to, he'd tell her. She had to believe that, no matter what.

* * *

Emanuel turned away from the window where he'd been watching the exchange between Carrie and Frank. Clara had just set his usual mug of coffee on the table.

"Frank seems to be taking some tentative steps toward finding his way, and Carrie has had some of her memory return," Clara said.

Emanuel took a seat and sighed. "Yes, but Alvin still seems to be fighting off his own resolutions." He curled his big hands around the mug and looked deep into the dark liquid it held. "I'd so hoped that he and Frank could help each other."

Clara straightened her mobcap and sank into the chair next to him. She patted his hand. "It's not over yet. Perhaps one has to heal first to be able to help the other."

"Perhaps," he said distractedly. "Perhaps. And perhaps

Alvin needs a gentle nudge."

Emanuel went silent. Clara waited. A deep frown creased his broad forehead, and he fingered the end of his long white beard, a definite sign that he was thinking about some way to give Alvin a shove in the right direction. She smiled. If she knew Emanuel well, and she did, probably better than anyone in the village, she was sure he'd find his answer before too long, and when he did, Alvin would not even know he'd been nudged.

She wisely left him to his thoughts and went into the pantry to get some fruit to add to the picnic lunch she had decided to pack for Frank and Carrie. Emanuel wasn't the only one who could deliver a discreetly aimed nudge to fate.

* * *

"Oh my!" Carrie was astounded at the beauty of the spot where Clara had directed her and Frank to enjoy the surprise picnic she'd packed for them. Now Carrie knew why Clara had urged her to bring along her paints.

High above their heads, a waterfall cascaded in silvery sheets over granite rocks and then plunged into the large, crystal-clear pool below. At its base was a wide area of soft, brilliant green grass dotted with yellow dandelions and purple and white dog-toothed violets. Surrounding the clearing, like sentinels, stately pine trees swayed in the warm, gentle breeze, and at the foot of the trees and encircling the entire setting grew bushes heavy with blueberries that provided a barrier between Frank and Carrie and the outside world. It was as though they'd found a private haven, safe and secure from everything that had twisted their lives into unmanageable chaos.

Frank spread the blanket Clara had given them, and Carrie laid out the food: two large, ruby-red apples; a loaf of golden, crusty bread still warm from the oven; a wedge of cheese; and two slices of dark chocolate cake, coated with thick, white icing. They ate silently, both surprised at the degree of their hunger.

When they'd finished, Frank lay back on the blanket, his arms folded beneath his head, while Carrie cleared away the remnants of their meal. He sighed contentedly and gazed at the treetops above him. Carrie finished up her chore, then sat beside him.

"I don't remember the last time I felt so at peace," she said, then laughed. "Of course, since I don't remember much of anything, that's really not saying much."

Frank turned to her. He frowned.

"What?" she said.

"Nothing. I'm just surprised you can laugh about it. Not being able to remember anything about yourself has to be very frustrating for you."

"It was at first, but it's better now that I've decided to let it come back at its own speed. Besides, it's so lovely in Renaissance; I almost don't want to ever leave." She drew her legs up to her chest and tucked her skirt around her, and then rested her chin on her knees. "And I do remember some things, like that," she pointed to an orange and black butterfly sitting atop a dandelion, its wings gently beating the air, "is a monarch butterfly. And that flower it's sipping the nectar from is a dandelion." She shrugged. "Unfortunately, the things I recall are not the important things. At first I was frustrated and eager to remember everything, but now I am trying not to force the memories to return. I know the dreams have something to do with my past, but right now, I don't know what. I'm content to wait until it all falls back into place."

Frank sighed. "I wish I had your patience. I want this over with so I can get back to my practice. I even tried talking to Alvin about it today, but I just can't." Nor was he ready to tell Carrie about the worst night of his life.

Carrie reached for his hand and pressed it reassuringly. "It'll come. Just give it time."

Pushing himself upright, Frank looped his arms around his bent legs. "How much time? Nothing is happening. Alvin comes and goes and says next to nothing. Emanuel said Tripp was my mentor and was supposed to help me, but he hasn't." He made a sound of exasperation. "Hell, he barely speaks to me at all."

Seeing that this subject was just getting blacker and blacker and that Frank had again scooted around the edge of his problem to avoid talking in specifics, Carrie rose to her feet and held out her hand. "Let's explore the clearing."

Glancing up at her, Frank's expression was very serious, and then the tension drained from his features, and he pulled himself to his feet and took her hand. "Okay. Lead on."

"Bring the napkin, and we'll pick some berries."

* * *

Over an hour later, Carrie and Frank were back on the blanket with a napkin holding a couple of handfuls of plump blueberries spread out between them. Frank picked up a particularly large berry and held it out to Carrie. She leaned forward and took it with her lips. Her mouth grazed his skin. It tingled where her mouth had touched him. He sucked in a breath.

"Mmm. That's so sweet," she said, and then her tongue darted out to lick away the juice.

Frank's groin tightened. His gaze was glued to her

wet lips. Quite suddenly, he had an overwhelming urge to gather her in his arms and see if her lips had retained the flavor of the berries.

Her naïveté was one of the things Frank liked most about her. She had no idea how sexy she looked. Other women strutted and preened to get a man's attention, but without even trying, Carrie exuded sex appeal as unthinkingly as a flower gave off perfume. Not one of the nurses who ogled him and vied for his attention on a daily basis at the hospital could hold a candle to Carrie.

With a toss of her head, she threw her long hair behind her. Very slowly, as she leaned toward him to get another berry, her hair slid forward again. Frank found himself wishing it were his hand that had just caressed her shoulder. He had to fist his fingers to keep from reaching for the long strands, to feel their silky texture and smell their seductive aroma, to have them wrapped around their naked bodies. . .

His groin grew tighter. The vein in his temple pulsated in time to his increased heartbeat.

He set his jaw. *Forget it, Donovan.*

But as quickly as it had come, he blocked out the warning. He wanted to do more than hold and comfort Carrie. He wanted to make love to her, right there beneath the heavens, surrounded by the untamed beauty of nature. If just for today and only for a few hours, he wanted to make her his.

"Carrie." He said her name so softly she almost didn't hear him.

She lifted her gaze to his face, and the desire in his expression stole her breath from her lungs. Even though a cool breeze caressed her skin, she could feel heat building in her. It started at the very core of who she was and spread until it throbbed in every one of her nerve endings. Even before he spoke the words, she could read the silent question in his eyes.

"I want to kiss you."

Should she let him? God knew, she wanted to kiss him, to have him hold her again. Before she could fully process the pros and cons to becoming involved with Frank, she nodded, her brain having ceased to function on a level competent enough to make rationale decisions and verbalize words.

Very slowly he reached for her. Cupping his hands around the back of her head, he held her gaze with his and drew her toward him. Resistance never entered her mind. Soon his lips were so close she could feel his berry-scented breath brushing her mouth. Her lips parted of their own volition.

As he pulled her the last few inches, she gave way completely, and collapsed across his broad chest. The heavy beat of his heart joined hers. Their lips met, and sparks zinged through her. The kiss started out as gentle as a butterfly's caress. Little by little it became hungrier, more demanding, more intoxicating.

Caught in a whirlpool of emotions, her thoughts swirled in a kaleidoscope of sensations. She had no memory of having done any of this with a man before and was surprised when her body took over and responded naturally on its own. Needing to be closer, she slid nearer yet to him and entwined her legs with his.

A hard ridge dug into her lower stomach. Automatically, she moved against it. When he groaned into her mouth, she smiled inwardly. Frank wanted her, and for some reason that brought happiness bubbling up in her like a mountain spring; she wanted him, too.

Frank rolled to the top, freed himself, and knelt in front of her. Gently, he drew her to her knees. As they knelt face to face, mere inches from each other, Frank slipped his hands beneath the hem of her blouse. With excruciating care, he slid the material upward, his hands skimming her sensitive flesh, until his palms cupped each of her straining breasts. With the pad of his thumbs, he circled the tips, stroking and teasing them into hard nubs.

Carrie gasped. Heat radiated out from where he touched. Her head grew light, and she thanked God that she was already on her knees. Had she not been, she would have collapsed in a pile of passionate bliss.

Cool air caressed her skin. Her fever-soaked mind was vaguely aware that Frank was removing her blouse. For a moment, shyness overtook her. She wanted to stop him. Then she looked into his eyes and saw that the perpetual sadness that always lurked there had disappeared and been replaced by desire. Nothing on this earth could make her do anything, even if she wanted to, to bring that back.

That she was the one who had caused that desire in his gaze made her swell with a strange sense of pride. Joy spread through her and mixed with the longing that Frank's touch had stirred to life. Slowly, he pulled the material over her head. He placed the blouse on the blanket beside them, and then turned back to her. Her bra came next, and then there was the caress of the breeze against her bare flesh.

He said nothing. He moved away from her. Then he frowned.

She knew that look. She'd seen it before. She couldn't remember where, but in her gut she knew what it meant.

"You think I'm repulsive," she whispered on a shuddered breath, and then she crossed her arms over her chest to hide her nakedness, to hold on to her hurt.

Before she could struggle to her feet and escape his scrutiny, he grasped her arms and held her in place.

"Repulsive? You think you're repulsive?"

"Isn't that what you think? You'd expected someone better, prettier, more—"

"No, absolutely not." He scooped her into his arms and held her close. "You are exactly what I expected and more." He set her at arm's length and stared at her as if something had just become very clear to him. "You have no idea how lovely you are, do you?"

She could feel her cheeks burn. "I am? Really?"

"Really."

"Then why did you frown?"

"This puzzled me." He traced her shoulder with the tip of his finger. "How did you get this scar?"

She twisted her head until she could see what he was talking about. A two-inch-long ridge of ragged, ugly flesh marked her shoulder. "I. . .I don't know."

"It doesn't matter." He kissed it. "It's as beautiful as the rest of you."

Her cheeks colored, and she averted her gaze.

It amazed Carrie that Frank saw her as beautiful. But why should it? She had eyes in her head. She was not a homely woman. Her figure was a bit thin, but curved in all the right places. Her hair was a vibrant shade of auburn, and her eyes were an unusual shade of green. There had been a time in her life when she'd considered herself attractive. . .

A memory. She had retrieved a bit of her memory. But as quickly as it came, it was overshadowed by another half memory.

Someone screaming how ugly she was erupted in her mind, but instead of encouraging it to come out into the open as she'd done so many times before, Carrie pushed it back into the darkness. Later she'd call it forth. Right now, Frank thought she was beautiful, and that's all that mattered.

He cupped her face. "You are the most desirable woman I have ever met. I want you," he whispered.

From somewhere in her annoyingly selective memory came the definition of *want*. Frank was proposing that they make love. Fear rose in her. Could she remember how? Of course, she could. But then, she couldn't remember much of her past life, what made her think she could remember this? But she'd remembered how to paint. Maybe she'd remember how to make love, too. But what if it was as ugly as the first painting?

She couldn't look at him. "What if I don't remember how?" she finally said, her voice a mere whisper.

He tilted her chin up and lowered his mouth to hers. "I'll teach you," he said against her lips.

As he explored her mouth with his tongue, Carrie gave in to the waves of delight washing over her and stopped thinking.

Feel, she told herself, *just. . .feel.*

Frank grew impatient with his clothing. He needed to savor Carrie's naked flesh against his own. But that little warning voice of reason kept holding him back. He shook it from his mind. This had nothing to do with reason, nothing at all. It had to do with wanting, aching, needing to be a part of this woman. To taste her charms, to make love to her until her soul believed she was good and beautiful and worthy. And maybe, through her, he could feel worthy again, as well.

He knew when she finally released her inhibitions. Her arms snaked around his neck, and her fingernails dug into his flesh. A whimper escaped her lips.

Frank stood and removed his clothing. The fresh breeze coming off the waterfall did nothing to cool his burning body. When he looked down at Carrie's nakedness spread out before him like a sumptuous, seductive feast, he smiled. Her emerald eyes overflowed with a woman's passion. Her moist, slightly parted lips swelled invitingly from his kisses and silently begged for more.

Carrie raised her arms. "Teach me."

CHAPTER 11

Frank sank to his knees and then lay down beside Carrie on the blanket and enveloped her in his arms. For a time he just held her, reveling in the feel of a woman in his arms. He'd held only dreams and ghosts for so long he'd forgotten how life-giving holding a flesh-and-blood woman could be.

But this wasn't just any woman. This was Carrie, which made the sensation of life returning to his soul all the more poignant. Was what he was doing right for her, or was it just going to add one more layer of complication to her life? To his own?

He drew away and looked down at her. "Are you sure you want to do this?"

"More than I want to take my next breath." She cupped his cheek and smiled. "Love me, Frank Donovan. Please."

He didn't need a second invitation. He was more than ready to become Carrie's teacher. His body was begging for the pleasure.

Carrie closed her eyes and waited for Frank's touch. When his warm hand closed over her breast, she sucked in her breath. Pleasure cascaded through her. Every part of her came alive. Heat radiated from his hand and engulfed her entire body.

She squirmed, trying to get closer. When it seemed that even the breath of air separating them was too much, Carrie wrapped her legs around him, imprisoning him against her sensitive core. She could feel his arousal, rigid and hot. Sliding her hand between them, she grasped it.

Frank's body stiffened. He sucked in air as though his lungs were starving for it. Then he let out a gust of ragged breath on a deep moan.

"My God." When she began to move her hand, he covered her hand with his. "It's been so long. I don't want it to end too quickly."

Deep inside, Carrie smiled. That she could bring Frank to this height of passion delighted her. Only a desirable woman could do that. She had no idea why, but it was important for her to know that.

Her delight turned to sweet, aching agony when Frank moved his hand over her stomach to the V of her thighs. Carefully he inserted a finger into her heat and began to imitate the age-old movements of love.

Carrie's body arched to meet each thrust. Each time she felt herself quiver on the edge of completion, he stopped, waited, then when the pressure subsided some, he'd begin again. Over and over he brought her to the brink of climax. And over and over he pulled her back from the edge.

Mindlessly, she groped for him, and when she found his arousal pressing against her thigh, she wrapped her hand around it and guided him to the spot where she longed for him to be.

He looked down at her. "Now?"

"Now," she whispered on halted breath, her voice weak with desire. "Please. . .now."

With the utmost care and gentleness, Frank slipped inside her, filling her up so completely, she couldn't think, couldn't breathe, couldn't. . .

Frank could never recall another experience like this. She may have doubted herself, but he was sure she needed no instructions on making love. She had it down to a fine, tantalizing art. Being inside Carrie felt as if he were surrounded by hot coals, searing her into his heart and soul. Every movement of her body sent blood pulsing through him. Every throb of her body around him magnified the need for fulfillment. When his lungs began to burn, he had to remind himself to breathe.

He was precariously close to losing control, and

he had to fight to keep from concluding long before he should. But each time Carrie squirmed or arched her body or dug her nails into his skin, he had to start the fight all over again. She was like a starving, wild woman. She responded to his every move with an untamed abandon that made him grit his teeth and fight once more to hold off his own climax.

His taut muscles screamed out in protest. Sweat slicked both their bodies, heightening the sensuality. Still they thrashed against each other, both fighting for the final satisfaction that would throw them over the precipice of desire and into the valley of completion, but neither of them wanted it to end.

When they could hold off no longer, it was if a bomb exploded inside Frank's head. He felt Carrie tighten around him and then arch her back one last time. Together they soared above the earth on ricocheting starbursts of light. Slowly the lights dimmed, and like a feather coming to rest, they drifted back to earth, spent, exhausted, and utterly satisfied.

Carrie snuggled against him. He held her close and waited for that reprimanding voice to tell him that he'd betrayed Sandy yet again. But it never came. What did come was an image of Sandy on the stream bank, smiling and nodding her approval. Deep down, he knew she would not hate him for finding happiness with Carrie.

Still, the joy was bittersweet.

But one scar was still there, one pain that would never go away. That Sandy seemed to approve of Carrie did nothing to lessen his guilt at having caused his wife's death and that of their unborn child. He knew that guilt would never go away, no matter what Steve said and no matter what tricks Emanuel conjured to make it otherwise. That scar would remain on his heart until the day he died.

Frank's silence disturbed Carrie. This time with him had been so sweet, so. . .wonderful, she wanted to store it in her memory, untarnished, to be treasured for always. She thought she'd die if he didn't feel the same way. But she had to know. She had to have the courage to ask him the question she wasn't sure she wanted answered.

"Are you sorry?" she asked timidly.

He roused, as though from a daydream, shook his head, and brushed back the hair that clung to her damp forehead. "Never. What about you?"

She raised herself to her elbow and looked down into his dear face. "Since I have no memory of making love with anyone else, I can't tell you why, but right here," she took his hand and laid it on her heart, "there is joy and happiness unlike anything I've ever known."

A smile curved Frank's lips. "You sure are good at bolstering a guy's ego."

"I didn't notice your ego sagging."

Frank rolled to his back and laughed out loud. The sound delighted Carrie. Could this day get any better?

Impetuously, she jumped to her feet and threw her arms out to either side, then spun in a circle, totally oblivious of her nudity. "I am a new woman!" she cried to the heavens.

Frank stood and caught her in his arms. "Let's go swimming."

Carrie nodded and happily followed him into the water, knowing this was going to be the happiest time of her life—even if it ended tomorrow. It could. It might. Who knew what would happen then—especially here? But she had today—right now. This moment. And she wasn't going to waste a second of it.

* * *

Dressed and refreshed from their swim, Carrie and Frank walked hand in hand along the pool's edge. Carrie felt a peace unfamiliar to her—but not because she couldn't recall another day such as this. In the core of her soul, she knew with a certainty that she'd had few days in her life filled with this degree of happiness.

Not for the first time, she wondered if her life had, indeed, been that sad and empty. If it had, did she want to remember it? Wouldn't she be happier not knowing the truth?

The words Irma had spoken to her back in the cabin nudged at Carrie's conscience. *There is no future without a past.*

Irma was right. Carrie wanted a future more now than ever before. Glancing at Frank's profile, she smiled. Especially now. If she had to recall a past that she'd rather forget in order to have that future, then she would do it. But not now, not today.

"Why so quiet?"

Frank's voice brought her out of her thoughts.

She grinned at him. "Just enjoying the company."

He squeezed her hand, and then kissed her cheek. "Let's go up there." He looked up to the top of the falls.

Carrie followed his gaze. Her stomach dropped, and her knees weakened at the thought of climbing the rock face to the top. Why was she afraid? She couldn't tell, but the fear was real and deep and strong. "I don't know."

Frank turned to face her. "I'll be with you all the way. Promise."

Still she hesitated.

It's important to him. Look at his eyes. They're twinkling. Do you want the sadness to come back? Well, do you? You can do this, Carrie.

Her head snapped toward Frank. Instantly, she

knew it wasn't Frank who would have said the words. Who, then, would be with her all the way? Something in her pocket tapped against her leg. She slipped her hand in to see what it was. Her fingers closed around the tiny bear talisman she'd left on her night table.

She'd barely had time to wonder how it had gotten from Clara's cottage to her pocket when the bear warmed to her touch. Instantly, she knew the answer.

"Well?" Frank asked. "Do you trust me?"

She still wasn't sure she could do it, but with Frank beside her, she'd try. "Absolutely."

"Let's go."

Up close, the rock face was even more treacherous looking than it had been from below. But Carrie was determined. The first few feet, she held tight to Frank's hand, allowing him to guide her over the rough spots and pulling her up when the height seemed beyond what her shorter legs could manage to span.

"I've got you," he reassured her over and over, holding tightly to her hand. And she knew he did.

At first, each step she took demanded concentration and guts. Each glance down to the pool below left her stomach bottomless. But as time wore on and they climbed higher above the pool, Carrie gained confidence. She could do this, and suddenly, she wanted to do it herself. She wanted to prove to herself that she could make it without relying on Frank. Without relying on anyone.

Reaching deep down inside, she found a new determination and strength. She let go of Frank's hand and began making her way over the slippery rocks and through the narrow crevices. Sometimes her foot slipped, but she grabbed on to the rocks and continued the upward climb.

Before she knew it, she and Frank were standing on the overlook above the falls.

"We did it!" She grinned up at Frank and felt a surge of accomplishment so strong that she wanted to declare it to the world.

"Yes, we did," he said, gathering her close against his side and kissing the top of her head. "But more importantly, *you* did it, Carrie."

Lifting her gaze to his, her smile widened. "I did, didn't I?"

She'd reached down inside and found a courage she'd forgotten she had, and then she'd conquered her fear and moved upward. For a reason she couldn't put a finger on, she knew that was important.

But she barely had time to think about it. Frank was kissing her again, and she gave herself up to the rapture of it. Her knees gave way. They sank to the soft, spongy, damp grass and made love again with the roar of the falls echoing the passion of their joining.

* * *

Alvin stood outside Ellie's door with his hand raised, trying to decide if he should knock or just head back to the fringes of the forest. Before he could make up his mind, the door swung open. On the other side of the threshold stood Ellie and Emanuel.

Emanuel was smiling at him in that secretive way he had when he was up to something. Alvin hoped it didn't involve him, but he was afraid it did. Still a bit miffed at Emanuel for forcing the memory of that dreadful night in his New York apartment, Alvin gave the Elder a curt nod.

"I can come back later," he told Ellie and turned to leave.

"No need," Emanuel said and stepped around Alvin. "Clara has coffee brewing for me. Mustn't keep her waiting." He smiled at Ellie, inclined his head at Alvin, and then ambled down the path toward Clara's cottage.

For a while, Alvin watched Emanuel's progress up the path. Why, when Emanuel had always called him his friend, had he forced such a hurtful memory on him? When an answer was not readily available, Alvin wasn't surprised. Emanuel was a complicated man who kept his own counsel and very often did things the rest of the village didn't understand. Alvin doubted if anyone, with the possible exception of Clara, knew why the village Elder did anything.

"Alvin?"

Ellie's voice drew his attention back to her. She had stepped out of the cottage and stood beside him in a pool of sunlight. The beams glinted off her blond hair, creating a faux halo around her head. His heart leaped into his throat, and he had to swallow hard to dislodge it.

"Would you like to come inside?"

He nodded, not yet trusting his voice. She reentered the cottage, and he followed her into the living room and sank into his favorite chair beside the blazing fire. As he searched for the right words to broach why he'd come to Ellie, his endless questions about himself and Frank, the hands-less grandfather clock in the corner ticked away the minutes. At other times, he found the soft *tick tock* soothing. Today it rubbed his nerves raw.

He was so deep in his thoughts about the clock's irritating noise that, when Ellie slipped a cup of fragrant herbal tea into his big hands, Alvin started.

"Thanks."

Normally, tea was not his beverage of choice, but he was so preoccupied that he sipped it and started in surprise at the sweet, unusual flavor and the warmth it brought to his body.

"Odd thing about tea," Ellie said absently as she swirled a tea bag around in her cup, "the longer you drag a tea bag through the water, the more intense the tea becomes. If you let it stew too long, the tea becomes bitter and unbearable to drink." She glanced at him. "Very counterproductive, don't you think?"

He nodded absently. "I guess."

"Much like the troubles humans let stew inside them."

Alvin frowned at her. What was she trying to tell him? "Your point?"

"Why have you allowed your troubles to stew inside you for so long and turn you so bitter?"

Since Ellie normally used the same subtlety, sometimes to the point of ambiguity, as Emanuel often employed, Alvin was taken aback at her frankness. His mouth dropped open in shock.

She set her cup on the table at her side, then leaned forward and grasped his hands. "Alvin, do you enjoy all this pain you keep bottled up inside?"

For a long time he stared down at her small hands. Next to his they were so fragile looking, but he knew that they were strong enough to hold the tattered souls of the Assignments who came into the village.

Ellie tilted her head. "Well? Do you enjoy the pain?"

He glanced at her and then shook his head. "Of course not."

"Then why not get it out where you can look at it and see what you can do to get rid of it?" She sighed and dropped her gaze to their clasped hands. "It hurts me so much to see you in such misery. I want to help. Emanuel wants to help, but you won't let any of us get close enough."

Alvin pulled abruptly from her grasp and stood. "I shouldn't have come here today."

"No, you shouldn't have," she said quietly. When he swung back to frown at her, she smiled gently. "You should have come here months ago."

The room went silent. Except for the crackle of the fire blazing in the hearth and the endless tick of the clock, only the sound of their breathing could be heard. Ellie looked pointedly from Alvin to the recently vacated chair. He sighed and returned to his seat.

When he glanced at the cup of tea, Ellie giggled. "Would you rather have coffee?"

He let a smile sneak through. Ellie knew him so well. And her point was made, so there was no need for him to drink the tea just to be polite. "Yes, please."

A few minutes later, they were both sipping a cup of strong coffee. Ellie set hers aside and looked at him expectantly.

He knew what she was waiting for. He leaned forward, rested his elbows on his thighs, and clutched the mug in front of him. Slowly he began telling her of the argument he and Alice had had on the phone, then of his return to New York with his exciting news about the lucrative deal he'd closed with Grayson Tech. When he got to the part about what he'd found waiting for him inside the apartment, he stopped talking.

"There's more, isn't there?" Ellie asked quietly.

He nodded, not trusting himself to say the words.

She took the mug away from him and set it aside. Then she grasped his big hand in hers and looked him in the eye. "Remember, faith and trust, Alvin. Have faith that, though it may be painful at first, getting it out will ease your burden. And trust that I'll always be here to listen."

The warmth in her eyes flowed through him like life-giving blood. At that moment, he finally admitted something he'd known for a long time. He loved Ellie Stanton. He had for a very long time. That love gave him the strength to go on.

Alvin cleared the emotion clogging his throat and allowed the memories to wash over him.

* * *

When he found the apartment door ajar, Alvin got a sick feeling in the pit of his stomach. Alice was fanatical about locking the doors at all times, whether or not they were at home. This was not in any way typical of her. Something was terribly wrong.

He pushed the door wider and stepped into the

room. The scene that met his eyes made him want to vomit. The room was in chaos: furniture upturned; books ripped from the bookcase and scattered over the rug; curtains half-torn from the windows; lamps broken and bent on the floor.

Everywhere he looked was blood: smears of it, drops of it, and puddles of it. The furniture and walls were splattered with bright, red spots. Across the beige carpeting were bloody footprints too big to be Alice's.

"Nooo!"

The scream ripped from him. Like a man demented, he raced through the apartment screaming his wife's name. But she was nowhere to be found—until he reached their bedroom, the room in which so much love had dwelt.

There, half in the closet and half on the bedroom floor, as if she'd been trying to hide from the intruder, lay Alice's body, covered in blood. On the floor beside her lay the bloody statue of Venus, the Goddess of Love, a gift he'd brought back last year when he'd gone on a business trip to Italy.

* * *

Alvin blinked away his tears and roused himself from the memory. He expected to be doubled over with what Ellie had forced him to face. Instead, although still weighted down with the reality of his wife's brutal murder, he felt a strange surge of liberation. As if a huge weight had been lifted from his soul.

Sometime, while he'd been talking, Ellie had moved from her chair and sat at his feet, her cheek rested against his knees, and her hands still clutched his. "I'm so sorry, Alvin. What a horrible thing for you."

"Don't feel sorry for me." He pulled free of her grip and threw himself back in the chair. "If I had. . ." He sniffed loudly, then drew a handkerchief from his pocket and blew his nose.

"Alvin, I'm sure there was nothing you could have done. It was all over by the time you got home."

He almost laughed. "Yes, by the time I got home. By the time I dragged myself away from my almighty important business deal."

Ellie blinked. "I don't understand."

"Don't you?" he asked, his voice dead. "If I had come home when I should have, instead of staying for another day to close a business deal, I would have been there. I could have saved her."

Pushing herself to her knees to be on eye level with him, Ellie frowned. "But you don't know that. There are all kinds of things that could have happened. Your plane from California could have been delayed or cancelled. You could have missed the plane—"

"But none of that happened."

"How do you know? Did you check with the airline to see if the plane you should have been on arrived on time?"

Alvin shook his head. He'd barely been able to think clearly enough to call 911 and give the detectives the details of what he knew. Why would he have thought to check on a flight he hadn't even been on? To his dismay, he realized that Ellie's arguments made perfect sense, but they did nothing to relieve the guilt he'd lived with for almost six years.

"No matter how many ifs and buts you dream up, the fact is, Ellie, *I wasn't there*. And I wasn't there because I thought my business was more important than being home with my wife."

"You said she was fanatical about locking the door, so how did the killer get in?"

He sighed. Ellie was like a dog with a bone, and she was not about to stop gnawing. "The police said that they found a cap with a messenger-company logo on it on the living room floor. They figured she opened the door, thinking it was a message either from me or for me."

"Is that how they found him?"

He nodded. "He was trolling for something he could sell for drug money." Alvin gave a short laugh that lacked humor. "The funny part is, while he was fighting with Alice, he destroyed most of the things he could have sold." He shook his head and then buried his face in his hands. "Alice died trying to save the damned stereo and TV, and the bastard who killed her ended up with nothing. It was all so senseless." Alvin raised his head and looked at Ellie. "She was a good, loving, gentle woman who didn't deserve to die like that."

Ellie stood and walked back to her own chair. She sat and clasped her hands in her lap. "No, no one does." She paused and looked at him, her gaze steady and strong. "Neither do you."

What was Ellie trying to say? "I don't—"

"If you had been there, couldn't you have been killed right along with Alice?" Ellie didn't wait for him to reply. "Everything happens for a reason, Alvin. Destiny. Yours, like mine, was to come to Renaissance."

Alvin studied her, trying to let her words sink in. Was she right? Had his destiny never been to raise a family with Alice and head up a thriving computer chip business? Had he been intended all along to come here and wander the woods of a tiny village that only appeared when needed? Was he never meant to save Alice from the man who took her life? Was his own destiny to come here, to help others because he had endured and could readily relate to them?

Not that he'd been doing a stellar job of it. He'd done nothing as yet to help Frank. . .

He looked at Ellie's sweet face, and contrarily, although a part of him still wished he'd died with Alice, it hit him that if he hadn't come to Renaissance, there would have been no Ellie in his life, and that would have been almost as tragic as Alice's death.

So maybe his destiny was here, with her. Maybe he was to mentor others. What did that mean about Frank? Was he not supposed to have saved his wife and unborn child? Was he meant to be here, too? Definitely possible, with him being a doctor and all. If so, then what was Frank's destiny? What higher purpose was there for saving his life and taking his wife's? Then Alvin thought about all the tiny souls Frank held in his hands each time he entered the operating room. Was that why? Or was there more, another purpose that none of them realized as yet? Whatever it was, Alvin knew he had to do his damndest to find a way to help Frank, to free him from his self-imposed prison of guilt.

Unsure of exactly how he'd handle it, Alvin stood. He thanked Ellie and then left the cottage.

She watched him walk across the square and head toward his home. His shoulders, though not as stooped with the burden his conscience had carried as they'd been when he'd come to her, were still bent. However, she thought she detected a lighter step and a purpose in his stride that she'd never seen before.

Chapter 12

Frank lay on his bed staring at the painting Carrie had given him. The opening and closing of the front door grabbed his attention, and then he heard what could only be Alvin's footsteps crossing the outer room followed by the muffled *thud* of his bedroom door. This was the first night since Frank's arrival in the village that he'd actually heard Alvin come home, and it took Frank by surprise.

Other than the one instance when Alvin had prodded Frank about Sandy's death, Alvin had been like a ghost in Frank's life, coming and going without being seen, leaving food for him and then disappearing. Basically, doing his best to avoid contact with Frank. What had changed all that?

Frank blinked and pushed his concerns about Alvin's unusual appearance from his mind. He had more important things to think about than the sudden change in the demeanor of a man he barely knew. He'd just had a day with Carrie at the waterfall that was unlike any other he'd ever lived through, and instead of savoring it, he'd spent the last hour or more trying to justify his feelings about it.

On the one hand, he'd spent an entire afternoon making love to a beautiful, desirable, passionate woman and had experienced the joy of seeing her draw on a strength she didn't know she had to climb to the top of the falls. On the other hand, he knew nothing about her. Had he had the right to make love to her, or had he been encroaching on some other guy's territory? Was she married? Engaged? Did she have children? Had he opened the door to a relationship with no future?

Worst of all, had he complicated Carrie's life even more than it already was?

He sat up. *Dammit!* Ostensibly he'd come to Renaissance to sort through his problems, not add more to the pile.

His gaze was drawn back to the painting. Though he'd waited and watched, Sandy did not appear again, and as more and more time passed, he became more convinced that the first time had been his imagination. Maybe. . . Even though he'd seen her three times now, he still wondered if it had been real or if his imagination had been playing tricks on him. He wanted her approval, her forgiveness, not so he could live guilt-free—that was impossible—but so that he could bear to live.

Outside a breeze rose suddenly, moving the trees beyond the window. A sliver of moonlight shafted through the glass and centered on the dresser top. Something glittered in the reflected light.

Frank slid from the bed and went to see what it was. When he got there, his breath caught in his throat. Lying in a halo of moonlight was a gold chain. Hooked to the chain was a small gold locket—the locket he'd given Sandy as a wedding present.

He vividly recalled what he'd said when he'd clasped it around her neck in their Jamaican honeymoon suite.

"I give you my heart for all eternity."

Sandy had turned and kissed him, then smiled. "Eternity is a long time. So I won't hold you to it. If the time ever comes when you need it, I'll give it back to you."

He had sworn to her that he was sure that time would never come. Now, here he was, holding it in his hand. She had always known him so well. Then he noticed a small chunk missing from near the bottom of the heart. He smiled. She'd kept a piece of it, as was right.

No matter how long he lived or who he loved, Frank knew that a very small part of him would always belong to Sandy. A part of his heart and the guilt of killing her.

* * *

Carrie thrashed about in her bed. Her dreams of a lovely waterfall and Frank making love to her had morphed into a nightmare.

* * *

The rough carpeting burned where it rubbed against her stinging cheek. Carrie lifted her head and tried to stand, but her feet became entangled in the material imprisoning her legs and hampering her escape. Beside her on the floor was a huge pile of. . .snow?

How could that be? Snow? Inside?

Hoping to grab some of the cold, white stuff to hold against her burning cheek, she reached for it, but her hands closed around not snow, but a silky, slick material. Blinking several times to clear her blurred vision, she finally realized that what she was clutching was white silk. She dragged the material closer and realized she was holding the hem of a wedding gown.

A wedding gown? Whose? Hers?

She looked down at herself and gasped. The front of her nightgown was covered in blood. Hers? From the throbbing in her temple and the blood oozing from several cuts on her arms, it had to be hers. Besides, there was no one else—

Suddenly an indescribable sense of urgency seized her. She had to get out of there, wherever "there" was. Awkwardly fighting off the tangles of nightgown and pulling herself to her hands and knees, she began to crawl toward the door. The sudden appearance of a pair of obviously male legs encased in black pants and feet in shiny, black shoes, stepping in front of her, stopped her.

A dark shadow fell over her. Above her a deep voice emitted an evil laugh. "Is my bride going somewhere?"

Bride? Was that really her gown? Was she his bride? Chills shivered up and down her spine. Terror, cold and icy, gathered in a tight ball inside her chest.

Slowly, Carrie raised her gaze. Above her hovered a man. Him. As before, his features were blurred as if she was seeing them through water. But the bone-chilling fear his voice evoked was the same.

"Who are you?" she choked out on a wave of unexpected courage. "What do you want from me?"

"Your life," he snarled. "I want your life."

* * *

Carrie bolted up sharply in bed, her eyes stretched wide, her gaze darting around the room. Her pulse raced, and her heartbeat throbbed in her aching temple. She looked down at herself and found the clean, pink nightgown she'd put on the evening before. *A dream. It was all just another dream.*

A sigh of relief gushed from her. Though she felt better knowing it had all been a nightmare, the terror she'd felt remained behind. When would this end? When would she finally be able to put a meaning to her dreams and a face to her tormenter?

But was it a dream. . .or a memory?

She left the bed and went to the window seat. Sitting down, she drew up her legs and circled her arms around her knees, then rested her chin on them. Below her, shadows played over the garden. Moonlight sprinkled the stream with slivers of silvery light. Where the light hit the banks of the stream, it could have been mistaken for snow.

Snow. Not snow. It was a wedding gown. Hers?

Like a cold, black fog, the dream replayed itself in her head, and for the first time since the faceless man had started haunting her dreams, memories fought their way through the cobwebs cocooning her mind. Pieces of pictures from the far reaches of her lost memory came into sharp focus and flashed before her mind's eye like a slide show.

The wedding gown that had been her mother's. The

bouquet of white roses. The church decked out in white bows and stephanotis.

Then the motel, and then pain. A lot of never-ending pain.

Her entire body went icy cold. It had not been a dream. It had been a reenactment of her wedding night. Then a thought so horrible, so terrifying drained her of all strength.

Only one explanation for the dream made sense. She was married. The faceless man was her husband, and he wanted to kill her.

* * *

Still elated from the previous day, Frank bounded out of bed, washed and dressed, wolfed down the cheese and bread Alvin had left for him, and hurried out of the cottage. Automatically, he headed for the stream.

He couldn't wait to see Carrie again. His step was lighter than it had been in ages, and his heartbeat quickened with the anticipation of another day with her. For the first time in a very long time, Frank Donovan felt utterly and completely alive, and happy to be so. He was looking forward to life, to tomorrow, to all the tomorrows spread out before him.

Puffy clouds scuttled across a sky so blue it defied

description. Birds sang in the trees, and insects moved busily among the flowers bordering the path. The trees swayed gracefully in the soft breeze. His skin felt deliciously warm from the hot sun beating down on him. Life was good again. Determinedly, he set the guilt aside—just for today. He would not let it consume him. Just for a while. . .

He rounded the hedgerow that shielded Clara's garden from the rest of the village. There, gazing silently over the stream, was Carrie. His heart skipped several beats. He stopped and drank in her beauty.

The sunlight turned her hair to fire. The breeze swept it back away from her face in burning waves. He had never seen anything quite as beautiful as Carrie. She took his breath away.

"Good morning," he said softly.

She started, as if she'd been deep in thought and he'd surprised her, and turned to face him. "Good morning."

Frank took a step toward her, but she backed away. Puzzled, he halted. She was wringing her hands, and her eyes were red and swollen from crying. Her whole body seemed to be on edge, ready to bolt at the least provocation. What had happened between last night and this morning? Worse yet, he knew that his presence was the cause of her edginess.

"Carrie?"

"No." She sobbed and shook her head. Holding up her hand, she backed still farther away from him. "Please don't touch me."

Totally confused, Frank took a step toward her, but stopped when he saw that, along with her tears, something else filled her eyes. Lurking in their green depths was stark fear.

"Carrie, what is it? What's wrong?"

She took a deep breath, as though trying to pull herself together, and then sat on the rock, her eyes averted from him.

Something was terribly wrong. His earlier elation was replaced by a very sick feeling in the pit of his stomach.

"Carrie? Please tell me what's wrong. What's happened?"

"I. . .I can't be with you anymore."

As if a fist had slammed into his gut, Frank fought for breath. Of everything she could have said, this was the last thing he'd expected.

"Why?"

She raised an anguished face to his. "Because I know who the faceless man is. I had another dream last night, and I still don't know what he looks like, but I'm certain of who he is."

Frank squatted on the grass at her feet. He didn't try

to touch her, and he kept enough distance between them so as not to spook her.

Though he didn't really want to know, as if not speaking it would make it not so, he had to ask her. "Who is he?"

For the first time, she met his gaze head-on. More tears gathered in her eyes and then spilled over onto her pale cheeks. "He's. . . He's my husband." She blurted the last words as if to get them past her lips before she lost her nerve.

Frank rocked back on his heels, completely stunned by her words. "Your—"

He couldn't say it. He couldn't allow himself to believe that this woman, who had become so special to him, belonged to someone else. It just wasn't possible. But deep down he knew it *was* possible and that he'd subconsciously been hoping all along that, when she regained her memory, this would not be the case.

As though someone had pulled the plug from a sink filled with water, the happiness he'd felt upon waking drained away. In the space of time it took her to speak those few words, Frank's world had crumbled at his feet.

But this was not about him. Carrie was terrified, and the look on her face was one that mirrored the desolation lying in the pit of his stomach. He was not the only one hurting.

"So your memory came back." His voice sounded as dead as he felt inside.

"Not all of it. Only a few more bits and pieces."

Hope rose in him. He grabbed her shoulders. "Then maybe he's not your husband. Maybe it was just a crazy dream. Maybe he is someone else."

She didn't say anything. But she didn't have to. He could tell by her expression that she had already gone down the list of maybes and had rejected them all.

The weight of despair on his shoulders made him drop to the grass. "So what happens now? Will you be leaving the village?"

Carrie shook her head. "Clara said when it was time for me to leave, the mist would gather around Renaissance again." She waved her hand. "As you can see, the day is crystal clear. There must be more I need to know. Maybe when I finally see his face. . ."

Although Frank's brain had accepted what she'd been telling him, his heart refused. He couldn't lose her, too. Not now. Not when everything was turning around for them. Not after yesterday. He had to do something to stop the sharp pain ripping through him and blinding him to reason.

"Tell me about the dream. Maybe you're wrong, Carrie."

She knew she wasn't wrong. She'd thought about it all

night until the sun rose over the trees. Nevertheless, leaving nothing out, she told him about the dream. When she got to the part about the man wanting her life, she saw the blood drain from Frank's face and heard his sharp intake of breath, followed by a string of subdued curses.

"So, what do you think?" she asked when she'd finished her recounting.

He shook his head. "I don't know. But what I do know is that the wedding gown proves nothing, and as long as that bastard has no face, you can't be sure who he is or how he's connected to you, if at all."

She wanted so much to believe him, but down deep, she knew he was wrong. This dream and what it had disclosed to her meant the end of them.

CHAPTER 13

Three weeks later, Alvin sat next to Emanuel on a fallen tree situated near the cliff above the village. The Elder was making Alvin uncomfortable. He just sat there, silent and waiting. Alvin knew what Emanuel was waiting for. He wanted Alvin to tell him why he hadn't talked to Frank about his demons. Not that Alvin had tried all that hard to get Frank to talk, but he didn't seem eager to talk to Alvin about demons or anything else. Frank was too busy with other pursuits. Namely, the woman Carrie.

"I wish they could find a way to be happy," Alvin finally said.

He didn't look at the Elder. He didn't want to see the condemnation on his face. He didn't want to be reminded that he'd failed in his task. He'd never failed Emanuel before and now that he had, he found it unbearable. And he knew why. If he made Frank confront his problems, Alvin feared he would have to confront his own.

After he'd left Ellie that day, he'd felt good. His burden seemed lighter, his determination to help Frank firmly planted in his mind. But as the days passed and he'd made no effort to talk with Frank, Alvin knew deep in his gut that he had not found total forgiveness for himself. He could not get past the idea that if he'd only come home when he should have. . . To do that, he would have to walk methodically through that horrible day again, as well as the aftermath of Alice's death.

The selfishness of his failure ate a hole in his heart.

"Happiness is a fleeting thing, Alvin. A man can be happy on the outside and dying on the inside." Alvin had to think for a moment before he realized Emanuel was referring to his prior statement about wishing Frank and Carrie could be happy.

There was no condemnation in Emanuel's voice, which made it all the more painful for Alvin. If only he would get mad at him instead of this calm acceptance of Alvin's failure. But that wasn't Emanuel's way.

"Right now, Frank has his problem buried behind a thin veil. Soon, very soon, that veil will rip wide open."

"I know," Alvin said quietly. "But how can I help him when I haven't been able to help myself?"

Emanuel turned his wise gaze on Alvin. "Haven't you?"

Alvin rose and walked to the edge of the precipice on which they sat. He looked down into the glen without seeing it. The scenario he'd found in his apartment played through his mind. Blood. All that blood. Alice's still body cradled in his arms. And the self-hatred rising up and consuming him. The hatred that would send him running from all he'd once thought so important.

"Why?" he asked the Elder. He swung on him like an enraged beast. His voice hissed from between his teeth. "Why did this happen to me, to Alice?"

Emanuel rose. His long robes stirred languidly around his robust body. "Why does anything happen, my friend? When you know the answer to that question, you will also find the answer to helping Frank. Look into your heart, Alvin. Faith and trust."

Alvin looked away, unable to stand the compassion he saw reflected in the Elder's kind face. "Just this once, why can't you give me a straight answer?" He made no effort to temper the harshness of his tone.

When Emanuel didn't reply, Alvin looked up to confront him. But the Elder had vanished. The only things that affirmed he'd even been there at all were the footprints and the drag marks from his long robe in the soft earth.

Left to himself, Alvin sank back on the fallen tree and buried his face in his hands. God, how he hated himself. If only he'd come home. If only the burglars had gone to the apartment next door or down the hall or down the street. If only. . .

Alvin brought his thoughts to a halt. He'd just wished his excruciating pain on someone else. What had become of him that he could have such terrible thoughts? When had his heart hardened into the stone that lay beneath his breast? When had he begun drowning himself in so much self-pity that he could actually wish his pain and suffering on some other innocent person?

When you blinded yourself to your fellow man, Alvin. When your pain became the center of your existence and the pain of those around you ceased to matter.

The voice came from inside his head, but he recognized it immediately as Ellie's. Was she right? Had he become so absorbed in self-pity that he'd stopped seeing the pain that others suffered? Was that why he couldn't help Frank, didn't want to help Frank? Was he enjoying Frank's pain in some twisted way?

No. You've just become so fixated on your own suffering that you don't see the suffering of others. You took some positive steps toward that end. Don't stop now. Don't go backward. Open your heart, Alvin. Just forgiving yourself isn't enough. Learn to love yourself again, and you'll be able to empathize with others.

Love himself? How could he love a man who put more

value on his business than on the woman he loved?

Open his heart? He wasn't even sure he had a heart anymore.

As if checking to make sure, he placed his hand over the left side of his chest. A strong, steady beat pulsated against his palm. Okay, so he did have a heart. So what? All that proved was that he was alive. If that's what he could call this half existence he mimed from day to day.

He buried his face in his hands.

"Life has a way of stomping on a body's neck and holding their head to the ground until they can't breathe."

The familiar voice drew Alvin's head up sharply. Sitting beside him on the tree trunk was a woman, although it was hard to tell that she was a woman beneath the many layers of grimy rags she wore. Her rheumy, blue eyes twinkled merrily through a fringe of graying hair that had escaped the moth-eaten cap she'd jammed on her head. In her hand she held a sunflower. A smaller bunch of the same bright yellow flowers protruded from a packed grocery cart parked close beside her.

The last time he'd seen her or heard those words had been. . .

He looked around. He was no longer in the woods above the village. He was sitting on a bench in Central Park. The very bench where he'd first met. . .

"Irma?" Her gap-toothed grin lit up her face. "One and the same," the Guide announced. "Good to see you again."

He blinked. "But we. . ."

The wrinkles in her brow deepened. She waved a hand encased in a fingerless glove as grimy as her clothes through the air. "That's not important. What's important is what has you looking so down and out."

Again, those were the same words she'd spoken the last time they'd met. Then it hit him. Irma had been sent to talk to him.

"Life," he told her.

"Ah. Life. Yup." She nodded and the gray hair flopped back and forth against her forehead. "It sure has a way of takin' all the damned fun outta livin' it, don't it?" She slapped Alvin on the shoulder with a strength that was unexpected, coming from a woman as frail looking as Irma, and then laughed at her own joke.

Despite his gloomy mood, Alvin smiled. This Irma was so different from the Irma he knew now as Meghan's mother, a woman who had taken over the duties of librarian in Tarrytown. The librarian Irma was well dressed, well spoken, and wouldn't have uttered a curse word if someone held a knife to her throat.

"Ah, we always think our life is the worst. But when you look around, there's those that have a hell of a lot less to be happy about than we do." She pointed a dirt-encrusted finger toward a group of people on the far side of the park. "See that elderly couple over there?"

Alvin followed the direction of Irma's finger. "The two sitting on the park bench beneath the tree?"

"Yup," he said distractedly.

She shifted her position so she was looking directly at Alvin. "Do you recognize them?"

Alvin had expected a repetition of their initial conversation years ago when he'd first met Irma, before Alvin had come to Renaissance. But this was not what he and Irma had talked about that day. That day they'd talked about his aching soul and his need to retreat from the world. Today, she seemed bent on a new form of attack.

"Well?"

He shook himself and then studied the old couple for a moment. They appeared to be in their seventies or eighties. As he watched, the woman helped the old man put on his sweater and then tugged it snugly around his bent shoulders. Then she took out a handkerchief and dabbed at his mouth and kissed his cheek. The man continued to stare straight ahead, showing no sign he was aware of any of her ministrations.

"That's Mr. and Mrs. Albertson. Your neighbors. He's in the advance stages of Alzheimer's. If she had died instead of Alice—"

"How do you know about Alice?" He was certain

he'd never told her about Alice, never so much as mentioned her name to Irma.

Instead of answering his question, Irma ignored him and went on. "If she had died instead of Alice, what would have become of him?"

He didn't need Irma's illustration to remind him how selfish his wish had been—that the burglar had gone into the apartment next door instead of theirs. Shame smothered him. When had he become a monster that would shift this terrible burden to another's life just to find relief? How could he have wished for such a terrible thing to befall them?

"Not a monster, my boy. It's easier to bear your pain if you can place it on someone else's shoulders."

He'd gotten so used to Emanuel doing the same thing, that it no longer took him by surprise that Irma had read his thoughts. "I get your point."

"Sadly, I'm not sure you do, my boy."

He shook his head and stood. "I shouldn't wish my bad fortune on someone else because they might end up even worse off than I am."

"There's that, but there's more to this than thoughtless wishes." She sighed and smelled the sunflower. "People are like some flowers." She held up the flower. "This one is self-sufficient. It has all the parts in the blossom to reproduce. But this one. . ." She reached into her cart

189

full of junk, and to his total shock, extracted a perfect lavender and white orchid. "This one needs another flower to pollinate it to reproduce."

Alvin was confused. He didn't think they'd been talking about reproduction. "I don't understand. What does reproducing have to do with any of this?"

Irma tucked the orchid into a hole in her cap. "You're missing the point. Sit your buns down here." She patted the seat next to her.

Alvin had to fight back a smile at the comical picture Irma made with that elegant flower stuck into her moth-eaten cap. She reminded him of a destitute hula dancer. He bit his lip and took a seat on the bench.

Irma sighed and took a moment to gather her thoughts. "People need people. As a team, or with the help of a stranger they run into on the street. Whichever way it goes, no one can get along in a vacuum. Those two over there," she pointed to the elderly couple, "need each other. Just like this flower," she held up the sunflower, "needs the other parts inside that blossom to reproduce." She plucked the orchid from her cap. "This flower needs another flower to reproduce. Just as some humans sometimes need to call on the help of other humans to get over the rough spots." She stopped talking and studied Alvin. "No matter how you look at it, they cannot make it alone."

Again she waited for Alvin to absorb what she was saying.

He understood her point. Basically, misery loves company. What he didn't understand was, how could he use this lesson in botany to get Frank to talk?

"So how does this make Frank open up to me?"

She smiled and stood. "You've already taken the first step." Then she put the flowers back in the shopping cart, adjusted her cap, and walked away down the path. "You know, this is the first time you've thought exclusively of Frank," she said and then waved a gnarled hand at him over her shoulder and continued on her way. Then she stopped and turned back to him. "Maybe you should give some thought to what the police told you that night."

Alvin watched her go, feeling as confused as he'd been before she showed up. He looked toward the overcast sky, closed his eyes, and shook his head. When he opened his eyes, he was back on the tree trunk. He leaned forward, placed his elbows on his thighs, and shifted his gaze to the ground. Despite his confusion and frustration, what he saw made him smile.

There, between his feet, lay the perfect lavender and white orchid. The one flower that needed another to survive and reproduce. "You win, Irma," he whispered to the wind. "Point taken."

* * *

Clara stood beside her loom, watching Carrie sit silently at the table, clutching a cup from which she hadn't taken so much as a single sip in the past hour. The girl hadn't set foot outside the house or picked up her paintbrush in over four days. During that time, she hadn't even mentioned Frank's name, and she'd done all she could to avoid meeting him.

Although Clara knew it was necessary to have this empathy with an Assignment to help heal her charges, at times like this, when she could feel their pain so acutely, she had a hard time dealing with it. And right now, she could feel Carrie's anguish right down to the soles of her feet.

Unable to stand it any longer, Clara took the seat across from Carrie and then gathered the girl's hands in hers.

"Would you like to talk about whatever it is eating a hole in your heart?"

Carrie glanced up, withdrew her hand, and then shook her head. "You wouldn't understand."

"Don't tell Emanuel that. I'll get fired." Clara laughed, and then, seeing that Carrie had not even cracked a smile, immediately became very serious. "Understanding is a big part of what I do, dear." When Carrie made no move to comply, Clara again pressed her to talk. "Try me."

Instead of confiding in Clara, Carrie set the cup aside, rose from the table, and then walked out of the cottage.

Clara stared after her. Even after Carrie had disappeared from sight, Clara continued to study the closed door. Something had to be done. But not too much. Too much would undo all the good they'd accomplished until now. Perhaps just one of Emanuel's nudges would do it.

CHAPTER 14

Carrie meandered across Clara's backyard, not really seeing where she was going. Not that she cared. She desperately missed Frank and their chats. But since she'd called off anything between them, she hadn't seen him except from a distance. His absence left a huge hole in her life. At times, she almost felt as if she'd be willing to sacrifice her memory just to have him back.

It had taken several sleepless nights and a lot of thought on her part, but she finally was forced to admit that she was falling in love with the heart surgeon. Rather than bringing her peace of mind, it just turned her emotions into a tangled web of confusion fueled by unanswerable questions. One in particular.

How could she be married to one man she couldn't remember and love another she couldn't forget?

There wasn't much she remembered about herself,

but she didn't believe she could do something like that. Then she recalled what her grandmother had said when Carrie had asked her why she'd married a man so different from her. Grampa Bill had been a sweetheart, but he'd also been a rough and rugged outdoorsman, while Gram had been a homebody, elegant and steeped in refinement. He'd been happy tromping through his beloved woods. Gram had been equally as happy sitting in the front parlor and serving tea to her friends from a porcelain pot. But above all that, the love they shared had been very special.

Her grandmother's words rang through her mind: *What you see on the outside isn't always what's in the heart. Your granddad is a rough man on the outside, but soft and smooth as butter on the inside. Following your heart is a good thing, but don't forget to give some notice to what's going on in your head, as well.*

So what was Carrie's brain trying to tell her about Frank? And why wouldn't it tell her more about herself?

Carrie flopped down onto her stomach, her head facing the stream. The grass felt warm from the sun and emitted that special, just-mowed aroma that she always associated with summer. She hitched herself closer to the water and allowed the tips of her fingers to trail through its crystal ripples. The cool caress calmed her shattered nerve endings and even coaxed a smile to her lips.

Carrie slid closer and immersed her forearms in the stream up to her elbows. The cool water felt so good, and she amused herself by watching the water adopt new currents to flow gently around her limbs. She relaxed her arms and allowed the water to pull them along with it. What started out being gentle tugs on her arms grew stronger. At first she was alarmed and started to extract her arms from the stream, but then she allowed it to pull at her. Her body began to slip toward the edge of the bank, and she had no desire to stop it. Bit by bit she moved closer as though some unseen hand were pulling at her.

Almost in slow motion, her body slipped over the bank and into the stream. The water closed over her head.

* * *

The bathtub was so full that Carrie could hear the water splash over onto the floor. The problem had to be the water pouring from the faucets above her head. She tried to reach for them to turn them off, but something heavy pressed against her chest, holding her down and keeping her fingers from closing over the faucet handles. She fought to free herself.

The pressure increased, pushing her down. Her head went deeper beneath the surface. She held her breath until her lungs felt as if they'd burst from her body. Still the weight on her chest remained in place. With both hands, she clawed at hard flesh.

Through the water she could make out the blurred silhouette of a man. It was his hand holding her down. He was trying to drown her.

Panic flowed through her with a white-hot vengeance. Frantically she tried to free herself from his hold. Her fingernails dug furrows into his flesh. Her legs thrashed against the imprisoning water, her heels beating painfully off the tub's hard bottom. But as her body flailed about uselessly, he continued to hold her down.

Her lungs screamed for air. Her chest throbbed painfully. She had to breathe. No, her mind screamed. You can't breathe yet. Hold on a little longer. Just a little longer.

Just when she was sure she'd held her breath as long as she could, she was hauled to the surface. Gasping and choking, she inhaled huge gulps of air. Water ran into her eyes. She brushed it aside. Standing over her was the faceless man.

"You want to sneak off to the lake, bitch? You want to be near water that bad? Well, I can see to it that you get all the water you want right here."

With a violent shove, he pushed her beneath the surface again. Once more the water enveloped her. She barely had time to hold her breath. Instinctively, her need for survival overriding her logic, she fought against the hands holding her down. Once more, when her lungs were about to burst, he hauled her out.

She gasped for air and sputtered. "No. . . Please. . . No. . .more."

* * *

"I won't do it again."

"Carrie?"

"No," she cried, fighting frantically against the hands imprisoning her shoulders. "No! No more!"

"Carrie, it's me. Frank." He lifted her upper body into his arms. Her hands still flailed at the air. One caught his cheek, and her nails sliced a scratch across his flesh. He winced, but held her tight. "Carrie, baby. It's me. You're safe."

At last, she stopped struggling and really looked at him. Recognition lit her eyes, and she went limp in his arms. He cradled her against him, crooning softly to her.

"He. . .he was trying to drown me." Her whispered words feathered his ear.

Frank's blood ran cold. Before he asked, he knew what the answer would be. "Who? Who was trying to drown you?"

She drew back and looked at him. Her hair was plastered to her face as though she had, indeed, been submerged in water, but the rest of her was bone-dry. "The man from my dreams." She turned in his arms and grabbed his shirt in her fists. "He wants to kill me, Frank."

Frank grasped the only explanation he could give her. "Carrie, you were dreaming. You must have laid down here and fallen asleep."

As though he'd slapped her, she pulled from his arms, stood, and backed away from him. "Don't tell me it was only a dream. Nothing in this damned place is *only* anything." Her voice grew so loud that birds abandoned their perches in nearby trees. Spinning, she stared at Frank. Her eyes had grown large and brimmed with the fear she must be feeling. Her gaze darted around them. "Am I going crazy, Frank? Is that why all this is happening? Maybe I'm not even here. Maybe I'm living through some unending grotesque nightmare."

Suddenly, she collapsed in a heap in front of him. The moment he'd stepped through the bushes and seen her body flailing about on the ground, he knew what was happening. She was imprisoned in another of those hellish nightmares that had been haunting her dreams.

He'd never felt so helpless in his entire life. He wanted so much to take away Carrie's fear and pain, but he didn't know how. He went to her and knelt beside her.

"You told me once that Clara said everything that happens here has a purpose. These dreams have to be trying to show you something. Tell me about this one, and then we'll talk it out, see if we can figure out what it's trying to tell you."

She raised her face to him. "What's the point?" The tears had been replaced by a bleak, hopeless surrender that made his blood run cold. "I know what it's telling me. I'm married to a man who's trying to kill me. How much plainer could it be?"

Frank hauled her to him. He would do whatever he thought was necessary to protect her, to keep her away from this monster that wanted to hurt her, and, if her dreams were actual memories, a monster who had already hurt her. Saving Carrie was paramount for him, even if it meant giving up his life outside Renaissance.

"You never have to see him again. We'll stay here. He can't find you here. As long as we're in Renaissance, he can't hurt you." But wasn't he? Haunting her dreams? Wasn't he, by virtue of them, already there? She couldn't hide from the demons in her mind.

* * *

After Irma disappeared and Alvin found himself back in the forest above the village, he remained seated on the tree trunk for a long time, thinking about Irma's parting advice. He absently twirled the orchid between his thumb and forefinger. What had the police told him that night that could possibly make his guilt go away? Over and over, he ran their words through his head. And over and over he found nothing that would change his thinking. He still believed that if he'd gone home instead of staying for the business meeting, he would have been able to save Alice. But Irma had seemed so sure. Had he forgotten something the police had said? Was it something that could change his mind? So what had the police said that would change that?

Maybe Irma was mistaken. Yet he'd never known Irma to be wrong, so Alvin had to be missing something. But what?

Once more, he played the detective's words through his mind.

The robbery and murder took place sometime around three in the morning.

So what significance did that have? Knowing Irma, it had to mean something. Alvin played the words again and again through his mind. And then it struck him.

His original flight from Los Angeles to New York had been a 12:15 a.m. red-eye. At 3:00 a.m. he would probably have been changing planes at O'Hare. Even if he had not stayed the extra day and he had taken the flight he'd planned to be on, he wouldn't have been home in time to do anything to prevent the crime. He *couldn't* have saved Alice.

With that realization, he felt as if a weight had been lifted off his shoulders. For the first time in a very long time, Alvin stood straight and inhaled fresh air untainted by the coppery smell of Alice's blood.

All this time, he'd had the answer right there in his head, but he hadn't been able to see past the guilt to find it. He looked down at the orchid. Was Frank doing the same thing? Was he so mired in the fog of blaming himself that he couldn't see where the true fault lay?

Below him in the village, a woman walked slowly down the path toward her cottage near the footbridge. *Ellie.* Her white blond hair lay on her shoulders like freshly fallen snow. His heart swelled, and he knew that now he'd finally be able to tell her what he'd kept hidden in his heart for so long.

But first, he had to see Frank.

CHAPTER 15

"Y ou can't stay here forever."

Frank pulled Carrie closer to the protection of his body. Then he jerked his head toward the voice. Relief washed over him when Alvin stepped from the bushes and into Clara's garden.

Even taking into consideration the orchid clutched in Alvin's huge hands, the rugged woodsman looked different, happier. He seemed to stand straighter, and a soft smile curved his normally set mouth just slightly. Frank couldn't help but wonder what had happened that had changed him. But right now, he had more important things on his mind, like what Alvin had just said.

"Why can't we?"

Alvin walked to where Frank and Carrie sat huddled together on the grass. He folded his long legs beneath him and sat opposite them.

"Because once you're ready, you have to leave to

confront whatever sent you here to begin with."

Frank was again struck by the change in Alvin. His voice was soft and considerate and lacked the edge it had had the last time they'd talked. Then Alvin's words sank in. They'd have to face whatever sent them there in the first place. Carrie would have to face this bastard who was trying to kill her?

Frank stiffened. "What if we refuse to leave the village?"

"You won't have a choice. The mist will gather, and the village will enter its Transition stage and disappear. You'll find yourself on the banks of the Hudson River in a glen filled with snow in the Hudson Highlands."

"But—"

Alvin held up his hand. "There are no buts, Frank. That's the way it is. Once you've left the village and faced your problems, then you can return as a Guide, but only as a Guide and only after you've made peace with yourself."

Carrie stirred in Frank's arms and sat up. She turned to face him, her expression resigned. "He's right. What kind of life could we have with your problems and mine hanging over our heads?" She looked down at her hands. "Besides, we can't have a life anyway until I find out what these dreams mean and who the faceless man is. If he's my husband, then I can't be with you." But regardless of whether or not she was married or engaged to the dream man, she couldn't be with Frank anyway. The dream man was a brutal monster who would not stop short of killing both of them, and she couldn't put Frank in that kind of danger. She took a deep, shuddering breath. "Either way, hiding from my problems is not the answer."

Frank felt as if he'd taken a sucker punch to the gut. He wanted to scream and rage about the injustice of it all, but there was no one to scream and rage at. He didn't care that Carrie might be married. If the faceless man haunting her dreams was her husband, then the bastard should be locked up somewhere in a prison for hurting her.

But even if they could get past that, Carrie was right about one thing—his emotional baggage. He couldn't ask her to share a life with him while he was being dragged down with his own problems. It would destroy anything they could ever have together. His hands balled into impotent fists of frustration.

Carrie laid her hand on his. "I know we can figure this out. We just need time."

Frank gave a short, humorless laugh. "We've had weeks. You're still having indecipherable dreams, and I'm no closer to an answer than I was when I walked in here. How much time is it going to take?"

"Time is relative," Alvin said.

Carrie squeezed Frank's fingers. "We can do this."

Frank looked into her eyes. She had such faith that this place would heal all wounds, answer all their problems. She reminded him a lot of Meghan and Steve and their unshakable faith in Renaissance. He just wished he could share her certainty. "And in the meantime—"

She shook her head. "We can't go on the same way." Then she locked her gaze with his. "Will you continue to be my friend?"

He forced a smile he was far from feeling. "Always." And he meant it, with all his heart.

Frank glanced at Alvin. "What now?"

Alvin pushed his burly body to his feet. "You and I talk."

* * *

Carrie stood beside the stream and watched Frank and Alvin make their way down the path toward Alvin's cottage. They made an odd-looking pair. Frank was not a short man by any means, but Alvin's extraordinarily towering frame dwarfed Frank's. The woodsman's shoulders were twice as wide as his companion's, and his stride equaled two of Frank's steps. Yet there was something about him that bespoke gentleness and kindness, something that made Carrie smile. She prayed that Alvin would be able to help Frank to lift his burden and finally free his soul.

But when they disappeared into the cottage, Carrie was once more faced with her own dilemma. She sank to the grass again, this time staying away from the edge of the stream. She had no desire to repeat her near-drowning experience.

Over the last few days, there had been no more nightmares, and she'd thought herself free of them at last. But then this. . .

When she recalled the suffocating feeling of being beneath the water and not being able to breathe, Carrie shuddered. What in God's name did it all mean? Was it her fears, or had those things actually happened to her? Not knowing was driving her crazy.

Suddenly, she thought about the blood that had been spattered all over her the night she'd found herself wandering the streets of a strange town. Had it been his? Had she. . .killed him—the man who could be her husband—for his cruelty?

Oh, God. *A murderess?* Her knees went weak, and she wobbled. Could she really be a murderess?

* * *

Frank sank onto the chair at the table in Alvin's keeping room. He studied the rugged man as he made a pot of coffee, then freshened the fire in the hearth. His shoulders seemed straighter. His face less lined. Even his lips hinted at a smile. What had happened to change Alvin from the man who would go to any lengths to avoid his houseguest into a man who sought Frank out to talk to him?

Frank eyed the orchid Alvin had placed gently on the table. Orchids didn't grow here, so how had he gotten this exotic flower? Then he chided himself. This was Renaissance. The place where anything was possible, or so they told him. Anything except finding a way to banish Carrie's nightmares and to ease Frank's guilt.

As long as his guilt hung around his neck like a dead albatross, Frank could never go to Carrie, even if she were free to start a new life with him. And he wanted that desperately. Since she'd been avoiding him, he'd come to realize that what had started as a need to protect and care for her had turned to love. That he could feel this way about a woman after having loved and lost Sandy took him completely off guard. Sandy had been the center of his life, and because of that, he had never expected to be able to feel the same way about anyone else.

But Carrie had proved him wrong. She'd snuck beneath his emotional shield and buried herself deep in his heart.

If he was to be able to love her freely and without conditions, he would have to make peace with himself and lighten this millstone he'd been carrying for far too long. To do that, he would have to do what Alvin was urging him to do—talk about a night he'd done his best to forget for a very long time.

"Alvin?"

The woodsman turned from his chore and looked at Frank. He gave a faint nod. "You're ready." It was more a statement than a question.

Frank sighed heavily. "No, not really, but it's way past time."

Throwing one more log onto the fire, Alvin turned, brushed his hands off, and then sat across from Frank. "Then let's do it."

Gripping his hands together tightly in front of him and then taking a deep breath, Frank started talking.

"It was late in November, the week after Thanksgiving. Sandy wanted to start shopping for the holidays. When we left the house, the sky was clear, full of stars." Frank laughed. "Sandy said they looked like an angel had broken her necklace, and the tiny crystal beads had been scattered over the heavens. She loved angels. We had an entire bookcase filled with her angel collection."

He cleared his throat of the choking emotion and went on. "We drove into the city and hit a few stores, then stopped at our favorite restaurant for Italian food. After dinner, we made our way home. But by that time a nasty snowstorm had blown in off Long Island Sound, and the traffic was crawling out of the city. The farther north we went toward our home in Westchester, the heavier the snow got. By the time we were about ten miles from our house, it was nearly a blizzard. I couldn't see more than a few feet in front of the car."

Frank looked at Alvin. He nodded. "I've seen those whiteouts. I've driven through them, too."

Alvin rose and stirred the fire, rearranging a few of the logs. The logs crackled loudly and threw sparks up the chimney like a miniature fireworks display.

Alvin, Frank decided, was using the time to allow Frank to collect his thoughts and diffuse some of the emotion building in his voice. Before returning to the table, Alvin got them both a cup of coffee from the pot he'd put on to brew when they'd first come home.

Frank stirred sugar into his cup. The *clankety clank* of the spoon hitting the sides of the cup and the crackling of the new logs Alvin had added to the fire filled the tense silence that had taken over the room. When he finally stopped stirring, he played with the spoon for a moment before placing it on the table and then going on.

"The plows hadn't come through yet, so distinguishing the road from the shoulder was somewhere between difficult and impossible. We came upon a steep rise in the road. I was afraid we wouldn't make it, so I tapped the gas to give us a head start. We made it up the hill okay, but at the peak of the rise, we hit a patch of ice. The car skidded down the other side, gathering speed as it went. It zigzagged crazily from one side of the road to the other. I kept steering into the skid, but nothing worked. The car just continued on its crazy path. I couldn't control it."

Frank stopped and ran his hand through his hair. He could feel tears running down his cheeks, but he made no effort to suppress them or to wipe them away.

A large hand covered his. He looked up to see Alvin smiling at him. "Go on. Get it all out. Once you do, then we can look at it with unblemished eyes and start you on the road to healing."

He knew Alvin was right, but every word he spoke felt like he was tearing off his flesh one piece at a time, leaving his heart raw and bleeding.

"A car was coming the other way. I tried to swerve to miss it, but I still couldn't steer. Finally the tires caught, but I had the wheel turned too far, and we headed into the oncoming car's path. I jerked the wheel, and the back end fishtailed. We missed the oncoming car, but by then, we were heading for a big oak tree. I tried to turn away, but it was as if someone else had control. The car just kept hurtling toward the tree. Then Sandy screamed and then there was the crunch of metal." He took a deep, shuddering breath.

Frank clamped his hands over his ears to shut out the echo of the smashing metal as they collided with the immovable tree trunk, and then the shattering of glass. And then her terrified voice. Then silence. God, the silence. The never-ending, deafening silence.

With an almost inhuman effort and eager now to get it all out and over with, he pulled himself together and began again, his voice flat and lifeless.

"I looked over at Sandy. She wasn't moving. Her head was covered in so much blood I couldn't see her face or where the blood was coming from. There was a big hole in the windshield where I assumed she'd hit her head. I tried to get to her, to help her, but I was trapped behind the steering wheel. The impact had pushed the engine back and pinned my legs against the seat. I couldn't move." His voice broke. "All I could do was sit there helplessly and look at my dead wife, aware all the time that I had done this to her, and then I blacked out."

Sobs tore from him in great, wrenching torrents.

Alvin sat quietly and waited while Frank cried the tears Alvin suspected had not been shed back then. His heart went out to Frank. The pain of what Frank had lived through that night would have killed a lesser man. At least Alvin had been spared the torment of being there and not being able to do anything but stare helplessly at the lifeless body of the woman he loved.

As he'd listened to Frank relate the events of a night that had altered his life forever, Alvin could not see that any blame should rest on Frank's shoulders. Under the circumstances, he'd done everything he could to prevent the accident. Now, he would have to make Frank see that truth.

"It wasn't your fault." No sooner had the words passed his lips, when Alvin remembered how many times he'd heard those same empty words and how many times he'd thrown them back in the face of the person speaking them. "I know you don't believe that now, and I'm not going to be foolish enough to ask you to, but the time will come when you will believe it." He gripped Frank's arm tightly. "I promise you that."

Frank raised his tear-streaked face to stare at Alvin. "She was a good woman, a loving wife, and she would have made a wonderful mother. Why? Why did she have to die? Why not me?"

Alvin took a deep breath. "How many young lives did you save in surgery after the accident, Frank?"

Frank shook his head. "I don't know. Dozens maybe. What does that have to do with Sandy's death?"

"How many of those lives would have been lost without your knowledge and skill?"

"I know where you're going with this. If I'd died, then those kids would have died. Well, that's not so.

There are other heart surgeons just as skilled as I am, maybe more so, who could have stepped in and performed those operations. But suppose you are right. Maybe I was spared so I could save those kids. That doesn't tell me the reason Sandy had to die."

Alvin sighed and released his grip on Frank's arm. "Perhaps there is no reason, Frank. Perhaps it was just. . .time."

Jumping to his feet, Frank glared at Alvin. "Perhaps it was time"? Is that the only reason you can give me?" Anger, hot and uncontrollable, flared inside him. "I thought you people had all the answers. I thought if I just spilled my guts to you, that you would have something for me. I guess I was wrong. So we're back to square one. *I* drove the car into that tree. *I* killed my wife and unborn child. And *I* have to live with that." He turned and strode into his bedroom and slammed the door behind him.

* * *

Alvin walked slowly down the path toward Ellie's cottage, the orchid clutched incongruously in his large hand. As he walked, he reran Frank's story through his mind. Try as he might, he could find nothing to point at to prove to Frank he was blameless. As far as Alvin could see, Frank had done everything anyone could have done. That the other car had come at the wrong time certainly could not be construed as Frank's fault.

No one could take ownership. It was simply fate. But Frank was not going to be convinced that fate had been the culprit. Not when he'd been the one at the wheel.

But how could he make Frank see past that without self-condemnation?

He paused outside Ellie's door. Although he wanted desperately to get on with his own life, he wanted almost as fervently to help Frank get on with his. That he didn't have an answer to that dilemma brought a bit of the old slump back to his broad shoulders.

Heaving a sigh that came up from the soles of his feet, he knocked on the door.

Seconds later the door swung open. The sight of Ellie's beautiful, smiling face lifted some of the weight off his mind. For a moment, she just searched Alvin's face, then her smile widened.

"He told you, didn't he?"

Alvin nodded and slipped inside, heading immediately for the chair by the fire.

CHAPTER 16

I t wasn't until Alvin had sprawled out his large body in her chair and then placed the orchid on the table that Ellie noted the flower. "Where on earth did you find an orchid in these parts?"

Alvin glanced first at the flower, then her. "Irma."

Ah, Irma. No further explanation was needed. "And why would she give you an orchid?"

Adopting his usual pose, he leaned forward, elbows resting on his thick thighs. "She told me a story about how some flowers are self-contained and have all they need to survive without mates."

Confused, Ellie picked up the flower and brought it to her nose. There was no scent forthcoming. She put it back. "And her point was. . ."

"Her point was that everything depends on something else to be complete." She thought his ruddy complexion pinked a bit. "The orchid can't reproduce without another orchid."

She shook her head. Sometimes, although the explanation became clear after a lot of thought, Irma's comparisons often left her floundering for an interpretation. This was one of those times. And most times, Alvin's explanations left her even more confused. She knew he was making a point, but it totally eluded her. "I'm afraid I'm missing something."

He ran a hand through his hair and sighed. Then he picked up the orchid and handed it to her. "I've been alone for a long time." When she would have spoken, he held up his hand to stop her. "I know. You don't have to say it. It was of my own choosing. I made that choice because I believed that I didn't have the right to inflict my problems on anyone else. As long as I felt guilty for not having been there to save Alice, I couldn't give myself or. . .my heart to anyone else."

She wanted to tell him that she didn't believe that he could have done anything to save his wife. That she'd never believed that. "Alvin—"

"Please, let me finish before I lose my nerve." He smiled at her, and she felt a bit better about what was to come. "Ever since you came to Renaissance, I've. . .well, I've been aware of you. As a woman, I mean. In the last few months, it's become more than just awareness." He swallowed hard, and his color deepened. "Damn. I haven't done this in a long time."

Ellie was finding it quite amusing that a big man like Alvin was finding it so difficult to express his feelings. At the same time, it finally occurred to her what he was trying to say. Her heartbeat sped up. It seemed as if she had waited her entire lifetime to hear Alvin say he loved her, and she was not about to let him wiggle out of it now.

She rose and went to sit on the arm of his chair. "Alvin, just say what's on your mind."

He looked up at her, and then took her hand. He covered it with his other hand and, sandwiched between his bearlike paws, her little hand disappeared.

"I guess what I'm trying to say is, I love you, Ellie. I have for a long time."

Her heart was so full she thought it would burst. Leaning forward, she brushed his lips with hers. "I love you, too," she whispered against his ear.

With one swift movement, he scooped her off the arm of the chair and into his big lap. Tenderly, he cradled her against his chest.

Alvin buried his face in her hair, satisfying himself about something he'd thought of for a very long time. Yes, her hair did smell like wildflowers. He inhaled deeply and kissed the top of her head.

She shifted her position, leaned away, and linked

her fingers behind his neck. Her blue-eyed gaze burned into his. The lower part of his torso stirred. Something it hadn't done in a very long time. He could feel heat spreading through him. It seared its way upward until he felt like his entire body was on fire.

He was sure she could feel his arousal against her soft bottom cheeks, but he didn't care. He wanted her as he'd only wanted one other woman in his life. But he held himself back. Ellie was so small, so fragile. He feared injuring her.

"Ellie, I—"

She laid her fingers over his mouth to stop the words, and then replaced them with her lips. Slanting her mouth over his, she pried his lips apart. He felt her silky, smooth tongue slip inside.

Desire swamped him. He was drowning in the pent-up passion of months of wanting. He was lost. He pulled her to him and feasted on her mouth like a man who hadn't eaten in years. Ellie's mouth was warm and moist, and his brain immediately went to wondering about other parts of her body.

Was she as warm and smooth there, too? Would she grip him in a glove of velvet and test his power to last until the end? Would she moan his name in the throes of passion? Would she—

Sanity seeped in, and he forced her from him. "No.

No. We can't do this."

"Why not?" Ellie searched his eyes for an answer. "Don't you find me desirable?"

The blue in her eyes had grown languid with the same wanting burning through him. The sight made him want to throw caution to the wind, and he pulled her back as if to continue where they'd left off.

When he didn't answer, the desire slowly faded from her eyes. Her white teeth tortured her kiss-swollen, trembling bottom lip.

With the pad of his thumb, he pulled it free. "Not desirable?" He smiled and tucked a long strand of golden hair behind her ear. "If you were any more desirable, I'd have been lost a long time ago. God knows, I want to make love to you more than I want my next breath."

She frowned. "Then what's stopping you?"

He kissed the tip of her nose. "You're stopping me. You're so. . .delicate, and you've probably never—I'm—" He swallowed. Next thing he knew, he'd be asking to meet her after study hall in the broom closet. "I might hurt you."

Her eyes softened. She stroked his cheek with her fingers. "Yes, I'm a virgin," she said frankly. "You would be my first man. And yes, it probably will hurt." She took his face between her hands. "But if you don't make love with me, that will hurt me much more."

Sincerity and longing shone from her sparkling blue eyes. "Are you absolutely sure?"

Her tongue slid over her lips, leaving them moist and very tempting. Alvin felt a tug from somewhere behind his navel. She smiled. "I'm very sure."

Alvin hesitated for a scant moment before rising to his feet, cradling her in his arms, and then striding toward the back of the cottage.

As though he was handling fine china, he placed her on the bed. Straightening, he removed his shirt, then started to unbuckle his belt, but stopped.

"What's wrong now?"

He glanced down at the front of his trousers. He was a big man in more ways than one. Fear as to what she would think when she saw his nude body in a complete state of arousal flooded through him.

He sank to the side of the bed and took her hand. "I don't want to frighten you."

She took his hand and kissed his palm. "You could never frighten me. For all your size, you're one of the gentlest men I know."

Touched beyond words, Alvin kissed her gently. "I love you."

Ellie smiled mischievously. "Prove it."

Standing, he finished removing his clothes and stood silently before her, waiting for her judgment. Her eyes grew wide, but with appreciation, not fear. "You are magnificent."

Her whispered words sent relief rushing through him, followed quickly by renewed passion.

Holding his gaze with the heat of her own, Ellie sat up and pulled her blouse over her head. Alvin gasped. Her breasts lay naked before him. Their creamy white flesh and rosy pink tips made his engorged manhood throb.

Continuing to hold his gaze, she slipped free of her skirt and panties. In what seemed like seconds, she lay naked beneath his heated gaze. "My God," he breathed.

Lying back against the pillows, she held out her arms to him. Without thinking, Alvin slid onto the bed and pulled her close to him. The sensation of her naked flesh on his, her little breasts pressing into his chest, her legs entwined with his, and the heat of her thighs burning into his almost did him in, but he hung on to his control.

Breath rasped from him when he felt her hand close around him. His control slipped dangerously when her hand began to move. As much as he wanted her to continue, he knew he couldn't contain himself. Grasping her wrist, he brought her fingers to his lips. Without words, she seemed to understand.

Ellie took his hand and guided it to her breast. "Then you touch me," she pleaded, her voice hoarse. "Please, touch me."

He closed his hand over her. The small breast disappeared inside his palm. But the heat burned into him like a branding iron. Slowly and methodically he kneaded her flesh, glorying in the feel of the tip hardening against his palm.

Life flowed through Alvin, acute and strong. This gift Ellie had given him was more precious than anything he would or had ever received.

Carefully, he slipped over her. With his fingers he prepared her. She moaned and twisted beneath him. When he thought she was ready, he entered her.

Expecting unbearable pain, Ellie stiffened against it, but when it came, it was nothing near what she'd thought it would be. It hurt, but she almost welcomed it. Now she was Alvin's, as she'd wanted to be for so very long. His. Completely his. As he was hers.

Very slowly and, she was sure, after waiting for her to get accustomed to his size, he began to move. Never in her life had she ever experienced such ecstasy. Her entire body burned with an overwhelming, pleasurable heat that left her breathless. She strained to get closer, to get more, to give herself so totally that he would never leave her.

Inside, a pressure started to build, making her strain to release it. Little by little it increased until it was so strong she thought she'd die of the need to set it free.

Alvin buried his face in her neck, and she clawed at his back. More pressure. More need.

"Are you ready?" he asked against her lips.

Unable to verbalize her need, she nodded.

Moments later she felt as though she'd been lifted into the heavens and held there long enough to see the brilliance of the glittering stars, then she was eased slowly and gently back to earth.

* * *

When they could catch their breath, Alvin cuddled Ellie's body against his. Their sweat-slick bodies glistened in the silvery moonlight spilling across the bed. Their heavy breathing filled the silence of the darkened room. Outside, crickets chirped happily as though echoing the couple's elation.

Alvin's breathing evened out. He sighed contentedly. Her warmth and her nearness erased the last remnants of his pain over Alice's death and replaced them with a deep regret for the loss and a peace that he'd forgotten was possible, but which now permeated his heart and soul.

"I wish everyone could be as happy as I am right now," Alvin said, kissing the top of her head.

"You're thinking of Frank," Ellie said, then turned her head to kiss his chest.

He smiled. She could always read his thoughts. He had to wonder how much of that was due to the village and its mystical powers, and how much was due to the invisible thread that had seemed to bind their hearts from the very beginning.

"Yes, I am."

Ellie propped herself on one elbow and stared down at him. "You said when you got here that you'd talked to him."

"Yes, I did."

"What did he say?"

Alvin sighed. "He told me exactly what happened that night." As briefly as possible, he related what Frank had told him.

"But I don't see that it's his fault," Ellie said, drawing the same conclusion Alvin had.

"I know that, and you know that. How do I convince Frank? He's a doctor, a scientist if you will. He's used to seeing everything in black-and-white proof before he believes. I don't have that proof, Ellie." A terrible thought occurred to him. He turned his face to hers. "Have we lost him?"

"Lost him? No. Carrie is going to need Frank when the final horrors of her lost memory emerge. If we lose Frank, we'll also lose Carrie, and that can't happen."

Alvin sat up. "That was the whole reason behind me

making peace with my guilt, wasn't it?"

Ellie nodded. "If you didn't make peace with your problems, then you couldn't help Frank, and if you didn't help him, he couldn't help Carrie."

"Why didn't you just tell me that?"

Ellie smiled and kissed him. "Because *you* had to forgive yourself. No one else could do that for you. The same goes for Frank. He has to come to see that the accident was destiny."

Alvin sighed. "I don't think mentioning *destiny* to him will help. I tried telling him it was time for his wife to die, and he about bit my head off."

She thought for moment and then smiled. "You usually do your best thinking in the woods beyond the village. Why not go there tomorrow and sort it out?"

Alvin laughed. "I tried that and woke up in my cabin. I don't think Emanuel wants me to leave."

Ellie pulled him down to within a breath of her lips. "I think if you want to leave the village tomorrow, you won't be stopped." Then she tightened her hold on his neck. "But right now, I have other duties for you to see to."

CHAPTER 17

Emanuel stared intently out the window of Clara's cottage at the sad young woman sitting on a rock next to the stream. "Carrie is still fighting her memories. She's been here for weeks, and I thought she'd have been farther along by now, perhaps even ready to leave the village."

Clara moved to stand beside him. "I don't think she's fighting them. Unfortunately, she seems content to let them come as they will." She shook her head. "I've done all I can do. I'm afraid it's up to her now to *want* the memories to return."

The village Elder turned to Clara, his brow furrowed in concern. "I was not accusing you of not doing your job, my dear. I hope you know that."

"I do." She smiled up at his serene face, and then smoothed his sleeve. "Now, come have your coffee."

After patting her shoulder and returning her smile,

Emanuel moved past her and sat at the table. His habitual coffee mug waited for him. Long, narrow fingers of steam rose from the cup, carrying with them the rich aroma of the freshly ground beans Clara used to brew her coffee. He inhaled deeply, sipped at the brew, and then replaced the cup on the table.

Stroking his fingers the length of his long beard, he stared off into space. His lips moved as though he were talking to some unseen confidant. His thick, snowy eyebrows drew together in thought, cutting through his wide brow with a slash of white.

Clara was well acquainted with this procedure by now, and knew that talking to him or trying to help him would be as effective as talking to her loom. Therefore, she sat across from him, folded her hands on the rough tabletop, and waited. He'd process his thoughts, some aloud, some to himself, and eventually arrive at a solution. She had only to endure the process.

When he finally turned back to Clara, his gray eyes were alive with a sparkle that Clara had come to realize meant he'd found an answer to a perplexing problem. "Perhaps we're pacing the return of her memories too slowly. Bringing them closer together might help her to remember more, to prompt others and decipher them more quickly."

"Do you think it's wise to bombard her with too

many memories? That could be dangerous, not to mention confusing. She needs time to think about each of the memories, to fully understand what they're trying to tell her before another is thrust upon her. Those wicked headaches that come with each memory don't do much to encourage her to remember more, either."

"Those are essential, I'm afraid." He considered what Clara had said for a moment, and then favored her with a beaming smile that made her heart beat just a bit faster. "Yet, as always, my dear, your wisdom is my guiding light. What would I do without you?"

Clara smiled. Emanuel didn't need her to make any decisions. He possessed an inner wisdom that never failed to guide him along the right path. He didn't need her to show him the way. However, it warmed her to know that he valued her as a sounding board and advisor.

"Perhaps the problem is that her dreams have been too subtle. The dreams may need to be stronger, more forceful, clearer, so they make a deeper impact on her subconscious memories, make her more eager to regain her lost memory and with it find the truth of who and what she is." He mulled over his newest solution for a moment. "Yes, I think that's the answer, Clara. More forceful memories, more vivid."

Clara had to admit that Carrie wasn't as yet seeing the true depth of the problem she faced, nor was she displaying any urgency to find the missing pieces of her memory. It had worried the Weaver for some time that Carrie seemed content to let them come to her at their own pace.

Still, Clara wasn't sure she liked the sound of Emanuel's answer to the problem, but then, she reminded herself, he would never do anything to hurt one of the Assignments. His purpose was to heal, not to inflict more scars. And, it was true, that to reach true peace of mind, one sometimes had to endure a little pain on the way. Clara knew that whatever Emanuel decided must be done would, in the end, bring that peace to Carrie, a peace she so richly deserved and for which she'd been yearning for far too long.

* * *

Carrie allowed her fingertips to trail in the stream's cooling waters. Then, recalling what had happened the last time she'd done that, she quickly snatched her hand back and used the hem of her skirt to dry it.

Lifting her face to the clear, blue sky, she squinted against the sun's brilliant rays and wondered if it ever rained in Renaissance. She'd been here for weeks, and every day had been the same: sunshine, soft breezes, and no rain. Though enjoyable, the monotony of each day resembling the last was rubbing her nerves raw. Unbidden, she found herself longing for the change of seasons and the relief of a long, rainy afternoon to laze around and read before a blazing fire.

Rousing herself from longing for things that were not going to materialize until she had her memory back and could return to the outside world, she centered her thoughts on trying to recall more of the many things she'd forgotten. Though she'd decided early on that trying to force herself into remembering was not worth the painful headaches that accompanied the process, she had now changed her mind. She was impatient to learn more of herself, and if enduring the pain was the price she would have to pay for retrieving her memories, it was a small one, and she'd willingly pay it.

Closing her eyes, she summoned those lost memories. Minutes passed, and a blank canvas stared back at her. The only thing that she accomplished was another searing pain in her right temple. It was useless.

Standing, she decided to go inside and spend some time with Clara. She had no sooner straightened and taken the first step when her world started to spin out of control. A thick haze enveloped her. Her knees gave way. The damp grass cushioned her fall. Then an inky black tunnel sucked her down into nothingness.

* * *

He was there again. She could feel his presence. The evil that seemed to always surround him like a black cloud lay thick on the air. His heavy, shuffling footsteps drew closer. Huddled deep in the closet, she lay very still, holding her breath, hoping if he opened the door that the clothes would hide her. Her heart thudded against her chest. Fearing he would hear it, she pressed her hand over her right breast to muffle the pounding that echoed in her ears.

The door creaked open. Light spilled in. She could see the tips of his heavy work boots.

God, please don't let him find me. Please.

Pain, excruciating and sharp, exploded in her scalp. Hauled from the depths of her hiding place by her hair, he threw her across the bedroom floor. As her face skidded across the carpeting, she could feel the skin being ripped raw. Her body came to a stop when the dresser's corner cut into her side. More pain radiated through her body, but she was too busy trying to move out of his reach to give it thought.

"I'll teach you to run from me, bitch! Next time stand up and take what you've got coming!"

But she hadn't moved fast enough or far enough. His fist connected with her face. Her head jerked back on her neck. She felt her jawbone crack. More pain.

She cried out. Warm liquid ran from her nose, the corner of her mouth, and over her chin. Blood. She cried out again.

"Shut up, bitch!" He swung again.

The imprint of his knuckles as they battered her shoulders and back left behind more pain. A starburst of agony ripped through her shoulders and ran down her spine. She'd barely had time to register this new onslaught when his foot shot out. The toe of his work boot connected with her stomach. Air rushed from her lungs. White-hot pain knifed through her ribs.

This time, knowing what the punishment would be if she cried out, she didn't make a sound. Instead, she bit her lip until she tasted the coppery sweetness of her own blood. And then she waited for his next blow to find her.

But as suddenly as the punishing beating had started, it stopped. Through her tears, she could see him leaving the room. The door slammed behind him. She closed her eyes and lay back on the floor, her broken body racked with pain, her crimson blood soaking into the carpet.

* * *

When Carrie opened her eyes, she was lying on the soft, cool grass outside Clara's cottage. Unlike her other dreams, this one had been vividly real. Pain still pounded through her body, and when she looked down, her arms still bore the bruises he'd inflicted before she'd found refuge in the closet.

But as she stared at them, the bruises faded, and the pain ebbed from her body. Soon she felt as good as she had before she'd fainted. But, although the marks left by the pummeling she'd endured had faded, the memory of the brutal beating remained vividly engraved in her mind. If the faceless man was, as she suspected, her husband, then she'd married an inhuman, unfeeling, brutal beast.

Why had she allowed him to treat her like that? What kind of a wimp was she that she hadn't fought back? There were any number of things she could have used to split his skull open—

The last thought brought her up short. My God, what kind of a monster had *she* turned into? She was no better than that faceless, evil creation of the devil.

Then she recalled all that blood on her the night she'd wandered into the library, seeking help. Irma had said that a head wound bled a lot, but Carrie couldn't believe that the amount of blood that had been all over her had come from the cut she'd had on her forehead.

So where *had* the blood had come from? Had she had enough of his brutality and killed him? Is that why she'd wiped everything from her memory? Newspaper stories of wives killing their abusive husbands flashed through her mind. Is that what she was hiding away in her lost memory?

She pressed her hands against her temples, trying to force some kind of coherent thought into her brain.

Think, Carrie, think. What happened after he walked out of the room?

Had she followed him and bludgeoned him to death? Shot him? Drove a steak knife into his black heart? Try as she might, nothing came back to her.

One question, however, kept returning. Had there been enough blood on her to prove she had killed a man? Was she a murderess? Frantically, she tried to force her memory to recall something it might never have known. With a sigh, she ordered herself to relax.

Then it came to her.

She may have no idea how much blood a human being had to lose before life left the body, but she knew one person who might be able to tell her exactly how much blood a human could lose and live.

* * *

Frank listened at the door to make sure Alvin was gone. He didn't need to talk about Sandy or anything to do with her death any more today. When he heard no sounds coming from the outer room, he opened the door and stepped out.

The orchid was gone, and so was Alvin. Frank poured himself some coffee and was about to take a sip when the door burst open. Haloed in rays of the dying sun that concealed her face, Carrie stood statuelike.

"Carrie?"

"I need. . . I need to ask you. . .something." She stepped inside and closed the door.

Without the glare of the sun obscuring his view, he could now see the lines of worry creasing her beautiful face. Her teeth gnawed at her bottom lip. In front of her, her hands were clasped so tightly, he wondered if the blood could still circulate to her fingers.

Setting his cup aside, he took her hand and led her to a chair beside the table. When she was seated, he poured her a cup of coffee and sat across from her.

"What is it?"

For a moment he didn't think she would say anything, only continue to worry her bottom lip. Then she looked up and sighed.

"Remember I told you that when they found me, I had blood on me?"

He nodded.

"Well, there was a lot of blood. My skirt and blouse were almost completely red with it."

He said nothing, fearing if he did, given her state of nervousness, that she'd stop talking and never ask him whatever it was that had caused her state of nervousness.

"I need to know. . ." She swallowed. "I need to know how much blood someone can lose before they. . .before they die."

Frank had expected her to ask many things, but this certainly wasn't one of them. For a time, he stared at her openmouthed. "And you want to know this because—"

She dropped her gaze to her fidgeting hands. "Because I think I may have. . .killed the faceless man." The last four words fell from her mouth in a rush, as though she had to get them out or lose her nerve.

He almost laughed at the ludicrousness of it. Carrie? Killing a man? In his wildest, most twisted dreams, Frank could not imagine Carrie doing anything that violent. "Why would you even think that?"

Carrie stood and walked to the window. "Because a few minutes ago, I had another. . ." She glanced at him, shrugged, and then looked back out the window. "I don't know what to call them anymore. Since they're happening when I'm awake now, they can't be dreams. Visions, I guess."

Frank got a sick feeling in his stomach. She'd had another bout with the faceless bastard, and he hadn't been there to help her through the aftermath. He moved to the edge of his chair. "Visions" will do for now. Will you sit back down and tell me about it?"

At first she hesitated, and then she retook her seat across from him. Before she could say a word, he scooped up her hands and enclosed them in his. Then he smiled at her. He wanted her to feel as much at ease as possible, to feel his presence and his protection.

She took a deep breath. "I was going to go inside and help Clara with supper. But before I could, I had this weird sensation, like when you step on a stair that's not there. Only it wasn't just a quick jolt. I felt like I'd stepped into a bottomless hole and kept falling and falling and falling. . ."

"You're absolutely sure you were awake?"

Yanking her hands away, she stood and glared down at him. "You think I'm crazy or that I'm making this up, don't you?"

She started to leave, but he grabbed her wrist. "No, I believe you. I'm just trying to find out everything."

After studying his sincerity for a time and evidently deciding he had spoken the truth, she sat down again. "No, I was not asleep. I told you, I was going inside to help Clara." Carrie wrapped her hands around her coffee cup. "Anyway, when I hit the bottom of the hole, I was in a closet. I knew someone was hunting for me. I knew it. I could hear his footsteps coming closer and closer."

As she talked, her voice had begun to rise. The building tension showed plainly in her features.

Frank took her hands again. She made no move to pull free. "Easy. Just tell me what happened."

Carrie found his touch very soothing, enabling her to recount her visions. She told Frank the whole thing, leaving nothing out. "Then as suddenly as he'd come, he went away, and I woke up on the grass. I still had the painful bruises, but while I sat looking at them, they disappeared."

"That son of a bitch," he mumbled when she'd finally stopped talking. He fisted his hands on the table. "If I could get my hands on him—" His voice had become a growl that sent chills racing down Carrie's spine.

"That's not why I told you all this. I don't need anyone to fight my battles for me." Surprisingly, she believed that down to her toes. If anyone was going to go up against the faceless man, it would be her. If she hadn't learned anything else about herself during her time in Renaissance, she'd learned that she was not a coward. She was an individual with enough wherewithal to fight her own demons. "What I need to know is, was the amount of blood I had on my clothes the night I wandered into the library enough to verify that someone had died?"

Frank searched her face. "My God, you actually think you killed someone. You think you killed the faceless man."

She simply nodded, not trusting herself to speak.

Firmly shaking his head, he rose and went to grab the coffeepot. She was sure it was to have something to do rather than because either of them wanted more. But he never poured any coffee. Instead, almost absently, he set the pot on the table and fairly fell back into his chair.

"Carrie, you could never have killed anyone, not you."

She loved him for believing her incapable of such a horrendous act, but. . . "Then how do you explain all that blood?"

"You said you had a cut on your head," he said, grasping at anything to explain it.

She shook her head. "The cut was minor enough to be closed with a bandage. It would hardly have caused the amount of blood on my clothing." She took his hand in hers. "You haven't answered me. Could that amount of blood have come from someone being killed?"

Frank turned away, but she took his chin in her hand and forced him to look at her. "I can take it. Please, be honest with me. You're a surgeon. You must have some idea."

Nausea churned in Frank's belly. He'd rather cut out his tongue than tell her what she wanted to hear. But he could see the need to know in her eyes and that she was not going to give up until she did.

He swallowed hard. "The amount of blood you described on your clothes could mean the person it came from had been critically injured or. . .that they could have died."

CHAPTER 18

Carrie could feel the color drain from her face. Instantly, Frank rounded the table and pulled her into his arms.

"That doesn't mean you killed him or anyone else. It might have been—" He couldn't think. All his brain registered was her intense fear and overwhelming distress. Still he fought for words. "It could be that—"

She laid her fingers over his mouth. "Don't. Please. If I did it, then when I leave here, the thing I have to face is my punishment."

"No!" Frank's booming denial seemed to fill the room. "I don't believe you're guilty of this. Some people are able to kill, but not you. Not you."

She leaned back and searched his eyes. "And you? Are you one of those who can kill?"

For a moment her question threw him off balance,

and then he realized to what she was referring. The accident. "It's not the same thing," he said quietly. "It was not on purpose, but I am still guilty."

"So you say, but I don't believe you're guilty of that any more than you can believe I killed that evil being from my dreams."

Then she laid her lips on his, and all thought flew from his mind. Willingly, he allowed himself to drown in a kiss for which he'd been longing for days. Carrie felt so good in his arms, so right. How could they not belong together? Could fate truly be heartless enough to bring them together only to rip them apart?

Feeling desperate, he pulled her closer and let his tongue delve deep into her mouth, tasting and savoring the sweetness he found waiting for him. Sweetness that had become a life-giving force for him, a forbidden elixir that drove him relentlessly to crave more. Carrie was his drug of choice, and he was a willing addict.

She moaned deep in her throat and pressed herself against him. "I want you," she whispered into his mouth. "I want you one more time."

God help him, he had neither the strength nor the desire to deny her. If this was all they were to have, then he'd take every last moment and treasure it. Frank scooped her into his arms and carried her to his bed.

Frank laid Carrie gently on the bed. Knowing the

trauma of her most recent vision still lay heavy on her heart, he'd decided to take it slow, but Carrie seemed to have other plans.

She pulled him down beside her and then rolled him onto his back. Before he could blink, she'd unbuttoned his shirt, pulled it off, and then tossed it carelessly to the floor. The rest of his clothing quickly followed the shirt. Naked and dazed by the speed and brazenness of her movements, Frank could only stare fixedly as she disrobed.

Moments later, she slid her naked flesh over his body. Her skin was hot and slick. Anticipation and desire sparkled in her heavily lidded eyes. Her warm, sweet breath fanned his face, and then her mouth claimed his in a hungry kiss.

The hesitant, insecure woman he'd first made love to was gone. In her place was an untamed wanton who would have her way with him, a woman who did not want to wait for foreplay. He sensed that right now, at this very moment, she needed the assurance of being the one in control. She needed to know that she could be the one in charge of their lovemaking. And he let her.

Though it took every ounce of his control, Frank let his hands fall to his sides and gave her free reign. As Carrie kissed every inch of his body and explored every curve and valley as though committing them to memory, he held his breath and prayed he'd be able to hold himself in check.

She straddled his middle and played her fingertips over his skin. It felt as if a million butterflies were caressing him. Where had she ever learned to stretch a man's endurance to the breaking point, and then stop just before he plummeted over the edge of pleasure? Wherever she'd learned it, he didn't care. That it was him who was the recipient of her desire made his arousal intensify, and he throbbed with a sensual pain that nearly drove him mad.

Then he felt her mouth on him, sucking, kissing, and laving him until he was sure the end would come without his bidding. But again, she knew the exact moment to stop him just short of completion.

She slid up his body and leaned over him, enclosing them in a curtain of fiery hair. The tips of her hair skimmed his chest. He moaned and squirmed beneath her. Still, he forced himself not to touch her, instinctively knowing she needed the assurance of being in control.

Finally, when he was convinced he could stand no more, she positioned herself above him and then slowly lowered her body onto him. Frank sucked in a huge lungful of air, certain he'd never breathe again.

Unable to hold out any longer, he cupped her breasts in his palms and massaged them until her nipples pressed hard against his palms. Carrie moved her hips in a circular motion.

The most incredible spirals of heat started at his toes and rushed upward. His groin tightened. Past control, he gripped her hips and guided her frantic movements. Carrie threw her head back and cried out his name. A flash of brightness exploded in front of Frank's eyes, and he felt as if the world had shattered into a million tiny shards of blinding light.

* * *

Several hours later, the glow of their lovemaking still clinging to her body and mind, Carrie slipped from Frank's bed, dressed, and then placed a kiss on his lips. She stole a moment to look at him. He's a good man, she told herself, with his own trials and tribulations with which to come to terms. He didn't deserve to shoulder the extra burden of her mistakes.

She would lay down her life for Frank, but, if she'd done this terrible thing, if she had, indeed, murdered the faceless bastard haunting her, then her life was no longer hers to control. By taking a life, and now she was almost certain that she had, she'd given up that right.

Brushing away the tears streaming silently down her cheeks, she whispered, "Good-bye, my love." Quietly, she slipped from the room and then from the cottage.

In the outer room, Carrie found Alvin sitting in the

pale dawn light. He looked up at her as she approached the table, but said nothing.

She laid her hand on his shoulder. "Help him, Alvin. Free him of his burden."

Alvin nodded wordlessly. Carrie forced a smile she didn't feel, and then walked out of the cottage.

* * *

Knowing she didn't want him to see her leaving, Frank had pretended sleep. But moisture burned hotly behind his closed eyelids. This was the end for them. Still, even knowing that in the depths of his soul, he wanted to snatch her back, hold her close, and never let the outside world come between them. But he knew that was impossible. A cavity, filled with nothing but emptiness unlike any he'd ever known, opened inside him.

Long after Carrie was gone, Frank lay staring at the darkened ceiling. What kind of God waved complete happiness in front of an emotionally starving man and woman and then snatched it away? How many times would he have to endure the pain of losing the women he loved? This place was supposed to make him feel better, not inflict more pain. Why in hell had he let Steve talk him into coming here?

Because you needed to be here, a disembodied voice

reminded him. *Because until you're free of your own guilt, you won't be any good to yourself or anyone else, including your patients and your friends, but most of all to Carrie. She's going to need you very soon. You can be there for her—if you dare to hope. But you won't be there for her if you don't shed this mantle of guilt.*

Frank knew that. God, he knew it. But shedding something you had earned was easier said than done. So far, she'd at least found some answers. He, on the other hand, had found none. At least her demon sort of had substance and form. Guilt didn't have a form that you could scream at or punch. Guilt simply hung on to your soul until you were so exhausted from carrying it that you gave up and allowed it to pull you under and consume your life.

Frank was tired of his burden, and he refused to allow it to take any more of his life from him than it had already. He wanted to get out from under it. But God help him, he had no idea how to make that happen. Talking about it to Alvin had only opened the wounds and intensified the knowledge that his lousy driving had taken the lives of his wife and unborn child.

Running out on Alvin, and then hiding in his bedroom spending the next few hours staring at the ceiling trying to think, had produced nothing more than a never-ending reenactment of what had happened on that snowy night on a deserted back road. And what had that gotten him? Nothing but more pain and an intensification of the guilt he already found impossible to bear.

He sat up, placed his pillow against the headboard, punched it once, then leaned against it and stared at the painting Carrie had given him. As before, a moonbeam slanted through the window and fell on the canvas as though spotlighting it for his benefit. The breeze moving the trees just outside the window made the silvery light shimmer across the canvas, falsely animating the one-dimensional painting.

Once again, as he gazed fixedly at the painting, he noticed a faint movement among the trees. *Sandy?* He sat up and watched it intently. His heart rate increased. He held his breath, fearing he'd frighten away whatever was happening.

As he watched, a flash of white appeared to flit in and out among the tree trunks. When Sandy, if indeed it had been Sandy, didn't appear as she had before, he decided it was nothing more than a trick of the flickering moonlight. He blinked, thinking that, when he opened his eyes, it would be gone.

But it wasn't. The tantalizing, phantom wisp continued to tease at his imagination, never fully revealing itself, but always there, moving around, darting in and out, disappearing and reappearing. Frank blinked repeatedly, this time trying to dispel the taunting ghost, but it didn't go away.

He slid to the foot of the bed and reached for the painting. As he did, the room began to spin crazily. He felt as though he were trapped inside a tornado. Colors, blurred, swirled around him. Nausea rose up in his throat. He swallowed repeatedly to control it. Just as Frank was sure he'd lose it, the spinning stopped.

Dizzy from the motion, his eyes closed, he dropped back onto the bed. But it wasn't his bed. Whatever it was, it was cold, hard, and wet.

Very slowly he opened his eyes and looked down. He was sitting on a big rock covered with snow. Dazed, he stood unsteadily and then raised his gaze to see where he was. What he saw caused him to suck in his breath sharply and fight back the sudden burning in his eyes and throat.

At first glance, the scene before Frank seemed chillingly surreal. Steam poured from the crushed radiator of a black sedan that was smashed accordion-like against the broad trunk of a large oak tree. Snow was falling at a blinding rate, muffling the already-deadly silence and turning the car white. On the opposite side of the road he could just make out the indistinct outline of another vehicle, a white van perhaps, parked on the snowy shoulder of the road. A man stood outside the vehicle alternately wringing his hands and running them through his hair. Faint footprints in the snow led from him to the smashed car and then back to the van. He began to pace, stopping periodically to look up the road.

Quite suddenly, the stillness of the night exploded with the scream of a wailing siren and the intermittent *whoop whoop* of police cars. Red and blue lights flashed against the wall of falling snow. Headlights cut through the darkness. Moments later, the entire scene had come alive with the sound of raised voices yelling instructions, emergency vehicle doors slamming, an ambulance backing up to the crash scene, and several New York State Trooper cars spewing forth uniformed officers.

Like having a brick heaved against the side of his head, Frank realized what this scene was—the accident he'd had with Sandy. With a cry of anguish, he turned away. A familiar hand came to rest on his shoulder.

"You must watch and see the truth of that night if you are to ever free yourself of your guilt, Frank."

Frank looked up into the tranquil face of Alvin. "I know the truth. Because of me, Sandy is dead, and so is my unborn child. What more truth can there be?"

The Traveler smiled. "Ah, what more, indeed? At times the real truth lies just below the surface until that moment in time when we see it with a clear eye."

"Riddles and more riddles," Frank spat. Sick to death of the vagaries of Renaissance and not in the mood to play Alvin's game, whatever it was, Frank spun to walk away. What he saw stopped him dead in his tracks. The accident scene was gone. Nothing remained but snow, a deserted road, and that huge oak tree. He shook his head and blinked. "Where—"

Alvin patted his shoulder. "You'll understand everything very soon, Frank. Right now, there's someone I want you to talk to." He swept his large hand through the air.

From the ground a wisp of snow began to swirl upward. Like a tornado being born from the bowels of the storm, it grew larger and larger, until at last it stopped, and the snow fell away.

The air seemed to grow thin. Frank's knees gave way.

Alvin caught him by the arm. "I trust there is no need for introductions," he said. A moment later, the Traveler had disappeared in another swirl of snow.

Frank was left to stare openmouthed at the figure before him—a woman in an ethereal, white, flowing gown; her dark hair cascading over her shoulders in soft waves; her blue eyes sparkling up at him.

"Sandy," Frank finally muttered.

Seeing her in the painting had been one thing. Having her standing within feet of him was another entirely.

Longing welled up in him. He stepped toward her, his hand outstretched, but when he would have grabbed her, his fingers went right through her image and clasped nothing but air. Disappointment and frustration welled up inside him. He wanted to scream out at the injustice of this latest of Alvin's tricks.

Then Sandy smiled the smile he'd known so well. "You can't touch me. I am without substance, Frank. A wisp of Alvin's imagination left behind to help you."

"Help me?" Frank laughed, but without humor. "How in hell can waving the specter of the woman I loved and killed under my nose help me?" He ran his hand through his rumpled hair. "You people have a really cruel streak in you."

His scathing words seemed to have bounced off Sandy like rain off a windowpane. "Perhaps you'll think differently after I show you something." She turned slowly toward the south, raised her hand, and pointed toward the deserted road.

Despite himself, Frank couldn't look away. As if magnetized, his gaze followed her pointing finger. In the distance, barely discernable through the thick snowfall, he could see the pinpoint of approaching headlights just cresting a rise in the road. He knew without turning that there would be a like set of headlights coming at them from the north. And he also knew what that meant.

He was about to relive the worst night of his life. Chills that had nothing to do with the cold snow raced over his body. He tried to close his eyes, but, as if they'd been glued open, he found he could not shut out what was about to happen.

Mesmerized, he watched the car, his and Sandy's car, creep over the hill's crest and then gain momentum as it careened out of control down the other side on the slick road. Unreasonably, Frank held his breath, hoping that this time the car would miss the tree and just end up in the ditch. But in his heart he knew that wasn't going to be the end to this.

He wanted to close his eyes and plug his ears to blot out the sights and sounds of what was about to happen, but his body still didn't seem to want to obey his wishes. He could not look away. He could not move.

Both vehicles hurtled toward each other, not knowing that tragedy lay only moments away. Instinctively, Frank opened his mouth to yell a warning, but like the rest of his body, his vocal cords refused to function.

"You can't change what's already been, Frank." Sandy's soft voice penetrated his anguish.

Inside, his useless voice screamed. *Stop! Don't come any closer! This can't happen again! Stop!* But no sound emerged. Instead he had to stand there, helpless, and watch Sandy die again. As if he hadn't relived it enough times in his dreams and as if it hadn't lingered in the back of his mind through every waking hour of every day.

The two vehicles grew closer. The one he was driving swerved and then righted itself, only to swerve again in the other direction. He saw himself steering into the skid in an attempt to right the car and succeed. At that moment, the other vehicle came toward them, and he watched as his car veered the other way and headed for the tree.

As if someone had suddenly turned off the power on a TV screen, everything went dark. When he could see again, emergency vehicles littered the accident scene. He relaxed. In his gut, he knew that Emanuel was behind this entire scenario, even if it had been Alvin who had brought him here, and the Elder had benevolently spared him from having to see the actual accident.

"Did you really think Emanuel would make you watch that all over again?" Sandy asked from just behind him as though she'd read his thoughts.

A wave of shame washed over Frank. He had known Emanuel to be nothing but gentle and wise. He should have realized the Elder would have never caused him to relive that horror.

"Frank."

He turned to face Sandy. "Yes?"

She pointed toward the accident scene. From what

he could tell, since the doors to their car were open and the EMTs were just closing the ambulance doors, both Sandy's body and his unconscious body had been removed from the wreckage and placed in separate ambulances. So what was it that she wanted him to see?

"Look at the van," she said, again reading his thoughts.

He directed his gaze to the vehicle that he'd swerved to avoid hitting. Painted on the side of the white van was a large, dark green oval. Inside the oval in white against the dark background were the letters *WHCRC*. Below the oval, smaller green letters read: *Westchester Handicapped Children's Rehabilitation Center*.

Frank was speechless.

Just then a boy of about four years hobbled out of the van on twin aluminum crutches. Shortly after that, a car pulled up beside the van, and a middle-aged woman scrambled out and swept the little boy into a tight embrace. Even from across the road Frank could hear her sobs of happiness.

Sandy's voice penetrated his thoughts. "That's Mrs. Gray. Her husband was on the town council. He died last year of a heart attack. Her son has been her whole life ever since then. If anything had happened to that boy, I don't know what she would have done." Sandy turned to him. "Because of your sacrifice, she'll never have to find out."

"It was your sacrifice, not mine," Frank whispered, his gaze still on the mother and child being ushered to a waiting car and then driven away.

"No, Frank, it was you. If you hadn't swerved, a lot of children who already had far too many health challenges to contend with would have been injured or worse. I gave up my life, but you saved the lives of all those children."

"But you—" Emotion clogged his throat and cut off the last word before he could get it past his lips.

"Died," she finished for him. "Yes, I died because it was my time, my destiny to die so that those children could survive. When you accept that, then your burden will be lighter." She frowned. "And, Frank, you still have your own destiny to fulfill. Carrie is going to need you soon. You can't help her if you aren't free of this unnecessary weight you've chosen to bear." Sandy's frown disappeared and turned to a smile. "She loves you, and you love her. Don't waste that love by wishing for things that can never be. The best memorial you can build for me in your heart is to be happy. I won't be able to truly rest until you are."

The snow began to swirl at her feet. A sick feeling invaded him. Sandy was leaving. Desperation drove him.

"No, don't go!" Even as the cone of swirling snow grew higher and denser, Frank snatched at her hand to hold her back, but as before, his fingers passed through her.

"I have to, Frank. You have your entire life ahead of you. Don't live it by feeding on guilt for something you had no control over and regrets that will suck the happiness from your soul." Her last words came to him as a fading echo. The snow swirl spiraled upward like a mini-waterspout, and then evaporated into thin air. Sandy was gone.

Before Frank could digest Sandy's disappearance, he felt a strange warmth replaced the chilling anguish of losing her again. In his heart, he knew he had seen his wife for the last time. Oddly, instead of sadness, a serenity that grew in intensity flooded him. He'd always love Sandy and miss her, but she didn't regret sacrificing her life for those of the children. She regretted him feeling guilty. He wasn't honoring her by doing so. He wasn't honoring her, and she should be honored. Now he understood. Now he knew that at last he was ready to go on, to go to Carrie a whole man. He could help her through whatever she had to face—and they would leave the mist together to do it.

CHAPTER 19

When Frank awoke in his bed the next morning, he had to lay there for a time to make sure he truly was back in Renaissance. Had he dreamed the entire thing the night before, or had it actually happened? Had his subconscious created it to assuage his conscience?

He sat up and swung his legs over the side of the bed. His bare feet hit something cold and wet. Looking down, all his doubts vanished. His feet rested in a small pile of melting snow. But more than just the material proof was the contentment that filled him, the lightness of a spirit no longer weighted down by unreasonable doubt and guilt.

Grinning, he climbed from the bed and quickly dressed, eager to find Carrie and tell her what had happened. In the outer room, he found Alvin sitting at the table with Emanuel. Both men looked somber.

"Is something wrong?" Frank asked, his good mood dampened by their expressions, and his thoughts going immediately to Carrie. "Is Carrie okay?"

Alvin and Emanuel exchanged concerned glances. "Carrie is fine, my boy," Emanuel finally said. "Please," he motioned toward the empty chair, "sit with us."

With trepidation Frank sat down. "If Carrie's okay, then what is it?"

Emanuel glanced out the window. Frank followed his gaze. A mist had begun to gather outside. As he watched, it slowly thickened. He could barely see Ellie's cottage across the square.

"I'm afraid it's time, Frank." Emanuel's voice was filled with compassion.

The Elder's meaning escaped Frank. "Time? For what?" He looked from one man to the other for an explanation. Neither of them seemed eager to fill him in. "Well? Time for what?"

Emanuel cleared his throat. Frank could never recall seeing the Elder uncomfortable about anything. "The village is going into its Transition stage. It's time for you to leave Renaissance."

For a moment what Emanuel said didn't sink in. Leave the village? But Alvin had said they couldn't leave until they were— Then the true meaning of what he'd said hit Frank full force.

"We're healed?" he said, including Carrie in his statement. "Then I'd better get Carrie." He started toward the door.

Alvin intercepted him with a hand on his shoulder. "No, Frank. *You're* healed. Carrie will not be going with you. She's not ready yet."

Frank couldn't believe his ears; there had to be some mistake. He couldn't leave without Carrie. "No. Carrie *has* to go with me." He pulled away from Alvin's hand and shifted his gaze from Emanuel to Alvin.

Emanuel stood and put his arm around Frank's shoulders. "Carrie has not come to terms with things. She can't leave yet."

"Then I'll stay and help her. Everyone says I'm supposed to help her." Even to his own ears, his voice sounded shrill and desperate. And he was. He could *not* leave without Carrie. He *would not* leave without Carrie. It would be like leaving a part of himself behind.

Emanuel squeezed his shoulder, then released him. "You will help her, but not here."

"Where then?" This was rapidly becoming far too confusing for Frank.

Emanuel strolled slowly toward the door, and then paused. "When the time comes, you will know it. Now, I'm afraid you have just enough time to say your good-byes. You have other tasks waiting for you."

* * *

Carrie watched Frank running down the path toward Clara's cottage. Behind him a thick mist was settling over the village. A sick nausea filled her stomach. Someone was leaving, and she knew it wasn't her. That left one person. *Frank.*

Instantly, the nausea, accompanied now by a deep and swamping sadness, grew worse. How would she get along here without him to lean on? But did that matter? When she left here, she would have only herself to depend on. She might as well get used to it.

But it wasn't entirely the idea of him not being there for support that upset her. She loved Frank more than she ever thought she could love anyone, and deep inside where her courage had been hidden, she knew she was strong enough to stand alone. But she didn't want to. Being separated from him would be the most intense torture she'd ever endured, perhaps even worse than the physical torment she now knew she'd endured under the faceless man's fist.

As he approached, he caught sight of her standing just behind the bushes bordering Clara's cottage. He stopped and stared at her for a long time.

Carrie, he mouthed.

With an anguished cry, she threw herself into his

261

waiting arms and clung to him. "Please don't go."

"Oh, sweetheart, I wish I could stay, but you know and I know that's not possible." He set her at arm's length from him and then wiped the tears from her cheeks with the pad of his thumb. "I'll wait for you. I'll never let you go. We will be together. I promise."

Something inside Carrie died. "We can never be together, Frank. Have you forgotten that I'm a—" She couldn't say the word *murderer* even though she was sure now that she was. She forced the word through her cold lips. "Murderess? A *married* murderess?"

His face grew grim. His fingers dug into her shoulders, but she was numb to any pain. "You don't know for sure that either of those things is true."

She shook her head, the hopelessness growing inside her. "No, not for sure, but there's little doubt. Until I do know, I'll be here." A sob escaped her. "And you'll be out there."

He pulled her back into his arms.

She glanced beyond his shoulder to the gathering mist. It had thickened until she could no longer see the footbridge over which Frank would cross back into the outside world.

"You have to go," she said.

But she couldn't let him leave without knowing. She had to say what was in her heart while she still had the chance. Cupping his face in her palms, she kissed him softly. "I love you, Frank Donovan."

He kissed her back, hard, hungry, and full of longing. "I love you, too, Carrie Henderson. I will until I die," he said, his eyes glistening with moisture. "Come to me when the time is right. Promise." She nodded, and then he turned and walked away.

Carrie kept watching him until he joined Emanuel and Alvin, and with the two men flanking him, he disappeared into the wall of white.

"Promise," she whispered to the wind, knowing in her heart that she'd never be able to keep her vow. That this would be the last time she'd see him.

Feeling as though her heart had been torn from her chest, she watched Frank until she could no longer see him, and then she went to her favorite place beside the stream and crumpled into a sobbing heap.

* * *

A long time later Carrie felt a hand on her shoulder. Tears blurred her vision, but she could tell by her warm smile that the woman leaning over her was the village Weaver. "He's gone, Clara."

The older woman squatted next to her and put an arm around her shoulder. "I know, child."

"He's gone," Carrie said again, the words torn from her heart.

Clara slipped her hand under Carrie's arm. "Come inside. It's going to rain, and you don't want to get all wet."

Rain? The likelihood of such a happening surprised Carrie enough to bring her upright.

Carrie looked toward the heavens, the pain of Frank's departure pushed aside for the moment. Boiling, angry, black thunderheads shrouded the normally unending blue sky.

Carrie dried her tears on the hem of her skirt and allowed Clara to help her to her feet. "Why is it going to rain?" she asked, sounding like a child who didn't understand why the weather could cancel a picnic.

"Don't you know?" Clara smiled knowingly. "Child, at some time or another rain falls into everyone's life. Without it, how would we enjoy the sunshine when it comes? The secret to enduring the rain is to remember that eventually, if we have faith and trust, the sun always comes out, and there's always a rainbow waiting somewhere just for us."

Overhead the heavens rumbled as though mocking Clara. Lightning sliced across the sky, followed by a burst of thunder so loud that Carrie covered her ears. Seconds later a deluge fell from the sky, soaking them to the skin. The two of them ran for the cottage.

Inside, Carrie stood in front of the fire, water dripping from her clothes, her hair plastered against her head. She wiped the rain from her face with her hands and turned to ask Clara for a towel, but the words never passed her lips.

Clara filled the black teakettle with water, hung it from the fireplace crane, and then swung the wrought-iron arm back in place over the flames. That process, however, was not what held Carrie's open-mouthed attention. While Carrie's clothing looked as though she'd been tossed in the stream, Clara's clothing was bone-dry.

"How. . ."

Clara waved her hand at the girl. "No time for silly questions. You need to get out of those wet clothes before you catch your death." She smiled slyly. "Won't do the babe any good if you get sick now, will it?"

About to climb the loft ladder to get out of her wet clothing, Carrie stopped dead. *Babe?* She shook her head, certain she had heard Clara wrong. "Did you say *babe?*"

"That I did," Clara said, placing two porcelain teacups on the table and measuring out a portion of loose tea in each, then adding a pitcher of cream and a bowl of sugar to the setting.

This was all coming at Carrie much too fast for her to digest. "I don't—"

"Never mind about that now. Get yourself into

some dry clothes, and then we'll talk." Clara nudged her toward the ladder leading to the loft. "Go on. Get along with you."

Mindlessly, her thoughts swirling in unruly circles through her brain, none of them making sense, Carrie did as she was told. She hurried through the process as quickly as she could, eager to return to the keeping room to hear Clara's explanation.

A few minutes later she emerged in dry clothes. As she stepped off the last ladder rung and onto the floor of the keeping room, Clara handed her a white towel.

"Now, sit down." She urged Carrie to the table. "The water just came to boil. You dry your hair while I get the kettle, and soon you'll be able to warm your insides with a nice hot cup of tea." When Carrie just stared at her, Clara frowned. "Go on, dry your hair," she scolded gently.

While she bustled off to the hearth, Carrie absently rubbed at her hair with the towel, her mind still a tangle of unsettled thoughts. After filling Carrie's cup and her own, Clara returned the kettle to the fireplace crane and then took her usual seat across from Carrie.

Carrie stopped rubbing at her hair and threw the still-damp strands over her shoulder, and out of her face and her line of vision. She couldn't wait for an explanation any longer. "Clara, what did you mean when you said it wouldn't do the *babe* any good if I got sick?"

With a look of surprise, Clara clicked her tongue. "Well, it won't, will it?"

"I suppose not," Carrie said. "But exactly what babe are you talking about?"

Clara's face melted into a radiant smile. "Why yours and Frank's, of course."

Carrie's jaw dropped, and her hand went automatically to her flat stomach. "Mine and Frank's? But—"

Clara said nothing. She just raised one eyebrow, and Carrie knew it was one of those things that Clara would never supply an answer to, like why her clothes were dry when Carrie had been soaked to the skin.

"This can't be true. Frank and I were only together a few times." She shook her head. "How could it have happened?"

A burst of laughter erupted from Clara. "Think about it, child. Mother Nature doesn't do things like this on her own, you know."

The blush of embarrassment heated Carrie's face. She dropped her gaze and folded her hands over her stomach. Mentally she counted back through the time that had elapsed since she'd come to Renaissance and then the time since she and Frank had made love at the waterfall. She supposed it was possible. But why hadn't *she* known? Probably because she'd had none of the usual signs. Since it wasn't time for her period yet, and she'd had one before she came here— that thought brought her up short. How did she know for sure that she'd had a period before coming here?

Suddenly, a terrifying thought struck her. Lifting her hesitant gaze to Clara, she asked, "This *is* Frank's child, right? You're sure?"

"As sure as I am that the sun will go down tonight and reappear tomorrow."

Relief flooded her. The baby was Frank's and not that faceless monster's. Not that she would have loved the child any less. She just couldn't bear the thought of having one more thing that would tie her to him.

Carrie pushed all thoughts of him from her mind and concentrated on the new life that lay safely against her breast.

Frank's child. Their child. A product of their love.

An overwhelming surge of elation filled her. Frank's baby. Inside her. A piece of him for her to love and care for. Then a wave of regret cast a dark cloud over her happiness. If only she'd known before Frank left.

"A baby. . . Mine and Frank's. It's—"

"A miracle? Yes, every baby is that, and," Clara laid her hand on Carrie's, "miracles don't usually come with an explanation."

That may be true, Carrie reasoned, but somehow,

when the miracle came about inside Renaissance, she had to wonder how much, if any, could be labeled coincidence.

Then, too, there was the problem of what she'd done before coming to Renaissance. If she'd committed the crime she thought she had, that would mean jail. Her baby would be born behind bars. The thought sickened her. Maybe this wasn't such a miracle after all.

Clara's warm hand covered hers. "Faith and trust, child. Faith and trust."

* * *

Frank stared into the Gateway Cabin's hearth. Meghan and Steve sat across from him. Neither of them said anything. The crackling fire filled the strained silence. The smells of Christmas: pine, cinnamon, baking cookies, the Christmas he'd left behind mere moments ago when he'd entered the mist with Emanuel, swirled around him mostly unnoticed. That he'd spent over a month inside the mist, and then come out to find mere minutes had passed baffled him. But right now, time being relative, as he had often been reminded, was the least of his worries.

He knew Steve and Meghan were waiting for him to speak, but what was there to say? That he felt as though his insides had been laid raw? That his heart beat solely to keep him alive? That tomorrow would just be the beginning of another day and a life without Carrie?

That without Carrie life seemed senseless, just a long parade of one empty day following another?

"Not all of them will be empty, Frank," Steve said. Frank's gaze flew to Steve. Steve laughed. "I'm sorry. I know that feeling. When Meghan used to read my thoughts, it infuriated me. Now, I've found that it has its benefits." He smiled down at his wife and winked.

Pain and intense jealousy of their happiness shot through Frank. "Maybe for you," he sneered.

Meghan leaned forward and touched his hand lightly. "It will have benefits for you, too. You need to have faith that Emanuel knows what he's doing."

Frank ran his hand through his hair, then leaned his elbows on his knees and gazed into the leaping flames of the fireplace. "But she's in there, and I'm out here. How can I help her? How will she get through this?"

Meghan stood and went to rearrange the logs in the fire. When she'd finished, she turned to Frank. "Every day Carrie is getting stronger. She's learning who she is and what she can do. She has to do that alone, Frank. No one, not even you, can show her the way. She'll come out of the village when it's time."

He could understand that, but there was still the big question he needed answered. "How will I know when it's time? I'll be off in the city. I don't even know where she lives. I'll never be able to find her."

Steve and Meghan exchanged glances.

Frank stood and paced the room, and then he stopped. "I'll just stay here. I'll wait for her right here."

Steve shook his head. "You can't do that, my friend. It's not over yet for you. You still have things to do."

Puzzled, Frank waited for him to continue speaking. When he didn't, Frank took his seat again. "What things?"

Steve spoke one important word. "Destiny. Why you were not killed in that accident along with Sandy."

Destiny. He'd grown so sick of that word. Shaking his head, he buried his face in his hands to gather his thoughts. When he could speak again without throwing his anger in the face of his friends, he looked at Steve and asked the one thing he most wanted to know. "How will I know when Carrie leaves the village?"

Steve glanced at Meghan. She inclined her head the merest fraction.

"I never told you why I ran out of Haverty's Bar the day we were having lunch, did I?"

Frank dredged his memory for the day Steve was talking about. Steve had just come back from his visit to the infamous Renaissance, and he'd been deeply depressed, much as Frank was right now. Worried about his friend, Frank had suggested they play hooky and meet for lunch at the Irish bar that the doctors from St Joseph's Hospital frequented. They'd just been served Haverty's signature platter of fish and chips when Steve had suddenly bolted from the place without explanation. The next time Frank had seen him, Steve had introduced him to Meghan and told him he was getting married.

"What about it?" Frank had no idea what their aborted lunch date had to do with Carrie, but he was willing to ride it out and see what Steve was leading up to.

"That was the day Meghan came to me from the mist."

Frank frowned. "But how—"

"How did I know?" Frank nodded. "I knew here." Steve laid his hand over his heart. "But even knowing didn't bring her through. It was when my absolute faith in our love took hold that she finally came to me, whole and with her memory of our love intact." He put his arm around his wife and cuddled her close to his side. "Have faith and trust in the love you share with Carrie, Frank, and you'll know when she steps off that bridge and back into this world. No matter where you are, your heart will tell you."

Frank nodded, but inside skepticism clouded his easy acceptance of Steve's prediction.

CHAPTER 20

A shutter banging in the night? The rain still pounding on the roof? Carrie wasn't sure what had awakened her, but she knew she would not find sleep again soon. One thing she was sure of was the nightmares that had ravaged her dreams for so long hadn't been the cause. Plagued by sleeplessness, she got out of bed and went to sit on the window seat.

With her fingertip, she traced the path of a raindrop as it skidded down the pane. Angel tears, her grandmother had called them. She picked up the tiny bear talisman from the table beside her and squeezed it tightly in her fist.

Courage, little one, her grandmother whispered in her ear. *Courage.*

"I'm trying, Gram. I'm really trying, but I miss Frank terribly, and I wish he were here so I could tell him about our baby." She laid her hand gently on her flat abdomen.

He'll know soon enough, child. Right now, you need to finish your journey here and find the answers you need so you can go back and do what needs to be done.

"But what is it that needs to be done?" she asked. Silence. "Gram?" More silence.

She sighed. No easy answers ever came her way either from Clara or her grandmother. Just this once she wished someone would give her a straight answer. With her memory still a blank, how was she to do whatever it was that everyone said she needed to do?

Her gaze shifted to the dresser where she'd propped up two of her paintings. One of the faceless man and one of Frank. Oddly enough, Frank's painting seemed to have taken on a life of its own. The sadness she'd painted into Frank's eyes originally was gone and had been replaced by a soul-deep longing that tore at her heart.

She let her head fall back against the wall and gazed at the inky darkness beyond the window. Out there, somewhere, was her future, and she flatly refused to think of it without Frank.

"I love you," she whispered and prayed that wherever he was, he heard it. "I *will* figure this out," she vowed, imbued with a new strength of purpose, "and I *will* find you." She laid her hand on her stomach. "*We'll* find you."

Knowing sleep would be elusive, Carrie lit the bedside candle and picked up her paint case. But instead of grabbing one of the blank canvases Sara had sent over from the store, she picked up the painting of the faceless man and settled herself in the window seat. Propping the painting in the opposite side of the window frame, she studied it for a long time.

Almost without knowing she did it, she found a brush in her hand. Taking a deep breath, she dipped the bristles into the paint and began to work. Time after time she replenished the brush and applied the paint to the picture.

By the time she laid the brush down, the sun was starting to seep through the window and illuminate the room with its pale morning light.

Carrie stared at her work. To her utter surprise, she'd painted a face on the man in the picture. His handsome features stared back at her through brown eyes dark with evil. Hair the same color as his eyes fell over his forehead.

To her further surprise, though she'd finally given a face to the man haunting her dreams, she had no idea who he was. Disappointment and frustration welled up inside of her. She'd been so positive that when he had a face, her memories would come rushing back. Instead, he was just another part of a puzzle of which she had no memory.

Giving vent to her anger, she threw the picture, the brush, and the paint box across the room and dissolved in a torrent of disheartened tears.

* * *

Frank pulled his scrub cap from his head and pushed open the swinging door to the operating room. It had been one long day after another of surgeries. Coupled with his nearly sleepless nights, exhaustion had become his constant companion.

Leaning on the waiting room window sill, he glanced outside. Night had fallen while he'd been in surgery, and the predicted, stiff northeasterner had blown a new snowstorm in off Long Island Sound. Already six to eight inches of the white stuff had accumulated on the sill.

Opting for remaining in the hospital and sleeping in his office instead of driving through the storm, Frank ambled toward the bank of elevators. He pushed the button and then closed his eyes and leaned tiredly against the wall while he waited for the car to arrive. The sound of the doors *whooshing* open roused him enough for him to make his way inside and push the button for the fifth floor.

No sooner had the doors closed than the lights dimmed. He sighed, hoping that didn't mean the storm had affected the electricity supply to the building. When they didn't come back up immediately, he assumed the generator had failed to kick in. Neither did the elevator budge. He mashed the button marked by the number five several times, but that did nothing.

"Son of a bitch," he muttered and resignedly collapsed against the wall. "What the hell? I'll just sleep here," he decided and slipped to the floor.

No sooner had he hit the floor than he heard a strange, high-pitched ringing in his ears. Clamping his hands over his ears, he looked around for the source of the sound. But there was nothing but the stark gray walls, the button panel, and a bright red emergency phone. He grabbed the phone and put it to his ear, but the line was dead. He slammed it back into its cradle and cursed.

"What the hell is going on?"

As suddenly as the ringing had started, it stopped.

"I love you. I *will* figure this out, and I *will* find you. *We'll* find you."

He knew that voice as well as he knew his own. "Carrie? I love you, too." But there was no reply. "What do you mean by *we*?" He waited. No answer. "Carrie, answer me." It was no use. The voice had gone silent.

Was this that time that Steve had warned him about? Did this mean that Carrie was coming out of the mist? He waited for the feeling Steve said he'd get in his heart, but the only thing he felt was desolation and pain and the familiar ache of the life being squeezed out of his soul. How long would he be able to stand this?

Hoping Carrie's voice would come again, he listened intently. With a jolt and a loud *whirring*, the elevator came to life. The lights grew bright, and the car climbed upward. With what must have sounded like a whimper of defeat, Frank slid to the floor in a crumpled heap, uncaring that when the doors opened on the fifth floor, someone might find him acting like a beaten puppy.

* * *

The following morning, Emanuel, Clara, Alvin, and Ellie were gathered around Clara's kitchen table. In front of each of them was a mug of steaming coffee. The previous night's rain had stopped, and brilliant sunshine streamed into the room.

Clara sensed something important was about to take place. With anticipation building by the second, she gripped her hands in her lap and waited. It didn't take long.

Alvin looked at Ellie, and then linked his hand with hers on the tabletop. "We'd like you to marry us, Emanuel," he blurted.

Clara noted that his rugged cheeks pinked, and he looked deep into his cup as though the secret to world peace lay somewhere in the depths of the dark, hot liquid.

"That's wonderful," she said, reaching out to squeeze

both his hand and Ellie's.

Emanuel smiled gently and nodded. "I'd be honored. When would you like the ceremony to be performed?"

"Now," Alvin said. "As soon as possible." He hesitated and turned to Ellie. "That is, if it's okay with you."

"Now is perfect." Ellie smiled up at him, her love bringing her blue eyes to life in a way Clara had never seen before.

"Now it is, then." Emanuel stood and positioned himself with his back to the window. The sunlight haloed his entire body. Alvin and Ellie stood in front of him, their hands tightly clasped together.

"Wait," Clara said. She grabbed her paring knife off the table and disappeared through the back door. When she returned, she carried a small bouquet of purple irises. "Here," she said, thrusting them into Ellie's hands. "Every bride should have a bouquet."

"How perfect, Clara," the Elder said, gazing down at the rich color. "If memory serves, irises mean faith, hope, wisdom, courage, and admiration. Very apropos. You couldn't have chosen better, Clara." Taking both Ellie's and Alvin's hands in his, Emanuel smiled at them. "Since only the two of you know what lies hidden in your hearts, I ask that each of you repeat your promises to the other. Ellie?"

Ellie turned to Alvin, and because she barely came

up to his shoulder, she tilted back her head so she could look him in the eyes. "Once, long ago, I came here as a child and saw you, and love took root in my heart. When I returned as a woman, that love had grown tenfold, and I knew this day would come. Now that it has, I pledge my heart, my soul, my life and my love to you and your happiness forever."

Clara sniffed loudly and dabbed at her welling eyes with the corner of her apron. Emanuel smiled at her.

Clearing his throat of what Clara thought had to be the same emotion that had drawn her tears, Alvin looked down at Ellie. "I never dreamed the day would come again when I would tell a woman I loved her, but you changed all that with your sweetness, your joy, and your wisdom. For that I thank you, and with all my heart I swear to protect you and do all I can to make you as happy as you've made me."

They both turned to Emanuel.

The Elder smiled. "I would advise you to kiss her and seal the bargain, my friend."

Alvin chuckled, then bent his head and kissed Ellie. Clara sighed and dabbed again at her eyes.

"Well, then, Mr. and Mrs. Tripp," Clara said, still dabbing at her eyes and sniffling, "I think this calls for a bit of a celebration." She hurried off to get the cake she'd baked that morning.

After they'd all taken their places at the table again, Clara refilled everyone's coffee cup and sliced large slabs off her special chocolate layer cake.

Emanuel cleared his throat. "Ahem. I'm assuming you'll want some time to get away on a. . ." He raised an eyebrow and looked to Clara.

"I believe it's called a honeymoon."

"Yes, a honeymoon."

Alvin and Ellie nodded in unison, then laughed.

"I wonder if you could put it off for a day or two." Emanuel waited patiently while they exchanged glances.

"Of course," Ellie finally said. "But why?"

Before he answered Ellie, Emanuel turned to Clara. "Where is Carrie?"

"She's in the garden."

Emanuel nodded, then turned his gaze back to the newlyweds. "I think Carrie might be ready to leave us by then, and I will need someone to escort her back to Tarrytown."

* * *

Carrie stretched her tired limbs and looked toward the sound of Clara's front door closing. Alvin and Ellie had just emerged. Hand in hand, they walked down the path toward Ellie's cottage. Ellie looked up at Alvin and said something that made him laugh out loud. Then he scooped her into his arms and headed for her cottage at a trot.

Jealousy knifed through Carrie. She dragged her gaze away. Though she was happy for them, she wished that they were her and Frank. They deserved happiness as much as Alvin and Ellie did. Why were they being denied that?

Unable to stand the loneliness of not having Frank nearby, she left the riverbank and meandered into the forest. She had gone quite some distance when she realized that her feet were automatically taking her toward the waterfall where she and Frank had known that one perfect day filled with love and happiness.

As she moved through the trees, she was suddenly aware of footsteps behind her. At first her heart leaped. *Frank!* But she immediately knew that it couldn't be Frank and that any hope that it was had been created by the desperate need in her aching heart.

Then, if not Frank, who could be following her into the woods? The first name to pop into her head was Alvin, but Alvin had gone with Ellie. Perhaps it was Emanuel.

She stepped behind the large trunk of an old maple tree and peered around it. Pressing her cheek against the rough bark, she scanned the trees. Sunshine bled through the upper branches in long, ghostly fingers.

Dark shadows crawled across the ground with each breeze that shifted the limbs.

A squirrel skittered down a limb near her head, causing her to catch her breath then straighten and spin around. The squirrel stopped and peered at her for a second or two through large, black, curious eyes. Then it scurried off into another tree. Could it have been just another squirrel she heard?

At that precise moment, the footsteps became audible again. They were heavy, decisive, and seemed to be getting closer. Definitely not a squirrel. Those footsteps undoubtedly belonged to a person. Quaking with inexplicable fear, she scanned the trees for any sign of a human being. But she saw nothing except trees and grass and wildflowers.

Had it been her imagination? Why had she been foolish enough to venture so far from the village alone? The thought almost made her laugh out loud. She was being stupid. No one in the village would harm her. Still. . .

Just as she was about to turn back, a long shadow fell across the ground a few yards from her. It had not been her imagination. Someone was following her. Despite the icy fear trickling down her spine, sweat beaded her forehead. She grabbed at the solid tree trunk for support. Her mind flashed back to her dream when she was hiding in the bushes from a pursuer.

No, this can't be the same. That was a dream.

Carrie knew she was awake, but the shadow still remained on the ground, as if the person throwing that shadow was waiting. . .waiting. But for what? Her?

A twig snapped, and her gaze flew back to the shadow. It had gained definition. It was a man—a very large man. Another twig snapped, this time just on the other side of the tree trunk to which she was clinging.

Then the oddest thing happened. Not far from where she was standing, a woman emerged from the trees. But not just any woman. This woman was. . .her. How could that be? Was she indeed dreaming again? Mouth agape, she stared fixedly at the woman as she moved toward the place where the person casting the shadow would be standing.

No time to decipher the hows and whys. Something inside Carrie told her that if the woman kept walking, she would be in danger. Still, her mirror image strolled closer, seemingly unaware of any danger.

"Don't come any closer," Carrie whispered very softly. "He's waiting for you." She had no idea how she knew that. She just did.

She'd stopped breathing. Her nerves drew tight. Her fingers dug into the tree's bark. Knowing the woman was walking into some terrible danger, she forgot about the

risk to herself and stepped from behind the tree, screaming, "Run! He's waiting for you!"

Oddly, the woman acted as if she hadn't heard her. But
Carrie knew she must have. She was just barely feet from
her. How could she not? Yet she made no sign of hearing the
warning and continued to walk in *his* direction.

Desperation and intense fear forced Carrie to try
again. "Can't you hear me? Run!"

Still the woman was oblivious to the threat awaiting her. Carrie spun toward the man to see if he was still
there. Not only was he there, he had stepped out of his
hiding place, and she recognized him as the faceless man
of her dreams. The difference was that this time, because
she had given him a face, she could plainly see the cruelty
in the set of his features and the almost animalistic anger
that twisted his mouth.

CHAPTER 21

Carrie couldn't understand why the woman wasn't listening to her. She was walking into certain danger, and Carrie didn't seem to be able to warn her away. If this woman who looked so much like her *was* her, then why couldn't she at least sense that there was a problem? Why wouldn't she listen?

Frustrated, Carrie ran up to her and looked her in the eye. "He's going to kill you one of these days!" she shouted into her face. The woman looked through her as if she weren't there.

Then what Carrie had said to the woman hit her. She hadn't said, he's *going to kill you*. She'd said, he's going to kill you *one of these days*. How had she known that? In her heart, Carrie was certain that this was not the first time she'd warned this woman. Nor was it the first time the woman had ignored that warning.

Carrie knew she wasn't imagining the threat. After

all, one had only to look at his face to see the evil and the anger that lurked there. She glanced back at him, as though reaffirming her thoughts.

To her surprise, his face had altered. He was now quite handsome, with a loving glint in his chocolate brown eyes. He held his hand out to the woman, and she took it. He smiled down at her, and she smiled back.

At that moment, the truth of what was happening hit her. Carrie was no more than a helpless, ignored onlooker whom neither of them saw or heard. *Why?*

Carrie grabbed the sides of her head. Pain unlike any she'd ever felt before sliced through her temples. She didn't understand any of this. Could more of her memory be returning in this scenario? If helping her remember was truly the reason for this, it wasn't working. Confusion and frustration filled her throbbing head.

Through the mist of pain, she watched the couple walk hand in hand, just as Alvin and Ellie had, into the trees.

"No! Don't go with him! He's going to—"

As they disappeared, the pain in her temples grew excruciatingly intense. Carrie sank to her knees, still holding her head as the pain finally subsided to a faint ache, and then disappeared completely. A sense of inevitability replaced it.

Then a woman's high-pitched scream rent the silence of the forest. The sound shivered over Carrie like the hand of death. Small animals scurried for cover. Birds squawked in protest and deserted their perches among the branches overhead.

Without thinking about her own safety, Carrie sprang to her feet and then ran toward the sound. As she rounded a large outcropping of rocks, she saw the woman on the ground, blood streaming from her mouth. The man was standing over her with fists clenched.

"Get up, bitch," he growled.

The woman whimpered, shook her head, and cowered against the dried leaves coating the forest floor, her hands shielding her face.

"I'm not telling you again." He grabbed a handful of her auburn hair, hair the same color as Carrie's, and dragged her up. "I said, stand up."

With little recourse, the woman scrambled to her feet, but her hands remained in front of her face. "Please," she begged, tears choking her voice, "don't hit me again."

"Don't tell me what I can and can't do." He hauled back his arm and hit her solidly against the side of her head with his fist.

Carrie thought she heard bone crack. She grimaced and hoped it was his hand. But the wail of pain from the woman told Carrie the cracking bone had been hers. The woman's body slumped and hung like a rag doll from his hand. He released her hair, and she fell to the ground in a heap, blood pouring from the corner of her mouth and from the new cut at her temple, most likely inflicted by the gold ring on his hand.

"Bastard!" Carrie screamed and rushed to the woman's side.

Frantic to help her, Carrie scooped her bloody body into her arms and cradled her against her chest. The woman didn't move. Carrie rocked her back and forth, praying that she was wrong, that the woman wasn't dead.

Looking down at her, Carrie wiped the blood away as her own tears fell on the woman's face. "You can't die!" she cried, keeping the rocking motion going. "Why didn't you leave him? Why?" She caressed the woman's face as she hugged it closer to her, oblivious of the blood seeping into her own clothes. "Please don't die. *Don't die!*"

But it seemed useless, and Carrie covered her face with her hands and sobbed. When she finally regained her composure a few minutes later, she dropped her hands. To her shock and surprise, the man had vanished, as had the woman whose head had rested in Carrie's lap. The blood from the woman's battered face that had stained Carrie's clothes was gone, as well.

High above her, birds twittered merrily from the treetops. All was as it had been before the man had appeared in the woods. Carrie shivered. What was happening to her? Was she going crazy? Why was she now seeing herself outside her body? What was any of this accomplishing except making her doubt her sanity?

* * *

Clara had just started supper when the door burst open. Carrie stood there looking bedraggled and shell-shocked. Her face lacked color, and she was chewing nervously on her bottom lip. Before the girl said a word, Clara knew her memory had started to return. Poor child. This was going to be an emotional time for her.

She went to Carrie and guided her to one of the chairs at the table, and then poured hot tea into a porcelain cup and set it in front of her.

"Drink this. It'll make you feel less shaky, and then we'll talk about what happened."

Carrie sipped gingerly at the tea and then nodded. "I think my memory is coming back." She looked at Clara, her eyes hollow and haunted. "But now I'm not sure I want to remember. It all seems too horrible to be true. How could anyone do that to someone they supposedly love? How could I love him?"

Brow furrowed, she sipped at her tea.

Clara shook her head. If she knew the answer to that, it would have saved a great many women years of undeserved agony. "No one can control or understand how love works, my dear. What happens to these women is like a homing pigeon that soars above the air currents, free and independent."

Carrie's frown deepened. "I don't understand."

"Well," Clara explained, "the pigeon gets caught on a violent upward draft, and for a time, it's nice to just soar there, free and relying only on the current to carry it from place to place. After all, to break free could mean its demise. Only when the bird realizes that although it may be easier to ride the violent current, it is not safer, and despite its loving the feeling, the current is battering it, throwing it around, harming it. If it wishes to ensure its survival, it must break free of the current. But in the end, the bird must make the decision to extract itself."

She refilled Carrie's cup and poured one for herself.

"You mean, I have to break free of him if I want to live."

Clara sighed. She shook her head. "I can't answer that, child." She wished Emanuel were there to help. This was one of the most difficult Assignments she'd ever handled.

The hand holding Carrie's cup paused midway to her mouth. "Why?"

Before Clara could answer, there was a knock at the door. She patted Carrie's hand and went to answer it. When she swung the door open, she was not surprised to find Emanuel on the other side. There had never been a time when she needed him that he didn't come. Most times she was grateful for his assistance, but this time his appearance brought humiliation with it. She'd never asked Emanuel for help with her Assignments before, and she should have been able to do this on her own, but. . .

Unable to meet his gaze, she dipped her head.

"I'm sorry. I—"

The Elder raised her chin so that his gaze fell upon her face. He smiled. "No need to apologize, my dear. This time your Assignment is not an easy one, and to not ask for help would have been foolish."

"I thought by now she would have realized. . . But she hasn't," Clara said, trying not to let her frustration show in her tone of voice.

He nodded, and then he swept past her into the room. She closed the door and followed him to the table where Carrie waited, her eyes wide and her face pale as snowfall.

This was the first time Carrie and the village Elder had come face to face. Clara had spoken of him, as had Frank, but even with their descriptions, Carrie still wasn't prepared for a man of such presence. In many ways, he reminded her of her grandfather. The same playful twinkle lit the soft gray eyes brimming with wisdom. His lips curved slightly in a perpetual gentle smile. Pink colored his ruddy cheeks, and lines crisscrossed his brow and fanned out from the corners of his eyes.

But that's where the similarities ended. The robe, the long white hair and beard, the way he seemed to be bathed in a light from an unseen source gave him the appearance of a man who should have been carved in stone and standing in a niche in a church.

Oddly, Carrie felt a surge of trust. She knew instinctively that this man would not lie to her or mislead her. For once, she just may be face to face with someone who could and would answer all the questions swimming through her brain.

"Who am I?" she asked Emanuel bluntly.

"Carrie Henderson."

"Where do I come from?"

"Tarrytown."

"Am I married?"

Emanuel didn't have an answer readily available as he'd had before. Instead he glanced at Clara. Clara shook her head, but wouldn't meet Carrie's gaze.

"She doesn't remember," she muttered.

"Carrie," he said, laying his large, warm hand on hers, "the woman you saw in the forest today—"

Carrie's head snapped up. "How did you know I saw a woman in the forest?"

He waved his hand dismissively. "That's of no importance right now."

She wanted to argue that everything he knew about

her was of importance, but she had more pressing questions for him than how he could have known what happened someplace he hadn't been.

"Am I married?" she asked again.

Emanuel shook his head. "No, my dear, you are not married."

Carrie's first reaction was a flood of relief that she was not tied to a monster by wedding vows. Her second reaction was one of near elation. She was free to be with Frank. Her hand went automatically to her stomach.

Then confusion set in and moved all other emotions aside. If she wasn't married, then who was that man, and why was she seeing such horrible scenarios?

Before she could voice her concerns, Emanuel patted her hand. "All in good time, my child, all in good time." He turned to Clara. "My dear, I think some of your excellent coffee is in order now."

"I don't want coffee!" Carrie exclaimed, jumping to her feet, her voice unnaturally strident and demanding. "I want answers."

Emanuel looked at her. He said nothing, just looked. Instantly, her impatience and anger drained away. Instinctively, she knew she would get nothing from this wise old man by making demands. She resumed her seat and folded her hands on the table.

Clara left the table and assembled the coffeepot for

brewing. Carrie watched her methodical movements. Pour water in the pot. Measure coffee into a basket. Place the pot on the stove.

In her mind a picture began taking form. She was in a pristine kitchen. Not Clara's. It was too modern. A woman was making coffee. She had her back to Carrie so she couldn't see her face, but her hair was the same color as the woman's from the forest. Carrie could hear her sniffling as though she was crying. She bustled about, but not haphazardly. Her movements were efficient and quick, as though she was driven not to waste time. When she'd placed the glass carafe beneath the basket in the coffeemaker, she turned and stared back at Carrie with red-rimmed eyes peering from a tear-stained face. Carrie caught her breath. The woman's face was the same face that Carrie saw in her own mirror each morning, except now a dark, ugly bruise rimmed one eye.

Instantly the image faded, and she was back in Clara's keeping room, sitting across from Emanuel.

"I don't understand," she said, still in shock from seeing the same woman again, and her battered face.

"Don't you?" Emanuel asked gently.

* * *

Frank scrubbed his arms while a nurse held up the chart

of the patient he was to perform heart surgery on. He scanned the chart again. He'd read it over the night before when he'd been told that Dr. Jensen was ill and he'd have to operate for him, but he always liked to refresh his memory by reviewing any patient's chart just before he went into surgery.

It was an operation he was very familiar with and had performed many times. When the child had gone for his pre-school physical, they'd detected a very faint heart murmur. On further investigation, they found a very small hole in the area of his heart between the right and left chamber wall. A fairly simple surgical procedure would close it, and the boy would be out playing with his friends in no time.

When he'd finished reading the chart and scrubbing up, he used his behind to push open the doors into the operating room. The patient was already on the table; the sight of an outline of a small body beneath the sheet always made Frank swallow hard. That such a young person should have to undergo surgery just didn't seem right to him.

He stepped to the side of the table and looked down into the child's face. His heart stopped. He made it a habit to read nothing more on the chart than the child's symptoms and the recommendation of Dr. Jensen. It made no sense to get attached in any way to a child that wasn't even his patient. He had enough small lives to worry about, enough names to put to the faces of children who needed his skills to live normal lives.

"What's this child's name?" he asked of no one in particular.

"William Gray," a nurse said after consulting the chart.

He glanced down at the outline of the boy's legs beneath the sheet. One was badly twisted, and no doubt would require the use of crutches for the boy to be mobile.

Frank hesitated before asking the next question. He wasn't at all sure he wanted to know what the answer was. Besides, he might be mistaken. It had been dark that night, and he'd been preoccupied. "Does it indicate where he goes to school?"

"Yes, Doctor. He attends the Westchester Handicapped Children's Rehabilitation Center."

The side of a white van with bright green lettering and the boy who hobbled out on crutches and into his mother's arms flashed before Frank. He took a deep breath. Inexplicably compelled to lift his gaze to the observation gallery that ringed the ceiling of the operating room, he noted a man with a white beard and a long white robe tied at the waist with a rope, looking down at him.

You have other tasks waiting for you. Emanuel's

words rang through Frank's head as if he were whispering in his ear.

He smiled up at Emanuel. *This is it, isn't it? This is the task I had waiting for me.*

The Elder smiled back, then gave a succinct nod. *It's one of them, but there's more you'll still need to do before your destiny is completely fulfilled, Frank.*

What?

You'll know them when the time comes. Emanuel smiled again, and then vanished, leaving Frank to wonder if his imagination had conjured the Elder or if he had, indeed, actually been there.

CHAPTER 22

Frank stepped back from the operating table and nodded to the doctor assisting him. "Close for me, please, Harrison."

The young physician, one whom Frank knew would one day make a superb cardiac surgeon, nodded and began the procedure.

Frank left the operating room and peeled off his surgical gloves and mask. Tossing them into the receptacles beside the door, he stepped into the hall and strode toward the waiting room. Inside the large, sunny room, he found a pasty-faced woman wringing her hands and pacing the floor. Her eyes betrayed the tears she'd been shedding while she waited.

When she saw him, she stopped dead in her tracks, her gaze searching his. "Billy? Is he alright?"

Frank smiled. "He's fine." She exhaled a long breath, then sank onto one of the leather sofas lining the walls. Frank sat next to her. "He made it through the operation with flying colors. He'll be out and running around with his friends in no time."

The woman looked at him, and although her lips smiled in delight that her son's prognosis was so favorable, Frank could see the sadness that lurked there, a sadness that had made its home there long ago. "I'm afraid he'll never run around with his friends, Dr. Donovan."

At that moment Frank realized his offhanded remark, which was meant to give her hope, must have cut this woman deeply. He recalled the twisted leg beneath the sheet. He knew a doctor who had worked miracles in the past on other kids in worse shape than Billy. Did he dare give her hope when there might not be any?

. . .there's more you'll still need to do before your destiny is completely fulfilled. . . You'll know them when the time comes.

Taking a deep breath, Frank smiled, knowing with a certainty that this was what Emanuel had been trying to tell him. "I'm going to give you the name and phone number of a doctor I know. I'll make an appointment for Billy to see him as soon as he's recovered sufficiently. I think he may be able to see to it that Billy *will* run around with his friends."

Her face transformed before his eyes. The sadness, while still there, was illuminated by the faint sunrise of hope. "Really? Billy may be able to walk without his crutches?"

"Not right away, but I believe there's a strong possibility." Frank had no idea how he knew that. Certainly it wasn't because of any extensive knowledge he had in that department, since it wasn't his field of expertise. He just knew, gut deep.

Faith and trust, my boy. Faith and trust make miracles, came Emanuel's disembodied voice in his head.

Without warning, Mrs. Gray threw herself into Frank's arms and sobbed on his shoulder. "How can we ever repay you?"

As he held her and patted her back, he thought about the accident and its repercussins: if Frank had died in it, if Billy might not have lived, and even if he had, he would have had a half life. But if Frank hadn't swerved, he'd have hit the van and this poor woman might have had to face her life alone without her son. For the first time, Frank could clearly see what Sandy had been trying to tell him.

Frank set Mrs. Gray away from him, but held her at arm's length. "Love him. Love is the miracle we all seek. You have yours in that little boy."

Someday soon I'll have mine, too. And his thoughts veered to a beautiful, auburn-haired woman with a smile that lit up his world.

* * *

Carrie lay on her bed, her gaze fixed on the rough-hewn beams in the ceiling.

Try as she might, she could not understand Emanuel's odd behavior. After she'd had the vision of the crying woman making coffee, she'd told him she didn't understand, and all he had to say to her was, *Don't you?* Then he'd just gotten up and left without explaining.

She'd been so sure that he of all people would put definition to these crazy visions she'd been having, but he hadn't. He'd just added to her quandary.

If it wasn't her, then who was that woman she kept seeing?

The click of Clara's loom told her the old woman had gone back to work and probably would not add anything to the brief conversation Carrie had just had with the Elder. Obviously, she was totally on her own to put definition to this tangle of events.

Lord, but she missed Frank. If he'd been here to hold her and help her sort through all this, she knew it would have been so much easier. One thing that had come from her conversation with Emanuel was that she now knew she wasn't married. Relief was a mild description for the wild rush of emotion and freedom that had ebbed over her with that affirmation.

She could leave here and find Frank with a clear conscience. She could tell him about her love for him and about their child. Then maybe, just maybe, they could have a future—if he hadn't already forgotten who she was. Her heart sank at the thought. She rolled over and buried her face in her arms. What would she do if Frank didn't want her or their baby? Where would she go?

She sat up abruptly. She was being stupid. She had no reason at all to believe that Frank wouldn't remember her or that he wouldn't want her and their child. The best thing she could do for herself right now was decipher that vision of the woman in the kitchen. Perhaps that would be the final piece to her puzzle and the key to her leaving Renaissance and getting on with her life.

Who was the woman with the auburn hair, and what did she have to do with Carrie Henderson?

The questions had no sooner passed through her mind than her bed felt like it had been sucked up in a giant whirlpool. Round and round it spun at breakneck speed. The room blurred and passed before her eyes in long streaks of indistinct light. Her head began to throb, and her stomach heaved. Her fingers ached from clutching the edge of the bed to keep from falling off.

Just as suddenly, the bed halted, throwing Carrie sideways. She reached out to catch herself and found her fingers wrapped around the edge of a kitchen table set for dinner. She blinked and the room came into focus.

Standing on the other side of the table, chopping a variety of salad vegetables, was the woman from before. This time Carrie could see her face quite clearly. Although she was still stunned by how much they looked alike, Carrie could now see a small brown mole just below the right nostril of the woman's nose. Carrie had no such mark. Nor did she have a thin scar over her right eyebrow.

So who was this woman?

"I can't leave him, Carrie. I love him. I know he hates what he does." She raised green, pleading eyes the same color as Carrie's to look at her. "He always says he's sorry."

She'd called Carrie by name. She knew her. However, even though she knew her well enough to call her by name, Carrie noted that she never quite met her gaze, as if she didn't want Carrie to see what was reflected in her eyes.

The eyes are the windows of the soul, her grandmother always said.

If that were true, then this woman was going to do whatever she could to ensure that the secrets she carried in her soul remained hers and hers alone. Why? Carrie believed that it had something to do with whomever she was talking about.

"Don't look at me like that," the woman said, turning her back.

She busied herself sorting aimlessly through a shelf in the refrigerator. When she'd rearranged the orange juice container and a milk carton for the third time, she closed the door. For a moment she remained facing the appliance, then she turned back to Carrie.

"You may be my sister, but that doesn't give you the right to come in here and tell me what to do and how to run my life. Now, I think you should leave. Dan will be home for dinner soon, and he doesn't like it when you're here or when his dinner isn't ready when he comes in."

Before Carrie could say anything, the room began to spin again, and moments later she found herself back on the bed in Clara's cottage. When everything calmed down and she had her balance, Carrie sat upright.

Her sister? She was this woman's sister?

A piercing, knifelike pain sliced through Carrie's temple. She groaned and collapsed against her pillow, clutching her throbbing head. The pain went on and on, pounding unmercifully at her skull until she thought she was dying. She tried to call out to Clara, but her vocal cords didn't want to work. Then she tried to get up, but each time she moved, the pain grew worse, to the point of being unbearable. She squeezed her eyes shut, hoping that if she shut out the light streaming through the window, it would help. But the pain persisted and increased.

Suddenly, as unexpectedly as it had come on, the throbbing agony was gone. Carrie took a deep shuddering breath and eased her eyes open. Not sure what to expect, she looked around the room. She was still at Clara's, so what had the pain been all about?

Then it came to her as clear as any picture she'd ever seen. The woman was, indeed, her sister, her *twin* sister. That's why they looked alike, except for that tiny mole that their mother had used to tell them apart. Her name was Cathy, and she was married to a brutal, self-centered, controlling jerk named Dan Carrington.

With that one memory slipping through the gates she'd erected to shut it all out, all the memories of the night, the time before she'd found herself wandering the streets of Tarrytown in a blizzard, rushed through on its heels.

* * *

She'd just left the art store after buying some extra paint to complete a picture she'd been working on for her sister, the first painting she'd done in years. Since it was Christmas Eve, she'd been lucky to catch them before they closed for the holiday. She stuffed her receipt into her pocket and hurried toward her car.

As she stepped to the snow-covered sidewalk, she

noticed Dan's car across the street. He and Cathy were in the front seat. Even from where she stood, she could hear Dan's harsh voice berating her sister.

"How did you ever live this long? I sent you to buy a simple lightbulb, and you can't even do that. Stupid bitch!" He swung his arm, and Carrie heard the distinct sound of his fist connecting with Cathy's face.

Before Carrie could react, he'd put the car in gear and sped off down the street. Fuming, Carrie jumped in her car, swung it in a wide U-turn, and followed them, determined that this time she'd get her sister to leave that bastard. She didn't have to guess where they were going. He was taking her home to their isolated farmhouse, where no one could see or interfere, and he could beat and batter her to his heart's content.

God, Carrie could scream when she thought of all the times she'd begged Cathy to leave him, and all her sister had been able to do was make excuses for the creep. Over and over she'd allowed Cathy to talk her out of calling the police because she was terrified of what he'd do to Cathy if the cops didn't cuff him and drag his sorry ass off to jail on the spot.

Carrie cursed and slammed her fist against the steering wheel. "Cathy, why didn't you let me stop him? Why?"

Thankful that the predicted blizzard had not yet moved in and that the smattering of snow that had fallen so far had not collected on the roads to slow her progress, Carrie floored the gas pedal. She pulled into the driveway of the farmhouse just as the front door was closing behind her sister and her husband. Wasting no time, she turned off the car and jumped out, not even taking the keys from the ignition.

She'd only run a few steps when she hit a patch of ice and went down, smacking her forehead on the cement walkway. For a moment she saw stars, then she blinked, and her vision cleared. She tried to push herself to her feet, but her head spun dizzily and her stomach heaved. She took a deep breath and gained some semblance of balance, then slowly struggled to her feet. Carrie could hear him shouting before she was fully erect.

"Don't stand there and lie to me. They must have had that bulb. You were just too lazy or too stupid to find it." The sound of flesh hitting flesh, followed by the crash of breaking furniture, exploded into the night. "Get up! Get the hell up, bitch!" Again the sound of flesh hitting flesh was followed by screams.

"Don't. . .Dan. Please don't. . .hit me any more." Her sister's pain-filled voice rang out.

"I'll do whatever I damned well please." Again the sound of Dan's fist connecting with what Carrie assumed was Cathy's face. "I. . .will. . .hit. . .you. . .and. . .hit. . .you all I want. Maybe then you'll. . .get. . .some. . .smarts."

Each word was punctuated by the muffled crunch of bone on bone.

This time Cathy didn't protest. Carrie's blood ran cold. Was it because she thought better of it and wasn't saying anything to anger him further? Or was it because she couldn't speak?

Ignoring the light-headedness that held her in its grasp, Carrie dashed up the steps, her heartbeat sounding in her ears, not knowing what she'd do when she got inside and was finally confronting Dan. All she knew was that this time he wasn't going to get away with it.

Carrie turned the knob, but the door was locked. Fisting her hand, she pounded on the wood. "You son of a bitch, open this door and let me in!"

"Go to hell!" he yelled back. "For once in your life, mind your own fucking business."

"My sister *is* my business, you bastard!" She pounded harder. "Open it!"

But it remained locked. Inside, she could hear the sound of scurrying footsteps. Fearful that he would attack Cathy because Carrie was trying to interfere, she renewed her efforts to get in, but to no avail. She looked around and saw a stack of fresh-cut firewood in a wrought-iron rack. Grabbing one of the logs, she smashed a living-room window, pushed the curtain aside, and climbed through.

Log held high, she was prepared to smash it against Dan's skull if he came after her or her sister. Quickly, she scanned the room, but Dan was nowhere to be seen. The freaking coward had run. Then she looked down and froze. The log fell from her limp fingers and hit the floor with a hollow *thunk*.

"Oh my God, Cathy!"

On the floor, her blood seeping into the beige carpet, lay Cathy. Blood was everywhere. Cathy's white blouse was smeared with it, as were the chair beside her, the wall behind her, and the floor beneath her. Her face was bloodied almost beyond recognition.

Carrie's knees went weak. The bastard had killed her sister. Tears stung her eyes, and she didn't even try to hold them back. They rolled in silent misery down her cold cheeks. Her head spun, and her vision wavered between clear and fuzzy. Nausea threatened. She leaned against the window frame searching for the strength to go to her sister.

Why hadn't she called the police despite Cathy's pleas not to? Why? Why? My God, her sister was dead, and it was as much her fault as it was Dan's. Sobs tore from her chest in wrenching anguish. Forcing herself to get control, she took a deep breath and managed to bring her vision into focus again. The cut she'd sustained on the sidewalk dripped blood down her cheek and onto her blouse.

Then she heard it. Cathy moaned faintly. Carrie ran to her and dropped to her knees. She scooped her sister into her arms and cradled her battered face against her chest. Cathy was alive, but barely breathing. If she didn't get help and fast, Cathy would surely die.

"It's okay, kiddo. Hang on. I'll get help. Hang on."

Carefully, she laid her sister back on the floor, then dashed for the phone. She picked up the receiver. No dial tone. Looking down, she saw the raw end of the wire lying on the floor. The son of a bitch had ripped it from the wall to make sure she couldn't call the cops on him.

Carrie glanced back at her sister's crumpled body. She had to get help. The sound of a car engine coming to life in the driveway drew her attention. Fighting dizziness, she raced to the window in time to see Dan pull to a stop beside her Toyota, jump out, and open her car door. A few seconds later, he emerged from the front seat, looked up to where she stood in the window, waved her keys and her cell phone at her, grinned, and then hopped back in his vehicle and careened out of the driveway.

"Damn you!" she screamed impotently after him. She smacked her hand on the windowsill. Dan had marooned them out here in the wilderness without any way to get help. "Bastard!" she yelled after his fading taillights.

Berating Dan wasn't going to help Cathy. But what

was she going to do? Her sister was bleeding to death, with God only knew what other injuries, and she had no way to contact anyone at all. Without a vehicle or a phone, she would have to walk to town for help.

After spreading the afghan from the couch over Cathy and placing a throw pillow beneath her head, she softly kissed the one small spot above her sister's left eyebrow that wasn't smeared with blood. "I have to go for help, Cathy. I'll be back as soon as I can. Hang on. Please, baby, hang on."

Reluctantly and with one last look at her sister, Carrie stepped into the cold, dark night and started walking. By now the storm had gained power, and snow was coming down in blowing sheets of opaque white. She had trouble staying on the road. Several times, she slipped off the side and into the ditch. Clawing her way back to the paved surface, she pushed herself on.

Fatigue and dizziness plagued her every step until she wasn't sure she could go on. The falls she had taken in the snow had soaked her clothing, and the freezing cold had seeped into her body, chilling every part of her. She shivered and pulled her coat tighter around her. Her steps dragged, slowing her progress. Dread filled her. She wasn't going to make it. Cathy would die on her own living-room floor, and Carrie would die out here on this frozen landscape. And that brutal bastard who had caused it all would go free.

"Please, someone, help me. Help me." Her sobbing plea was muffled by the falling snow. Even if someone had been around, they never would have heard her. Hopelessness overwhelmed her. Slowly, she sank to her knees in the snow.

Her head throbbed painfully, and her eyes wouldn't focus. Blackness began to gather around the outer fringes of her peripheral vision. Unwilling to give up, she pushed herself to her feet again and forced herself forward, stumbling blindly, falling time after time and dragging herself back to her feet. Her strength was quickly ebbing.

She stumbled and ended up face-first in the snow. Using the last bit of her strength, she pulled herself to her knees. Through her blurred vision, she thought she saw a man in a long, white robe coming toward her. Her muddled brain rationalized that she'd died, and this was the angel of death coming to claim her.

Chapter 23

Carrie's first thought, when she found herself back in Clara's cottage bedroom, was of her sister, Cathy. Was she still alive? If so, how could she save her? Carrie's second thought was that not only was she alive, but also she was now finally free to leave Renaissance, get Cathy help, and find Frank. She sprang from the bed and hurried down the ladder as fast as she could.

As Clara moved away from the loom, she turned to Carrie, a knowing smile curling her lips. "It's all come back, hasn't it?"

Carrie nodded. "But my sister. . . Is she. . ." She swallowed hard to rid her throat of the large lump of emotion suddenly lodged there. "It's been so long—"

"Time is relative, my child. Don't be too eager to break out your mourning garb."

Carrie felt a surge of hope. "Does that mean Cathy is still alive?" But Clara busied herself by folding the length of recently woven cloth, as if she hadn't heard Carrie at all. "Clara? Is Cathy still alive?" she asked, knowing in her gut that this was yet another of those questions that would go unanswered.

Before Clara could answer, *if* she had even been at all inclined to do so, a knock sounded on the door, and the Weaver hurried to open it. Outlined in the doorway by the sunlight pouring in behind him was Emanuel, flanked by Alvin and Ellie. Over his shoulder, Carrie could see a thin veil of mist gathering in the village.

At the sight of the Elder, hope rose anew. Emanuel would know about Cathy. He must. She immediately went to the village Elder. "My sister? Is she—"

Emanuel held up his hand. "All your remaining questions will be answered in good time, my dear. But you must be patient. It will happen as it is meant to." He smiled a greeting at Clara, and then took his customary seat at the table. Ellie and Alvin did likewise. "Join us, Carrie, please," he motioned to the empty chair beside Ellie.

Anxious and edgy, Carrie sat. She folded her shaking hands in her lap and gripped them tight to still their trembling. Impatiently, she glanced from one person to another, waiting for someone to speak.

"My child," Emanuel finally said, "it's time for you to leave us."

The mist!

Carrie glanced toward the window and could see that what had been little more than a haze before had thickened appreciably in the brief time since Emanuel had entered the cottage. The Transition that Clara had told her would mark her departure from here was beginning. She was really leaving. Thoughts of what she'd find outside Renaissance made apprehension swell inside her.

Please be alive, she begged Cathy silently. *Please don't die. I'm coming.*

Emanuel patted her hand. "You cannot alter destiny."

"What does that mean?" Carrie's body turned cold as ice. His elusive answer could mean only one thing. "Is Cathy already dead?" When he didn't reply, her anger rose to the surface. "Dammit, answer me. Is my sister alive?"

He smiled kindly. "Faith and trust, my child, faith and trust."

His calmness infuriated Carrie. "Why can't you people just answer a simple question? My sister may be dying or already dead. Can't one of you, for once, talk without riddles and tell me what's happened to her?"

Her strident tones filled the little room. She glared at Emanuel, and at that moment, came as close as any time in her life, aside from her encounters with Dan, to throttling someone. Carrie clenched her fists under the table and bit her tongue to hang on to her control. She just wanted to know how Cathy was. Was that so hard to understand?

The Elder's kindly smile never wavered. That he continued to show so little emotion should have brought her temper to a dangerous boiling point. Instead, when he laid his hand on hers, calmness invaded her. She leaned back in the chair.

"As soon as the Transition is complete, Alvin and Ellie will escort you out of the village and back to Tarrytown." He glanced in the direction of the rapidly gathering mist outside the window. "It should be very soon."

The five of them went outside. Clara handed Carrie her coat and kissed her cheek. "Be happy, child."

Carrie smiled weakly, nodded, and then hugged the Weaver. "Thank you. . .for everything."

After Carrie had said her good-byes, Clara stood beside Emanuel and watched as the trio crossed the footbridge and disappeared into the mist.

She turned to Emanuel. "All's well that ends well," she said with a sigh. But he didn't reply. His face was creased in a deep, worried frown. "What is it? Her memory has returned, and she's ready to go into the outside world and face what she left behind. What troubles you?"

"Not all of her memory has returned. She has one more to face that could be more devastating to her than what she just learned about her sister." Emanuel began to walk slowly back to Clara's cottage.

She hurried to catch up. "I don't understand. You let her recall all the memories you removed with the amnesia."

He smiled sadly. "That I did, Clara, but this is one memory that Carrie suppressed herself long before she came to us. A memory that I have no control over. She is the only one with the power to free it. When she does, she'll need someone." He paused. "I think I'd better pay a visit to Steve and Meghan."

* * *

Frank settled himself on his sofa with a beer and switched the TV to the Weather Channel to watch the local forecast.

"All you commuters better plan on leaving early for work tomorrow," the attractive young woman on the screen warned. "The blizzard that is just starting to hit the city is expected to last the rest of the day and into the night. Total accumulation should be in the neighborhood of ten to twelve inches before the storm system moves off to the northeast. The roads will be treacherous, so stay home unless you absolutely have to go out."

Frank glanced out the window at the inch or so of accumulated snow on his car. Not that he cared one way or the other. He had nowhere to go. He wasn't due back at the hospital until Monday. He had an entire weekend to do what he'd been doing constantly since he'd left the village: think about Carrie. Wonder what she was doing and if she needed him. Hope that she'd soon find the answers to her lost memory and come to him. Even after Sandy's death, he hadn't felt this lonely, this desolate. That was no disrespect to Sandy. Before Carrie came into his life, he hadn't believed love was again possible for him, and now he knew how precious it was. He knew what he'd lost with Sandy. Now he knew what he had found with Carrie. It was real, and he yearned for it. There seemed to be a gaping chasm inside him that couldn't be filled. He'd always loved his work, and it had always fulfilled him, but even that held no appeal for him now.

He took a long drink from the bottle of beer and set it on the coffee table. Steve had told him he'd know when Carrie left, and he'd been waiting every day for a sign with his nerves stretched out like a rubber band. Every flutter put him on alert to feel more. But more never came. Every day blurred into the next, and she was still there, and he was still here.

He started to lean back when it happened. A sharp tightening in his chest, almost like having a heart attack, but there was no pain. His heart clenched, then seemed to swell and pulsate harder. His chest grew tighter as though a steel band was wrapped around it.

He leaned forward and rested his elbows on his thighs, trying to catch his breath. When the pressure lessened a bit, he gulped in deep breaths, but the sensations persisted. His head grew light, and his vision seemed fuzzy and dotted with white specks of bright light. Seconds later, his vision went totally white.

My God, he thought, *I'm going blind!*

But just as suddenly as the whiteness came, it dissipated. When it had cleared, what he saw was not his living room. It was a small footbridge spanning a narrow, gurgling stream. Everything on his side was crystal clear, but on the other side, the fog was thick enough to walk on.

As though someone had jabbed him with a stick to prod his memory, he knew instantly what the scene reminded him of. The footbridge leading out of Renaissance. He stopped fighting whatever had come over him and waited, his breath held, his heart pounding erratically in his chest, his mind's eye glued to the bridge.

Then the fog stirred as though someone had run their hand through it. It swirled and pulsed. Light emanated from inside it. Then, looking like an invisible knife had sliced it open, it parted.

Three people stepped onto the bridge. He barely saw two of them. It was the third person who captured Frank's attention and held it unwaveringly.

Carrie!

She was leaving Renaissance. Frank grabbed his keys and jacket and ran out to his car. He had no idea where he was going. Hopefully, whatever was telling him that she was leaving the mist would guide him to her.

* * *

Carrie wrapped her coat around her shivering body. The snow blowing down her collar chilled her to the bone. She'd gotten too used to the perpetual spring of Renaissance. She squinted and peered into the night to see exactly where she was, but the driving snow made it hard to see much more than a few feet beyond her.

The brief stop Alvin, Ellie, and she had made at the Gateway Cabin had warmed her enough to get to Steve's car. Then his heater had kept her cozy until he'd deposited the three of them here on the deserted streets of Tarrytown. Alvin and Ellie had left her with a reassurance that everything would be okay, and then they hurried off into the night to start their honeymoon.

When she'd protested, they'd told her to stay there and wait. For what? If she had to wait too long, she'd surely freeze to death in the biting cold, and then she would be no help to her sister at all. She'd just about decided to start walking to find shelter when a car's headlights cut through the opaque wall of white.

The car crept along toward her, eventually coming to a stop beside her. For a moment her heart jumped into her throat. Was it Dan? Had he doubled back and found her? No. It wasn't Dan's car. Then who?

Then the door flew open, and Frank jumped out. A smile split her face.

Before she could even say anything, he had scooped her into a bear hug while he rained kisses all over her face. He set her away from him and looked at her as if it had been years since they'd last met. Of course, it hadn't been, but it certainly felt that way to Carrie.

"How did you know where to find me?" she asked, returning his kisses.

"Your love guided me, just like Steve said it would." Frank held her face in the palms of his hands and looked her over as though he was unable to believe she was actually there. When he touched her forehead, she winced in pain. "You're hurt." Frank ran his fingers gently over the cut in her forehead, then the rest of her face, as though testing her flesh to make sure she wasn't injured anywhere else.

She stopped his hand. "It's just a cut where I fell and bumped my head. I'm fine." Forcing her nearly numb fingers to work, she touched his dear face. "And you? How are you?"

He grinned. "Right now, I couldn't be better." He pulled her to him and whispered against her hair. "I was terrified that I'd never see you again."

Tears of happiness burned at the back of her eyes. She had so much to tell him, especially one very important thing. But it would have to wait.

Reluctantly, she gently eased away, then opened her mouth to speak just as a convulsive shiver vibrated through her.

"You're freezing. Get in the car," he said, wrapping his arm around her and guiding her toward his idling vehicle.

For a moment, after the car door had closed behind her, her skin tingled from the sudden onslaught of warmth. By the time Frank had joined her, her body had absorbed the warmth thrown out by the car's heater.

She swung around sideways to face him. Not giving him a chance to say anything first, she blurted out, "I need to get to my sister. I think she's dead or dying."

Confusion claimed Frank's features, melting away the happiness in his eyes. "Your sister?"

"Yes, my twin. She's the one I've been seeing in my dreams. Her husband is the faceless man, and he beat her badly. I was going for help when you found me."

At that moment, Frank's gaze dropped to her blouse. She looked down to see what had captured his attention. Her blouse and skirt were red with blood. Cathy's blood.

Her urgency grew stronger.

"We have to go *now*, Frank, before it's too late. Please."

"But the blood—"

"It's Cathy's. Please."

Frank took her cold hand in his. His skin was so warm it almost burned her. "First things first." He released her hand and pulled his cell phone from his coat pocket. As he punched in 9-1-1, he asked, "Where is your sister?"

"At the farm on Whitman Road." She knew once she could confide in Frank, things would be better.

"This is Dr. Frank Donovan; I need an ambulance to go to Whitman Road." He raised his gaze to Carrie. "What's the house number?"

"763."

He repeated the number sequence into the phone, then folded it, threw it on the seat, and put the car in gear. While he drove, Carrie filled him in on what had happened that night. He listened, his anger at this man even stronger now that the bastard had a face and an identity. He had no respect for or understanding of a man who beat up a woman just so he could prove his masculinity and dominance. He'd seen too many victims of such treatment.

He'd take care of the son of a bitch when he met him face to face. Right now, he had to get them to the farm in one piece. The roads were almost impassable, reminding him of another snowy night when he'd navigated through a blinding snowstorm.

Gaze glued to the road, Frank prayed silently that they'd make it safely to the farm and wouldn't end up being another pickup for the ambulance. Determinedly, he blocked that thought out. No sense borrowing trouble. Still, his heart raced so loudly he wondered that Carrie didn't hear it. His pulse throbbed in his temple. His tightly clenched jaw felt as though it would break.

"Frank."

He didn't look at her, but he could hear the hesitation in her voice. "What, sweetheart?"

"This is probably not the best time to tell you this, but in case anything happens, I want you to know."

Frank felt the blood drain from his face. *In case anything happens?* He gripped the steering wheel tighter. Dread settled over him in a dark, cold cloak. "Nothing's going to happen. Right now I need to concentrate on getting us to your sister. We can talk later."

"I. . .we. . . Okay. . .later." She cleared her throat and turned to look out the window into the dense snowfall.

For a moment, Frank lost all feeling in his body. What was it she had to tell him? That she really didn't love him? That their time in Renaissance had been an interlude during which she relied on him for lack of anyone else to cling to? That her love had been nothing more than gratitude?

He opened his mouth to speak, but the car caught the side of the pavement and slid sideways. He jerked the steering wheel in the direction of the skid, and the car righted its path once again. He exhaled a deep, relieved breath.

My God, how cruel could fate be to put him back in this situation again? The woman he loved more than his own life beside him, and the worst storm in history raging outside the car. Instinctively, he let up on the gas. Then his worst nightmare loomed ahead of them. His blood froze in his veins.

Barely visible through the thickly falling snow, a substantial rise in the road came into view. The rise was not unlike the one he and Sandy had driven up the night of the accident. Frank slowed the car even more. Now they were barely moving. He knew they'd never make the hill unless he stepped on the gas, but he couldn't get his foot to obey. He reminded himself that Carrie's sister needed them, but still his foot refused to move.

"Frank? Why are we stopping?"

He could hear Carrie's terrified voice coming from the far fringes of his mind. But he could not make his vocal cords work. All he could do was stare numbly out the windshield and curse the fates for letting this happen again. The wipers slapped back and forth in a monotonous rhythm, clearing a path so he could see that damned hill.

Faith and trust, Frank. Faith and trust.

Emanuel's reminder roused him from his fear-induced trance.

"Frank. Why are we stopping?" Carrie's voice had become panicky.

"We aren't stopping. I. . .I just slowed down because of the road conditions." Not totally untrue. How did he tell her he was too terrified to move? How could he tell her he was scared to death that he'd. . .

No! He couldn't think that way. What happened with Sandy was an accident, a separate incident that had nothing to do with Carrie. But he realized that the tension coiled in his stomach like a snake was not due to any residual guilt, but just plain fright. The roads were treacherous; it was perfectly reasonable that he'd be scared and cautious.

The apprehension coiled in the pit of his stomach eased. He concentrated on resuming their trip. After all, Carrie's sister's life might depend on them. Finally he pressed his foot gently on the accelerator, and the car inched forward. Little by little, it gained speed and managed to ease up the hill with little trouble.

When they reached the crest of the hill, Frank took a deep breath. So far, so good. Now to make it down the other side. As he stared down the hill through the blizzard, headlights of an oncoming car broke through the wall of snow.

CHAPTER 24

Very slowly Frank eased the car over the crest of the hill and started down the other side. The oncoming headlights grew closer and closer. Frank's sweaty palms clenched the wheel in a death grip.

Carrie said nothing. From the corner of his eye, he saw her stiffen as they started downward. Her hands were tightly clasped in her lap.

"We'll make it. I just have to take it easy. I know you're scared for your sister, and I really wish we could move faster." He wasn't sure she'd heard, but he kept talking in an effort to ease her apprehension. "It's just too dangerous, and we won't do Cathy any good if we get in an accident or end up stuck in a snowbank."

Casting a quick look in her direction, he saw her body relax and her hands come unclasped. Feeling his own nerves unwind a bit, he directed his attention back to the hazardous road.

She turned to him, patted his thigh, and said, "I know."

Those two words seemed to imbue Frank with the confidence he needed to get to the bottom of the hill and past the oncoming vehicle. As the headlights slid past them, he risked another glance at Carrie. She had grown silent, and her forehead was furrowed in a frown. Without taking his gaze from the road, he touched her arm.

"She'll be fine."

She nodded wordlessly.

A few miles later Carrie came to attention. "There." She pointed toward faint houselights set back a bit from the side of the road. Frank could barely see them through the blowing snow. "That's their house."

Frank swung carefully between the two stone pillars that seemed to appear out of nowhere and maneuvered the car slowly into the driveway. He parked near the side of the porch. Before he could turn off the engine, Carrie was out and running clumsily for the front porch through the knee-high snow. He jumped out and raced after her, catching her by the arm just before she grabbed hold of the doorknob.

"He might have come back. Let me go in first," he told her. For a moment he thought she'd fight him, but then she nodded and stepped away from the door.

He opened it and cautiously stepped inside. He

scanned the hallway and what he could see of the adjoining rooms, and then listened for the sound of anyone else in the house. It was eerily quiet, except for the ticking of a large grandfather clock in the hall.

"I don't hear anything. I think its okay."

Carrie grabbed his hand from behind and whispered close to his ear. "She's in the living room to the left."

He entered a room. Furniture and broken shards of all manner of bric-a-brac were strewn everywhere. The coffee table was overturned, and a lamp lay on the floor beside it. There had been one hell of a struggle here. If Dan had been trying to kill Cathy, as Carrie had told him in the car on the way here, her sister had fought hard for her life.

"Cathy!" Carrie ran toward a large shadow in the middle of the floor.

After scanning the room to make sure no one else was there, Frank followed her to the woman's body covered by a colorful crocheted afghan. The blood that had seeped into the beige carpeting had turned a dark brown.

He knelt on one side of her, Carrie on the other. Taking Cathy's wrist, he placed his finger on the pulse point. The beat was thready, but it was there. He then quickly did a cursory examination of the rest of her body. Her breathing was ragged and uneven.

"She's alive," he said and heard Carrie's gasp of relief

next to him. "But barely." What he didn't tell Carrie was that he suspected broken ribs and that one of them might have punctured her lung. He glanced over his shoulder at the window. "Where in hell is that ambulance?" He stood. "You stay with her, and I'll go out to the road and wait for them. They might miss the house completely in this storm."

Carrie watched him go. "Be careful," she called after him.

"Don't move her," he called over his shoulder. "We don't know what her injuries are."

Cathy moaned and snapped Carrie's attention back to her. At first, she started to gather her sister's body close to reassure her. Then, recalling Frank's warning, she opted instead for whispering to her.

"It's okay, Cath. The ambulance is on the way." Using great care not inflict more pain on Cathy than she'd already suffered, Carrie gently soothed her sister's hair away from her blood-streaked face.

"Dan?" Cathy's voice was so weak Carrie had to put her ear against her lips to hear what she said.

"I don't know. He took off."

Cathy grabbed at Carrie's coat lapel, but she was too weak to hang on. Carrie leaned over her mouth again.

"You. . .were. . .right. I should. . .have—"

"Shhh." Carrie laid her fingers over Cathy's lips to

stop her words. "Save your strength. Time for all that later. We need to get you to a hospital so they can get you fixed up and back on your feet again." She glanced nervously over her shoulder at the door and said a silent prayer that the ambulance would arrive soon.

It felt like they'd been waiting hours when Carrie heard a siren coming closer. Long minutes later, Frank and a team of EMTs rushed into the room.

* * *

Carrie paced the hospital waiting room, anxious to hear about her sister. Frank had told the nurses and intern who had met them that he was a doctor and had immediately gone off with the EMTs and the emergency room people, but not before he'd promised Carrie he'd be back soon to let her know whatever he could find out. That seemed like it had been hours ago.

While she'd waited, she'd passed some of the time by calling the police to alert them about Dan. They'd told her they would come to the hospital to talk to her, but they hadn't shown up as of yet.

She flopped down in one of the vinyl chairs and rubbed at her burning eyes. She couldn't recall the last time she'd slept. Leaning her head back, she closed her eyes. Instantly the burning sensation eased.

But just as quickly, a vision of what she'd witnessed in her sister's house passed before her. Her eyes snapped open. A reminder of the night's events was the last thing she needed right now. What she needed was a cup of the hospital's strong-enough-to-walk-on-its-own coffee.

Dragging herself to her feet, she pushed open the glass waiting-room door. One step into the hall she heard angry, raised voices coming from around the corner at the other end.

"She's my freaking wife, and I have a right to see her!"

Carrie recognized her brother-in-law's angry tones. What was that son of a bitch doing here?

"You gave up any rights when you beat her to a pulp. If you want to see Cathy, you'll have to go through me."

Frank? Carrie had never heard him that angry. His voice resembled the growl of an enraged animal. Chills shivered down her spine. Cautiously, she edged her way in the direction of the chaos.

"You think you're going to stop me, big man?" Dan's sarcastic laugh followed his question.

"Try me," Frank spat, his tone becoming more and more threatening each time he spoke.

"I want to see my wife, and you're not going to stop me."

"You can bet your ass I will. That woman's in the operating room fighting for her life because of you, and you are not getting near her." Frank's tone had grown menacing, colder. It sent an eerily familiar shiver down Carrie's spine.

Just as Carrie rounded the corner, she saw Dan lunge for Frank. Even from this distance, she could hear the sound of Frank's fist connecting with Dan's jaw. She couldn't believe her eyes. Frank had never given her any indication that he was capable of physical violence.

Dan staggered backward under the blow, but regained his footing and lunged again at Frank. Frank stuck out his foot and tripped him, sending Dan sprawling across the highly waxed floor. Before he could get up, Frank had straddled him and was pummeling Dan's face with blow after blow.

"Frank!" Steve Cameron appeared out of nowhere and grabbed Frank's arms. "Stop it. He's slime. He's not worth you breaking your hands on him."

With some effort, he pulled Frank off Dan, his fists still swinging. Frank was like a crazed man. It took Steve several minutes to get him under control. Just as he did, a security guard rounded the corner.

"Get him the hell out of here. But keep track of him," Steve commanded, gesturing toward Dan's crumpled, bloody body. "I'm making a citizen's arrest for domestic violence and attempted murder until the police get here and charge him themselves."

As the guard led Dan away, Frank glared at him. When the elevator doors had closed, blocking out Dan's glowering face, Frank straightened his clothes and then wiped a trickle of blood from the corner of his mouth.

During the entire incident, Carrie had remained frozen in place. Horror at what was happening flooded her. Though she understood the reason for his rage, the intensity of Frank's anger terrified her, and she had no idea why.

He noticed her for the first time. His features, softened now from the fury that had distorted them into someone she hadn't recognized, reflected his concern that she'd witnessed the fight with Dan. When he took a step toward her, she moved away.

"Carrie?"

She couldn't speak. She just held up her hand, shook her head and turned away. Before she knew it, she was running, running as far and as fast as she could—away from Frank.

Confused and hurt, Frank looked at Steve. "What the hell was that all about? Why did she run from me?"

Steve continued to stare down the hall where Carrie had disappeared. "I have no idea."

Suddenly, Frank realized whom he'd been talking to. "Where did you come from? How did you know we were here?"

"Emanuel sent me and Meghan to help." Steve ran a hand through his hair. "He said that you two would be needing us. Looks like he was right." He glanced down the empty hall. "Trouble is, I'm just not sure which of you needs our help the most—you or Carrie."

* * *

Carrie clutched her coat around her and walked faster, ignoring the snow and sleet stinging her face. She had no idea where she was going; she just knew she didn't want to be near Frank right now. She needed time to think.

Why had the fistfight upset her so much? She'd seen men fight before. She'd just never seen such rage on anyone as Frank had displayed. It was as if he'd become someone she'd never met before, an animal bent on killing his prey, instead of the man she loved, the father of her baby.

He certainly wasn't the man she'd lain on a blanket with next to a waterfall, and with whom she'd made long, passionate love. That man had been infinitely kind, gentle, and considerate. The Frank she'd seen in the hospital was. . .a mindless brute. It went without saying that Dan had deserved to be beaten within an inch of his life. If she thought she could have summoned enough strength, she'd have taken him on years ago. That Frank would do it and with such savagery had stunned Carrie beyond words.

"Carrie?"

A woman fell into step beside her.

"Meghan? What. . ."

"What am I doing here? Emanuel sent me and Steve to help."

"Help? With what?"

Meghan smiled softly. "You tell me."

Carrie stopped walking. She glared at Meghan, and then shook her head. "Can't you people ever be straight with us? I have no patience right now for your damned riddles and clever evasions. If you're really here to help, then, dammit, help! Tell me why the man I love turned into a monster before my eyes." The words had no sooner left her mouth than she wanted to snatch them back. "I'm sorry. It's been a hell of a night."

Meghan wrapped an arm around her shoulder. "I know."

Carrie began to ask her how she knew, and then silenced herself. There was no point in asking. Meghan probably wouldn't tell her anyway. She wasn't any more forthcoming with explanations than the rest of them.

"I don't know about you, but I'm about to freeze to death." Meghan shivered and then pointed across the street. "How about we slip over there and grab a cup of coffee to warm us."

Numbed by a combination of the cold and what she'd just witnessed, Carrie nodded, and allowed Meghan to steer her to a small diner tucked between two very large buildings. She didn't recall seeing that place before, but then she wasn't paying much attention to her surroundings. Still, how convenient, in this street filled with apartment buildings, that a diner just happened to be there when they needed it.

My God, Carrie. Get a grip. Your imagination is out of control.

She followed Meghan across the street and into the warm interior of the restaurant. The diner looked like it had dropped right out of the fifties. Though the place was spotless, the smell of old grease hung heavy in the air.

Long, rectangular glass cases holding an assortment of pies and Danish pastries lined the back edge of the counter. Vinyl and chrome stools stood sentinel down the black and white tile floor on the outside of the counter. On each of the pink Formica-covered tables rested a set of nondescript, glass salt and pepper shakers. A chrome napkin holder held up the food-stained, yellowed menu stuck between them. On the table at which Carrie and Meghan chose to sit was a glass holder containing a small votive candle that was burning with two flames. Odd place, Carrie thought, staring fixedly at the twin flames, but. . .comfortable, homey, and very welcoming.

They settled into a booth covered in cracked burgundy vinyl. A waitress dressed in an aqua polyester uniform, from which a crochet-edged handkerchief bloomed from the breast pocket, approached their table. She stopped beside them, and then hitched one hip higher while she vigorously tortured a piece of gum and opened a book of pale green guest checks.

Pencil poised above the paper, she smiled down at them. "Help you girls?"

Carrie stared at the waitress. She looked suspiciously familiar. . .like a younger Clara. Lord, on top of everything else, she was hallucinating.

"Just coffee," she finally said.

"What about you, sweetheart?" the waitress demanded of Meghan.

"Coffee for me, too." Meghan smiled at the waitress, and Carrie could have sworn the woman winked at her.

"Pie? Danish? Burger and fries?" the waitress offered while she continued to chew her gum, a periodic *crack* resulting from the tireless movement of her jaw.

Both women shook their heads. The waitress walked away, humming a Christmas carol. Carrie had totally forgotten that it was Christmas when she'd gone into the mist, but since time stopped for all intents and purposes in the village, it still was Christmas now that she'd emerged from it.

Merry Christmas, she told herself sarcastically. As if mocking her, the plastic Christmas tree on the cash register decked out in a garish red-tinsel garland began to slowly turn and play a tinkling rendition of *O Come All Ye Faithful*.

"So, you want to talk about it?" Meghan asked, folding her hands on the faded pink Formica tabletop.

"Talk about what?"

"What happened back there in the hospital that spooked you."

Carrie sighed. She didn't bother asking if Meghan was referring to the fight. But she wasn't at all sure she could put her fear into words. "I don't know. Seeing Frank like that did something to me, and I don't know why. He was so. . .so. . ."

"Angry?"

She nodded. "But it was more than that. I've never seen him like that, and it frightened me terribly. I don't know why it should."

"He was protecting your sister from an abusive man. Why should that frighten you?"

Carrie sighed. "It shouldn't. Hell, I should be grateful that he was there to run interference with Dan. That's why my reaction makes no sense."

"Doesn't it?"

Before Carrie could answer, the waitress returned with two cups of steaming, fragrant coffee. To forestall having to say anything more, Carrie sipped at the steamy liquid. Her eyes widened. There had only been one place she'd ever tasted coffee this rich and robust. She looked up at the waitress.

"Clara?"

The woman blinked. "Excuse me? The name's Millie, child." She flashed at Carrie the red and white plastic name badge hooked to her lapel. The white engraved letters read *Millie*. As the waitress walked away, she slid a sideways glance at Meghan. Carrie was not convinced she'd been wrong about the woman's identity, nor was she surprised that Clara was there to help, but at the moment the waitress's identity was the least of her worries.

Meghan stirred sugar into her coffee. The spoon clanking against the cup magnified the silence inside the diner. It was then that Carrie realized there were no other customers, save her and Meghan.

"Do you recall the first memories that came back to you?" Meghan finally asked.

"Yes, but what has that got to do with Frank acting like a wild man?"

Meghan didn't say anything. Obviously she was giving Carrie time to think about what she'd asked.

What could her earlier recollections have to do with any of this? With Frank. With Cath—

"Does it have anything to do with my sister? Is she still in danger?" Carrie started to get up, but Meghan's hand on her arm stopped her.

"Cathy's fine. Steve and Frank are with her."

Carrie wasn't sure that having Frank there right now gave her much peace of mind, but Steve's presence did. She sat back.

"All right," she said, leaning back and trying to relax and concentrate on Meghan. "What do my earlier memories have to do with any of this? And please don't hand me a bunch of questions, riddles, and evasions. For once, be straight with me."

Meghan sighed. "Carrie, this is your memory. This is something you have to decipher for yourself. I'm just here to guide you."

"Memory?" She frowned at Meghan. This didn't make sense. Clara had told her that she couldn't leave Renaissance until all her lost memories returned. And they had. Hadn't they?

"I thought I'd recalled everything I'd forgotten."

Laying down the spoon she'd been fiddling with, Meghan locked her gaze with Carrie's. "You didn't forget this one. You suppressed it. I can't help you remember anything you've chosen not to. This time, I'm afraid it's entirely up to you."

Carrie cupped her forehead in her hand and racked her brain for anything she was pushing deep into her memory. Nothing came to mind. But then, if she'd been repressing something, could she just summon it to the forefront?

"Think about those first memories, Carrie. The ones you recalled while you were in the village." Meghan's voice seemed to come from far away.

From deep in her subconscious, Carrie deliberately summoned the awful memories of the man she now knew to be her brutal brother-in-law, starting with the dream in which she'd awakened to find a man without a face standing beside her bed. One after the other, they tumbled through her mind, until she came to the one in which she'd first seen the woman in the woods, the woman she'd later find out was her twin sister, then again in the kitchen. Those had been the only two in which she hadn't been the woman being pursued by the man.

Why? Why had that suddenly changed?

* * *

While Steve stood guard like some kind of watchdog to make sure he didn't flip out again, Frank sat beside Cathy's bed, determined to be there when Carrie came back. Besides, when Cathy came to, he didn't want her to be alone.

A heart monitor beeped rhythmically beside the bed. An intravenous system stood beside the bed, dripping blood slowly into a tube attached to the bend of her right arm. The dim bed light illuminated her swollen face.

He stared at her. She was so stark white against the sheets. A long white bandage covered the laceration that had received over twelve stitches and still oozed blood through the gauze. Traces of dried blood on her scalp were visible through her hair. A large bruise had formed around one eye and across the bridge of her nose. Her bottom lip was split and swollen out of proportion to the top one.

Even for a seasoned doctor, seeing another human being like this and knowing the cause was unnerving to say the least. Staring down at her identical twin was like staring down at Carrie. The thought of anyone hurting Cathy like this was unbearable, but the thought of Carrie being battered brought his rage to a boil again. He clenched his fists to harness his control. He was not a violent man under normal circumstances, but if anyone touched Carrie, he wasn't sure what he'd do. If the beating he'd administered to Dan was any indication. . .

Frank shook his head. "How could anyone do this

to another human being?"

Steve, who'd been prowling restlessly in front of the window, stopped and glanced at the woman in the bed. "It's usually to maintain a twisted sense of control."

"By beating them into submission?"

Steve nodded. "Most of these guys are insecure. The only way they can feel manly is to keep the woman in what they see as *her place*, which is tightly under their thumb."

Frank laughed without humor. "Kind of like that old saying? Barefoot in the winter and pregnant in the summer. And they call that love?"

"I'm sure that barefoot and pregnant would be preferable to what she's been through." Steve sat in the chair beside Frank. "Unbelievably, in their insecure, twisted minds, these guys do believe they love these women. At least that's what they keep telling them. It's all a part of the brainwashing process. They have the wife so convinced that she's to blame, that it never occurs to the woman to blame the man. She just continues to try to please him, to stop making mistakes in an effort to stop the beatings. She doesn't realize that no matter how perfectly she does things or keeps herself, it will never be enough." He stopped and shook his head. "Of course, the abuser punctuates the periods of abuse by what they call Calm Phases. During that time, he'll apologize abjectly and solemnly swear it will never happen again. Desperate to believe it's over for good, the woman doesn't believe there will ever be a *next time*. But there always is. And then the cycle starts again. It's all a rather complicated domino effect, but most abusers are experts at making it work." He glanced at Cathy again. "In this case, I'd say she was lucky she came out of it alive."

Getting up and going to the window, Frank sighed tiredly. He stared out into the night, wondering where Carrie had gone to. "I don't understand why someone didn't try to stop it. Why not Carrie? She was her sister, and she had to know what was going on."

Steve came to stand beside him. He laid a hand on his shoulder. "Not necessarily. Abusers are as good at covering up their crimes as they are at perpetrating them, and the woman is either too afraid or too ashamed to say anything, even to her relatives and closest friends. What doesn't help her confidence is that these guys present a different face to the public than they do to their wives. So she has to wonder if anyone would believe her if she did say something." He sighed. "Even if Carrie had known and had tried to talk Cathy into leaving Dan, there's every chance that Cathy was either too afraid to leave, or that she just didn't believe Dan was a bad man. She might have still been blaming herself."

Frank glanced over his shoulder, and then turned

quickly away again. "Every time I look at her, I see Carrie."

"You love her a lot." It wasn't a question.

For a long time, Frank said nothing. His silent hesitation was not because he didn't love Carrie. God knew, he loved her more than he did life itself. He just had never before shared those feelings with anyone but Carrie.

Outside the door, the muffled shuffle of people moving up and down the hallways, the hum of the elevator and *whoosh* of the doors opening and closing, and the rattle of late dinner trays being collected punctuated the thick silence.

At last Frank nodded. "I never thought I'd ever love a woman as much as I did Sandy, but Carrie is. . .well, she sneaked into my heart to stay." He looked at Steve. "I just don't understand why she ran away from me like that."

"You will," Steve said. "You will."

"And how can you be so sure?"

Steve said nothing. His face took on that closed expression that Frank had become very familiar with in Renaissance. There would be no answer to his question.

* * *

"I still don't understand what my early memory has to do with all this." Carrie leaned back. The brittle vinyl covering of the booth crackled beneath her. Millie refilled both coffee cups for the third time.

"Memories are funny things. Sometimes they just show up because of something you see or something you hear or smell. But if we think about them long enough, they'll tell their own story." Millie smiled kindly at Carrie, and then moved off.

Carrie raised an eyebrow and looked at Meghan.

"Listen to her. What she says is true."

Again Carrie combed her memory. While she delved into her past, she stared at the diner window. Her reflection stared back at her, reminding her of Cathy. Just then, a shadow fell across the windowpane as a man passed outside in the street.

Carrie jumped. Her father? It couldn't be. He'd died years earlier when she was twelve. She blinked and looked again. It was a total stranger who looked nothing like Gerald Henderson. Nothing. So why had her father jumped into her head? She'd made a concentrated effort for years to make sure he never invade her thoughts.

Why? He was her father. Why would she not want to think about him?

She squinted, trying to force through a memory that hovered on the fringes of her mind.

Millie refilled Meghan's coffee. Carrie stared at the cup as though waiting for it to move. Meghan picked up the sugar dispenser and turned it upside down. White crystals poured into her coffee from the hole in the top of the dispenser. Then, she deliberately moved the cup, and the tiny crystals cascaded onto the tabletop.

For a long time Carrie watched the tiny crystals skip across the Formica and then fall over the edge to the floor. They looked so innocent, but Carrie knew the kind of violence they could bring about. She jumped as if she'd received an electric shock.

In her mind's eye, a scene started to take form. Little by little, it became clearer and clearer. Then it was there, clear as any photograph she'd ever seen. It was the kitchen of the house in which she grew up. Her mother was pouring sugar from a paper sack into the sugar bowl. The sack split, and sugar spilled all over the table and onto the floor.

Carrie held her breath, and looked from her mother's terrified expression to her father's face, purple with rage.

"Stupid bitch! You're as stupid and ugly as your two brats. Do you think I work my ass off all week so you can throw sugar around like it was sand?" His hand flew up and caught her across her cheek.

Her head jerked backward. The sugar sack flew out of her mother's hands, hit the floor, and exploded. Bright red droplets of blood oozed from her split lip.

"Damn!" Her father's curse had nothing to do with his injured wife. His full attention was on the floor where the sugar sack had landed. Beneath it, white sugar flowed onto the tiles. "Just look at what you did!" His voice filled the room. He kicked his chair from beneath him and lunged for her mother.

Cathy shot from her chair and raced around the table. She grabbed her father's arm to prevent the fist he'd made from hitting her mother. "Momma didn't do it!" Cathy yelled. "You made her do it. It's your fault!"

Before he could retaliate, Carrie saw a younger version of herself step between him and Cathy. Carrie's jaw received the full force of the stinging backhand meant for her sister. She flew off her feet and backward into the corner of the stove. The sound of her head coming into hard contact with the appliance echoed through the kitchen.

Despite the pain in her head, she scrambled to her feet and once more put herself between her father and her sister. He swung, this time catching her off balance and sending her crashing into the corner of the counter. A deep, searing pain cut into her shoulder. She could feel the warm flow of blood on her skin, but she vaulted to her feet once more.

He turned back toward her mother. Cathy again inserted herself between her parents. Before her father could swing, Carrie pulled Cathy away. Again her father's hand found her instead of Cathy. This time she fell against the corner of the table, and blackness engulfed her.

Carrie started. She looked around, dazed, but with tears filling her eyes. She was back in the diner, sitting across from Meghan.

"You always got between them, Carrie, so Cathy wouldn't get hit." Meghan's voice cut through the haze that had enveloped Carrie in her harsh memories.

"That's why, at first, I saw myself as the woman being abused in my memories. I had always protected Cathy, and even in my recollections, I continued to protect her by taking her place and putting myself between her and Dan."

Meghan nodded.

Carrie could feel tears running down her face. She wiped them away. Cold fear gripped her. She raised her gaze to Meghan's gentle face. "Why couldn't I remember that in Renaissance when I remembered everything else?"

"Because you chose not to. It was not a part of the amnesia Emanuel used to keep you from the trauma of recalling everything too fast. If you had, the damage would have been inestimable. Something you may not have recovered from. But this memory of your father was something *you* had suppressed, and only *you* had the power to bring it back to the surface." Meghan's warm hand closed over her icy fingers. "But there was just enough residual memory there that when you saw Frank fight with Cathy's husband, you got scared and ran."

Carrie covered her face with her hands and wept.

How could she have hurt Frank like that? She knew in her heart that he could never hurt her. Still, he had been so very violent. How did she know he'd never turn that rage on her? She'd read that women who grew up in abusive households often married abusive men. Cathy had proven that to be true. Carrie didn't want to end up being the second notch on her father's belt.

"Don't allow your father to make you a victim again, Carrie. Don't give him that power."

Meghan's voice drew Carrie out of her thoughts. "What about Frank? I love him, Meghan, God knows I love him." Her hand automatically went to her stomach. "He doesn't even know about—"

"The baby?"

She nodded.

"Then you have to tell him."

Carrie felt as though a hand had reached inside her and was twisting her insides into knots. The pain was unbearable. A soft sob escaped her.

She loved Frank so much. But what if Frank *was* like her father? What if he appeared to be the angel she needed in her life, but turned out to be evil in disguise? She didn't want to expose her baby to that. Once she told him about the child, there would be no turning back. He'd be a part of its life forever. Did she want to take that chance?

"Carrie?" Meghan touched her hand lightly. "Think about the man you know and love. Do you really believe him to be evil?"

Forced to think about it by Meghan's words, Carrie remembered the times she'd been with Frank. She recalled the gentle man who had listened to her wild tales of a dream man she couldn't identify. She recalled the night he'd welcomed her into his arms to soothe her ragged nerves about a nightmare that had terrified her. The same man who had comforted her and never asked for more. The man who had held her so tightly because he had to leave the village without her. The man who was willing to give up his life in the outside world, a life he loved, to be with her forever.

But mostly, she remembered the man who had made gentle, passionate love to her at the waterfall. The man who had guided her up the cliffs and rejoiced in her being able to go the last few feet on her own because she'd conquered her fear of heights. Logically, she could never see this man doing the things to her that Dan had done to Cathy or that her father had done to his family. But she was sure that both Cathy and her mother had felt the men they married would never use them as a punching bag.

"I don't know," she finally cried. "I just don't know." Laying her head on her folded arms, she sobbed out her frustration.

Faith and trust, Carrie. Faith and trust.

Emanuel's words filled her head. Suddenly the fear, confusion, and apprehension that had claimed her mind and body lessened. The cloying fog cleared from her reasoning.

All these people—Emanuel, Clara, Meghan, Steve—they all knew Frank. If they felt he was a good man, could she do any less? He saved children on a daily basis. Why would he hurt their child? And hadn't he promised to protect her forever?

She raised her tear-stained face and looked at Meghan. To her surprise, Millie was sitting in the seat beside Meghan. Only it wasn't Millie anymore. Oh, she still wore that uniform with the ridiculous handkerchief spilling from the pocket and the name badge, but the face of the waitress was gone. In its place was Clara's grandmotherly countenance.

"Go to him, child. Tell him about the baby. Trust his love for you and yours for him."

"Love is a miracle with a power you cannot even imagine. Give it a chance to work its magic." Meghan rose and held out her hand.

What should she do? Carrie glanced toward the candle burning between them. The two flames flickered, twined around each other, and became one. She knew her answer.

Carrie nodded, rose from the booth, and took Meghan's outstretched hand. She offered both women a tentative smile, and then touched her tummy. "I think it's time you met your daddy, little one."

* * *

Frank awoke abruptly from the nap he'd fallen into in the chair beside Cathy's bed. Looking around, he found Steve gone. His gaze moved to the woman in the bed. She was asleep. The strident humming and beeping of the machines hooked up to her filled the silence of the room. Tubes ran from her swollen nose and an intravenous drip still ran from a bottle above the bed to her bruised, outstretched arm.

He looked out the window into a night lit only by a full moon and the streetlights in the hospital parking lot below. He checked his watch. 3:52 a.m.

His gaze returned to the battered woman who, aside from the blotches of bruises and the cuts on her face and neck, looked so colorless against the white sheets. He still couldn't believe the brutality she had endured and survived. From speaking to her doctor, Frank had learned that she had a broken nose, a fractured cheekbone, four cracked ribs, a long laceration on her forehead, and a bruised spleen. The X-rays they'd taken before surgery revealed innumerable bones that revealed old healed fractures from previous beatings. No wonder Carrie had chosen amnesia over the reality of knowing her sister was being used as a punching bag and being helpless to stop it.

He sat up in the chair, worked the kinks out of his body, and then leaned forward and buried his face in his hands. He missed Carrie so terribly. She'd become such a huge part of his life that he felt as if a gaping chasm had opened inside of him, a hollow place that could be filled with nothing but Carrie.

He could still see the look of horror on her face when she'd come upon him and Dan fighting. It had cut deep into his heart. Then the stark fear that replaced her horror as she'd backed away from him. He'd had to battle every bone in his body to keep from going after her. Logic had told him that was the worst thing he could do at that point. But that didn't stop the agony of knowing he'd frightened her, frightened the one person in the world whom he wanted to protect, to keep safe.

Didn't she know he'd sooner hurt himself than hurt her? That he'd protect her at all costs from anyone and everything?

When he became aware of someone else in the room, he'd been sorting through his jumbled thoughts for some time. He raised his head slowly. In the corner of the room, a shadow loomed.

His first reaction was to assume that Dan had somehow gotten away from the cops who had taken him into custody hours earlier. Then he realized that the silhouette was not that of a man.

The shadowy figure stepped into the meager light seeping in from the hallway. "We came to see you."

Carrie!

Frank sprang from the chair. It took everything in him to keep from going to her and pulling her into the safety of his embrace. Fearful of scaring her again, he held himself back. Instead, he hoped he could reach out to her with his heart.

"I'm. . .I'm sorry about. . .before." His cracking voice sounded foreign to his ears.

"I know. I shouldn't have run, but I'd never seen you that angry before and. . .well. . ."

He gave a short, humorless laugh. "I don't think I've ever been that angry in my life." He ran his hand through his hair. His bruised knuckles throbbed, but he ignored the pain. "Carrie, I love you, and I would never, ever hurt you. Please believe that. I know those are only words, and that Dan probably said them to Cathy many times before. . . well before their marriage had turned to hell on earth." Frank extended a tentative hand toward her. "Please give me the chance to prove that I'm not Dan."

She smiled. "If I didn't believe that, I wouldn't be here."

Then, without another word, she walked into his arms. He pulled her to him. His heart raced. His knees wobbled beneath him. Carrie was home in his arms for good. Setting her back just enough, he covered her mouth with the gentlest kiss he could manage.

Carrie clung to him, and putting her hands behind his head, she gently pressured him to deepen the kiss. He obliged. Soon he was raining kisses all over her face.

"I love you," he murmured between each kiss. "Marry me so I never have to lose you again."

"I love you, too," she said, tucking his words deep in her heart. "And yes, I'll marry you." He began kissing her again. Suddenly, he stopped and looked around the room as if searching for something. "What is it?" Carrie asked.

An expression of confusion came over his face. "When you came in, you said *we* came to see you. Who else did you bring?"

She smiled. Taking his hand, she laid it over her flat stomach. "Your son or daughter," she said simply, watching the look of surprise, followed by elation spread over his face.

"You're. . . We're. . ."

Carrie laughed aloud. "Yes."

Frank scooped her into his arms and twirled her around in a circle. Then he quickly set her back on her feet. "How? I mean, I know how, but. . .*how*?"

Carrie opened her mouth to speak, but before she could speak a word, another voice gave him the only answer that mattered.

Faith and trust, my boy. Faith and trust make love, and deep and abiding love makes little miracles.

EPILOGUE

Christmas Eve—The Gateway Cabin—Two years later

A freshly fallen snow from the night before glistened like tiny diamonds on the ground all around the Gateway Cabin. The lights of an enormous Christmas tree spilled out through a bay window onto the white covering, turning the icy crust brilliant with a rainbow of mixed colors. A curl of gray smoke spun off into the night from the chimney above the peaked roof. Excited voices of a happy family emanated from the interior and spilled out into the silent evening.

Even as Carrie stepped from the car, her arms loaded with gaily wrapped gifts, she could already detect the welcoming mixture of aromas: burning logs and fresh baked cookies. On the other side of the car, Frank unbuckled David's car seat.

"Come on, sport," he said as he hoisted his small son

into his arms and sent Carrie a loving smile over the roof of the car. "I bet Aunt Meghan has some of her special sugar cookies waiting for you."

David cuddled into his father's neck and yawned sleepily.

Carrie returned Frank's smile, unable to believe that there had ever been a time when she had doubted Frank's gentleness.

The long hours of waiting for Cathy to recover in the hospital had been a time of renewal for Frank and Carrie, a time to open their hearts to each other. Frank had finally shared the details of the accident with her, and although it had been hard talking about it, she had shared her life with her father with him. The experience of sharing their pain had brought them closer together.

During the length of time they'd been married, she could not have asked for a more loving and considerate husband than Frank. Nor could eighteen-month-old David have wanted for a more attentive, adoring father. These had, indeed, been the happiest two years of her life.

Together, the little family trooped to the cabin's front door and knocked. Seconds later, the portal opened to reveal a grinning Meghan.

"Hi. Merry Christmas! Come on in out of the cold." She stepped aside to allow them entry. "We were afraid you'd been in an—" She cut herself short and sent Frank an apologetic smile.

He kissed her cheek and smiled down at her. "It's

okay. I came to terms with that long ago, Meg."

She touched his sleeve and nodded, then took a suddenly fully-awake David from him and began to remove the child's winter clothing. When the boy had been divested of all his winter wear, she placed him in the playpen in the center of the room with their youngest daughter, Anna.

"Is Faith in the village?" Frank asked when he didn't see Steve and Meghan's six-year-old eldest daughter.

Steve scooped the gifts from Carrie's arms and deposited them beneath the shimmering tree in the large window. "Yes, with Irma. Just because Irma took over as the village Healer for Ellie doesn't mean she would allow her Christmas Eve tradition of decorating her tree with her granddaughter to fall by the wayside." He straightened. "Because of the time thing within the village, she'll still be back here for Christmas morning. Speaking of time, did the bad driving conditions slow you down tonight?"

"No. We would have been here hours ago, but the first gallery showing of Carrie's masterpieces ran late. The people just didn't seem to want to leave." Frank gathered Carrie against his side, his face glowing with pride in his wife. "I guess I have to finally admit that I'm married to a female Rembrandt." He smiled down at her and kissed the tip of her nose. "And I couldn't be prouder."

Steve laughed. "Gee, Frank, one would never know."

Carrie giggled and then snuggled against Frank. Ever since her paint box had mysteriously shown up in their car, Frank had been her biggest supporter, encouraging her to paint and then contacting a friend who was more than thrilled to promote the debut showing of her work.

"If Irma's taken over as the Healer in the village, where's Ellie now?" Carrie asked, taking a seat on the couch in front of the blazing fireplace.

Meghan settled next to her. "She's joined with Alvin as a Traveler." She chuckled. "They are inseparable." Her expression grew serious. "How's Cathy?"

Carrie beamed. "She's doing great. The therapy has helped enormously. Divorcing Dan helped a lot to push her along the road to healing. He's no longer in her life in any way, and it will be a long time before he can play the bully with another woman. She's even met a very nice man who adores the ground she walks on."

"Wonderful news." Steve came to join them. "How long was the jail term Dan got?"

It had taken over two years for Dan to come to trial. Thank God that in that time, the judge had refused to grant bail, so he spent the time awaiting his trial date behind bars. Last week, the trial finally ended, and that part of their lives was over for good.

"Let's just say, he will be spending many of his future

Christmases looking through bars. The DA went for attempted murder, and once the jurors saw the pictures of Cathy's face and heard my testimony and Frank's, there was no trouble getting a guilty verdict."

Meghan rose and disappeared into the kitchen. Moments later she returned with a tray of her signature sugar cookies and hot chocolate crowned with peaks of white whipped cream. Carrie sipped the steaming, sweet liquid and remembered the night she'd first come to the cabin, lost, lonely, and terrified and without a memory to call her own. What a blessing that night had been. Without these people and Emanuel and Clara, she would have never gotten her sister away from that animal she'd married, and she'd never have known the blessings of being loved by a man who treated her with dignity, respect, and gentleness.

She looked from one dear face to another. It was way past time that she told them. "You are all such a blessing in my life. Although I didn't think so at the time, in retrospect, losing my memory and wandering into the library that night was the best combination of coincidences that has ever happened to me."

Meghan and Steve looked at each other. Carrie could have sworn they giggled. She looked from one to the other. "What?"

"I would have thought you'd have figured out by

now that there was nothing coincidental about either your amnesia or your finding us at the library that night." Meghan laughed again. "Think about it. It was almost midnight, two days before Christmas. Why on earth would the library be open, and what would we be doing there at that hour?"

Confusion fogged Carrie's thoughts for a moment. Then it hit her. "Emanuel?"

Steve and Meghan nodded.

Carrie turned to Frank. "Did you know?"

He put down his cup of hot chocolate and grinned sheepishly. "Not for sure, but I did put two and two together and suspected."

She jabbed him in the ribs with a well-aimed shot from her elbow. A soft *oomph* accompanied by a laugh emitted from him.

"Why didn't you tell me?" she demanded.

"I thought you'd figured it out for yourself. Besides, as I recall, we weren't talking all that much back then." He winked at her while he rubbed at his side. "Forgiven?"

She glared at him, fighting back a smile, and lost the battle. "Forgiven," she said and kissed him.

For a while, a happy silence settled over the room. The only sounds came from the barely intelligible chatter of the two children in the playpen, the crackle of the logs being consumed in the fireplace, and the occasional clank of a cup being replaced on its saucer.

"When are you going to give Steve and Meghan their gift?" Frank whispered to Carrie.

She'd been so content just enjoying the company and the atmosphere that she'd forgotten that she had a very special gift for their friends. "It's in the car. Would you mind getting it?"

Frank nodded, stood, slipped on his coat, and went outside.

"Where's he going?" Steve asked.

"Oh, I left something in the car. He's getting it for me."

A few minutes later, Frank reappeared, carrying a thin, rectangular package wrapped in silver paper and tied with a huge red bow adorned with holly.

"Merry Christmas, with much love from both of us," he said, placing it on Meghan's lap.

For a moment, Meghan just looked at the package. Finally, Carrie said, "Well, are you going to open it or stare it down? And please don't tell me you're one of those irritating people who removes each piece of tape and carefully folds the wrapping paper before looking at their gift. I've waited far too long to see your reaction to sit through that ritual."

Without further hesitation, both Meghan and Steve grabbed paper and bow and tore them from the gift. Carrie heard Meghan's gasp of surprise.

"Carrie, it's beautiful." Steve carried the painting to the mantel and propped it up so all of them could admire it.

She had perfectly captured in oils the footbridge leading into the village, the stream flowing beneath it, and just beyond, the cottage in which Meghan had lived when she was the village Healer, the cottage in which she and Steve had found their love. Even more amazing was the mist that hugged the cottage and the trees in a thin white veil.

Meghan came to Carrie and hugged her. "Thank you so much. I will treasure it always."

Over Meghan's shoulder, Carrie noted something strange within the painting, something she had not put there. From the mist surrounding the cottage, the faces of Emanuel and Clara smiled down at her.

She smiled back.

Beside the painting on the mantel, a shimmering white fog began to swirl in the small green lantern.

Once more, some blessed soul was about to walk into the mist.

A special presentation of *Miracle in the Mist*
by Elizabeth Sinclair

PROLOGUE

―――――❧―――――

December—Tarrytown, NY

As Anna Hobbs maneuvered her walker to the front of the Tarrytown Library's main room, then lowered herself into the brown leather chair, Durward Hobbs' gaze followed the sure-footed movements of his wife. No longer did she baby herself and spend her days closed up in their small apartment because of her increasingly acute rheumatism. Since they'd come back from the village, she'd reverted to that emotionally strong, gregarious woman he'd fallen in love with over a half a century ago.

Nowadays, Anna Hobbs had a special glow about her that drew people to her. With her snow-white hair encircling her head like a halo, her blue eyes shining, her cheeks rosy with anticipation, and her smile so friendly, she reminded him of one of the angels in the stained glass windows at church. Her always cheery voice warmed him inside, just like a rainbow after a surprise summer shower.

He studied the children gathered around his wife's feet, waiting expectantly for the weekly story hour to begin. With a smile, he settled into the hard wooden chair at the back of the room and waited for Miss Anna, as the children called her, to start her tale. For a while, she thumbed through the worn volume in her lap, trying to decide where to start. As she studied the table of contents, she spoke to prevent the children from becoming restless while they waited.

"In the early 1800's, a boy named Washington Irving lived here in the Hudson Highlands. When he became a man, he wrote stories about his birth-place, which were published in a book called *The Sketch Book of Geoffrey Crayon, Gentleman*." She held the book aloft. The cover showed loving wear, but endured, as did the tales it held. "Some of them make us laugh. Some make us shudder." She shook, as though fright-ened. The children followed suit and giggled. "It's nearly Christmas and Mr. Irving's stories are more for Halloween. But I'm afraid there are so many won-derful Christmas stories that it'll be hard for me to choose. Do any of you have a favorite?"

"Miss Anna, please tell us the story of Emanuel." The request came from Elethia Stanton, a young girl with a quiet voice and the face of an angel. She cradled a worn teddy bear in her thin arms.

Though her smile seemed genuine to an observer, Durward knew her cheerful mask hid a deep and profound sorrow.

Anna glanced at the child, then looked at Durward and nodded almost imperceptibly, confirming what he already knew. This was the child they'd been waiting for.

Anna turned back to the gathering of young expectant faces. As always, when requested to tell the tale of Michiah Biddle and the mist, Anna's face broke into a beautiful smile. But Durward paid little attention to his wife at that point. He sat up straighter, stretching to see the girl better.

"That's the best tale of all," Anna said, laying the book aside, then leaning forward, warming to her subject.

Durward knew his wife loved telling this tale above all the rest.

She scanned the faces in the room. "Do any of you know who Michiah Biddle was?"

A unified "no" came from the children. The young girl listened intently to Anna's every word. Her grandparents stood beside her, her grandfather's hand resting protectively on the girl's slim shoulder. A bright red bandana concealed her hairless head, but nothing could hide the sadness that filled the old man's eyes.

Durward took comfort in the fact that the sadness would soon be a thing of the past. He and Anna would see to that just as soon as the story hour ended.

"Michiah came to the New World a long time ago, when the United States still belonged to England,

3

before New York became a state. He brought with him his wife Rachel, whom he loved more than anything else in the whole world. Together, they built a cabin out near the river."

Half listening to his wife's soothing voice, Durward concentrated all his attention on the girl and her grandparents. The girl smiled, but her grandmother and grandfather exchanged apprehensive looks above the girl's head. Clearly they doubted. Durward smiled to himself. He and Anna had doubted, too, but no more.

Anna continued with her story.

"Michiah and Rachel lived very happily in their little house. After a few years, Rachel had a baby. They named him Emanuel for Michiah's great grandfather. From the very first, Michiah adored his small, inquisitive son. Emanuel had a serious nature and asked questions Michiah, a man of little book learning, found difficult to answer. Where did the robins go when the snow came? Why did the river flow down and not up? Where did the clouds come from?

"When Emanuel reached the age of twelve, Rachel became very sick. Michiah was beside himself with worry that his beloved wife would die. What would he do without her? How would he go on? Searching for solitude to pray, Michiah went into the woods to the top of a hill, a hill where he often sat to think while he watched the Hudson River flow lazily to the sea.

"On this day, a mist had gathered in the glen,

blocking Michiah's view. An odd mist, thick and white, it glowed softly from the inside. He stared at it for a long time until his curiosity got the better of him, then, descending the hill, he walked into the fog.

"Later, when Michiah came out of the heavy mist, then climbed back up the hill, the mist had disappeared, but something wondrous had happened to him inside that white cloud. He knew in his heart things would be better. When he arrived home to tell his wife and son of his strange adventure, he found Rachel fixing dinner for the first time in weeks. In his joy of Rachel's recovery, he forgot to tell his little family what had happened in the glen.

"Michiah went back to the hill many times after that, but the mist never reappeared. One day he took Emanuel with him, and while they sat side by side on the top of the hill, Michiah told his teenaged son the story of the mist.

"The young boy questioned his father about what he'd seen in the mist. Michiah said he'd seen nothing, but he'd felt such overwhelming peace and love that, if it hadn't been for Emanuel and his mother, he would have been content to remain there forever.

"Emanuel, captivated by the story, returned time after time to the hilltop, waiting for the mist to reappear, but it never did."

The group began to stir, as if ready to leave. Anna put up a hand. "Wait. That's just the beginning of the story. The best is yet to be told."

Durward turned his attention from the child back to Anna. His heartbeat quickened in his chest. He slid a little farther forward on the chair. She smiled. Not outwardly. Her face didn't change, but Durward could feel Anna's smile inside him, as if he'd just walked into an open meadow filled with sunshine.

"Two days after his fourteenth birthday, Emanuel's parents died of a fever that swept the valley. Emanuel was very sad, and no matter what anyone said or did, they couldn't cheer him up. He buried his parents together on the hilltop overlooking the glen where his father had seen the mist.

"That same day, some said, the mist reappeared, and Emanuel walked into it. Others said he just ran away into the woods, unable to bear the sorrow of losing both parents, and the Indians got him. Whatever happened, no one ever saw Emanuel again." She paused. "Except for—"

"Except for who?" a young boy called out.

"Shh," his mother admonished. She sent Anna an apologetic smile.

Anna went on, undisturbed by the interruption. "Except for Josiah Reeve."

"Who's he?" asked a little girl in the front row.

"Josiah Reeve ran the local livery stable. A stingy man, he'd hoarded all his money and kept it stashed in a secret hiding place, refusing to give anything to the poor. 'If they can't earn an honest dollar, then let them die an honest death instead,' he'd say.

6

"Two years after Emanuel disappeared, one of Josiah's horses ran off, and he chased it into the woods. Josiah saw a glowing mist in the glen." The children gasped. "Yes, it was the same mist Michiah had seen. He went into the mist, thinking his horse might have wandered into it and couldn't find its way out.

"When he came out, finding that he'd only been gone for a few minutes astonished him. He thought it had been days. When the town's people didn't believe him, he tried to convince them by telling stories of what he'd seen in the mist. Wondrous tales of an entire village. He told of local people who had disappeared from their little settlement and who now lived inside the white cloud and had strange powers. *And* he had seen Emanuel, not as the boy who had vanished, but as a full-grown man." Anna's voice took on a wispy quality Durward knew well. "But, what he remembered most was the love he'd found there, a love so powerful that no man could resist its pull."

Durward smiled and glanced at the young girl. He knew about love. Love happened when Anna touched him, and he felt a peace beyond description. Love happened every time he looked into her face. Love happened in the heart of every child who listened to her stories.

"When asked to give the name of this village he claimed to have seen," Anna went on, "he said the people called it Renaissance, which means rebirth."

A collective "oh" rose from the children and adults

alike. No one remained aloof for long from the drama Anna put into her tales.

"His stories made the people of the settlement laugh. No such village existed near the river. Nothing could be found there except wild animals, trees, and grass. 'How, when Emanuel was only gone for two years, could he have grown to manhood?' they questioned, laughing harder still.

"But the laughter died when Josiah began to give the poor all the money he'd hoarded all those years. To their amazement, by the week's end, he didn't have a cent, and he was blind. Then they knew something *had* happened to him in the mist. They thought about it and discussed it amongst themselves. They could find but one answer. Something evil lived in the mist and had stolen Josiah's mind. The old man had gone crazy."

She paused and gazed expectantly around the room. "After that, fearing Michiah's glen to be an evil place inhabited by witches and demons, no one went near it. Those that did were never heard from nor seen again. Back then when people couldn't explain something, they always said that evil spirits were to blame. So, when other townspeople disappeared, everyone believed witches in the glen lured them into the fog, then pushed them over the cliff into the river."

"Why didn't they just ask Josiah what happened to the people?" ask a small girl, who had sidled up to Anna and rested her cheek against Anna's knee.

"Because, child, Josiah not only went blind, he

also never spoke another word after he told his story and gave away his fortune." Anna patted the child's head gently. "Some say a curse had been put upon him by the mist demons as punishment for telling their secrets. After a while, Josiah also disappeared. Everyone said his craziness had driven him back to the woods and that he'd grown confused and died out there somewhere in the wilderness.

"The cabin that Emanuel and his parents lived in still stands in the woods, but, sadly, their graves are no longer visible. Some say that the woodland flowers grow brightest on the hilltop, and even in the dead of winter, when the weather is bad, the creatures come to Michiah's and Rachel's cabin for shelter, knowing they'll find food, love and protection from harm. Since they loved the woodland creatures, I like to think that would please Rachel and Michiah."

Happy tears rolled down Anna's rosy cheeks. Durward nodded knowingly. Telling Michiah's story always exposed Anna's emotions. It brought back to her the secrets they'd discovered together in the mist.

Story time had ended, and Durward moved to his wife's side, then laid a tender hand on Anna's shoulder. She patted his hand, telling him in her own silent way not to be alarmed. Drawing from her pocket a white, lace-edged handkerchief, embroidered with a small, fancy "A" on one corner, she dabbed at the tears collected on her lashes. He recognized the handkerchief; he carried one much like it.

The young girl and her grandparents came forward. "Is the cabin ready?" the grandfather asked Durward in a low voice.

Touching her heart with the hand clutching the handkerchief, Anna whispered, "The cabin is *always* ready."

The girl pivoted toward her grandmother. "Nana, I'm tired. Can we go now?" Fatigue colored her voice. Her eyes, which should have sparkled with the excitement of life that all children had, were lifeless and sad. Her cheeks were pale and dark circles rimmed them. Her arms, embracing the teddy bear, had grown limp.

"Would you like me to take you to Michiah's cabin now?" Durward waited for the child to respond.

She stared thoughtfully at the teddy bear. Finally, she turned her face up to his. "Yes." Her voice betrayed her fatigue.

The girl's grandfather pulled Durward aside. "I'm not sure I believe all this gibberish about the mist, but if it'll help our little girl, I'll walk barefoot over hot coals." He glanced at his granddaughter. "She's all we have, and we love her dearly." He frowned, blinked back tears, and turned to Durward. "I pray you're right, but I think we need a miracle."

Anna, overhearing the end of the conversation, sidled closer with the aid of her retrieved walker. "If it's a miracle you want, sir, you must believe." She stroked the young girl's thin hand resting on the arm of the chair. "Only faith and trust can make a miracle."

The small group left the library and climbed into Durward's mini van. He steered the car carefully over the ice-encrusted streets and soon they were going down the main highway. Not far down the road, Durward turned into a narrow side road. They bumped over ruts and blown snow piles until they came to a half-hidden driveway.

At the end of the driveway stood a cabin, small and old, but spouting a welcoming curl of gray smoke from its chimney. In the front window a Christmas tree's lights scattered dollops of color on the snow that had collected on the porch.

For the first time that night, the girl smiled a genuine, from-the-heart smile. Durward thought he heard her whisper "I'm home," but it had been so soft that it could have been a bit of breeze blowing through the trees.

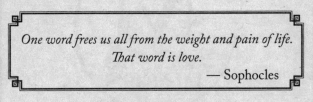

One word frees us all from the weight and pain of life.
That word is love.

— Sophocles

ISBN# 1932815651
ISBN# 9781932815658
US $6.99 / CDN $9.99
Romantic Fantasy
Available Now

For more information

about other great titles from

Medallion Press, visit

www.medallionpress.com

PRESS ®